The Private Life of
ɔrence Nightingale

RICHARD GORDON

The Private Life of Florence Nightingale

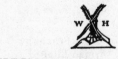

HEINEMANN : LONDON

William Heinemann Ltd
15 Queen St, Mayfair, London W1X 8BE
LONDON MELBOURNE TORONTO
JOHANNESBURG AUCKLAND

First published 1978
© Richard Gordon Ltd 1978
434 30253 8

Printed in Great Britain by
Cox & Wyman Limited
London, Fakenham and Reading

Author's Note

1915 WAS LIKE 1854 a year of killing. After Mons, the Marne and Ypres, Asquith's Government judged it unfitting to unveil Florence Nightingale's statue with ceremony. On the Wednesday of February 24, workmen folded the canvas and dismantled the scaffolding, one brushed the snow from the plinth, and they left her alone in Waterloo Place, in the middle of London's gentlemen's clubland.

On the corner of Pall Mall opposite, through the windows of the Athenaeum Club, her father once wrote with his quill pen – he abhorred the new, gimcrack Birmingham steel nibs – his exasperated surrender of £500 a year and her independence. Behind her stand figures of guardsmen, cast from the metal of Russian cannon captured at Sebastopol. To her left, she is matched by the statue of Sidney Herbert, Secretary at War for the Crimean campaign. Sidney Herbert was the only man she loved. Though in the flash of Miss Nightingale's mind, even love took an appearance as original as her theories on military sanitation.

She was emotional, she was vain, she was complex, she was incomparable. She was a passionate cultivator of new ideas on the compost-heap of long rotted ones. She had a genius for rubbing noses into facts right in front of them. She had infinite capability and little tenderness. Her antiseptic ghost today haunts every sickbed in the world, to which she was Britain's most valuable and useful gift.

She shares a cell in our folk-memory with Nelson and Wellington, she is the girl on the £10 note. She has been trampled by the fastidious footsteps of lady biographers and stamped by the cloven hoof of Lytton Strachey. She is much misunderstood. Everyone knows what she offered humanity. Few know what she offered humans. Even the Aladdin's lamp of her statue and popular imagination is not the sort which lit her fame in the wards of Scutari.

What was she like to work alongside, argue against, chat to, laugh with? Which way swung the lodestone of her sex? The long letters of a long lifetime print her personality. She had fragments of Elizabeth Fry and Elizabeth I, history's Joan and Shaw's, Jane Austen and Gertrude Stein, Lady Hester Stanhope and Amy Johnson, and nothing at all of Emmeline Pankhurst or Mary Poppins.

I have tried to introduce her by a novel in which most of the events happened, many of the characters lived and much of the dialogue is their own. The opinions of Tristram Darling are mine.

I

TOWARDS NOON ON the last day of June 1854 – as thundery
as any other that sultry summer – a young man bounded with
enviable confidence up the front steps of the Reform Club
in Pall Mall. His aggressive flourish swung open the pair
of brassbound oak front doors, his four strides were enough
for the eight inner ones which led up from the porter's
booth with its massive brass cigar-lighter. He came to an
abrupt, disconcerted halt in the club's great saloon,
breathless, with sweat dampening his upper lip, which
distressed him. He had feared being late as much as disproving the axiom that a gentleman is never in a hurry.

The young man was me – yet he was not me. Human
personality is not etched in the cradle and shredded in
the grave. It is more like a family portrait gallery. The
sprig who went to the Crimean War claims only kinship
with my portrait today in the library of my country house,
rich, robed, ennobled, in this first year of the reign of
King George V. I have sown the seed of charity and as
assiduously reaped the honours. In 1854, I was chubby
and chestnut-haired, the unmatured good looks which drew
glances under the parasols at Lord's or Henley, and I had
only two sovereigns in the world. I had embarked upon,
in Samuel Daniel's line, *The shipwreck of my ill-adventured
youth.*

'Page—' I stopped a pale elf in a cuirasse of brass buttons.
'My name is Mr Tristram Darling. My compliments to
Mr Wakley-Barlow, MP, and pray say that his guest has
arrived.'

The saloon, which no forthright Reformer would ever

call the *salon*, was vast, colonnaded, galleried, lit by a vaulted skylight of flint glass and lined with portraits of dead Whigs. The men who had stormed the Parliamentary Reform Bill into law in 1832 had demanded of architect Sir Charles Barry a clubhouse to outblaze Brooks's in St James's, which steadily blackballed them as Radical freaks. Barry had responded joyfully by incorporating in his plan not one Roman *palazzo*, but three. 'A building worthy of Michelangelo!' exclaimed Macaulay to Leigh Hunt. It still stands, a congenial monument to our early Victorian unquenchable vulgarity.

The saloon comfortably held a dozen groups of comfortable men, in full-skirted coats, clasping their canes, wearing their top hats, in animated or grave conversation about the war. Great Britain had been fighting Russia three months. 'Against unprovoked aggression,' ran the Queen's Declaration, 'a just, necessary and honourable war'. Whatever war was not? 'The finest Army that has ever left these shores,' according to *The Times*, had landed at desolate Gallipoli, sailed away in May to Varna on the Bulgarian coast and sat waiting to be attacked. Instead, the Russians had that June week abandoned the frontier town of Silistria and recrossed the Danube on their way home. It was unsatisfactory and unsporting.

I waited, not daring to feel affronted, hardly to feel irritated, leaning on a silver-headed cane as shiny as my boots, which were a little too tight, or my hat, which was a little too tall, while members mounted the steps for their lunch like salmon up a fish-ladder. After half an hour, a beef-faced man some ten years my senior hastened from the front door with a club footman in blue dress coat and buff waistcoat, the old Whig colours. He shook hands briefly and damply, cursed the scarcity of cabs at the height of the London season and hurried me across the terrazzo floor into the long coffee-room, which was misty with cigar smoke, its mahogany tables polished like mirrors, alive with the chatter and clatter of men eating wearing their hats.

'Well, Mr Darling, I can no longer offer you the artistry

2

of our great chef, Monsieur Alexis Soyer,' Wakley-Barlow said at once. 'You've heard of him?'

'Who has not? His *Shilling Cookery* embellishes every tradesman's bookshelf, and his Sultana's Sauce every tradesman's mutton chop.'

'He got too big for his boots, and had to go. It's the same in the kitchen as the House of Commons. Devilishly full today.' He scowled. 'Some finishing their breakfasts, I suppose. We fine 'em if they linger past noon.' We were wedged by a waiter at a table between pillar and corner. 'So you're a literary man, Mr Darling?' Wakley-Barlow jerked his head across the coffee-room, towards a square-faced, grey-haired man with small round glasses in a bottle-green coat, leaning in lively argument. 'Like Mr Thackeray?'

'The profession of letters, sir, has its ranks like the profession of arms.'

'That's prettily put. And you yourself are a corporal?'

'Might I remind you, sir, that I am only twenty-two?'

'Oh, at that age Byron had started *Childe Harold* and Keats was already dying.'

He laughed, showing a tongue which struck me as big enough for an ox. He spoke with a mixture of joviality and mockery, which I already found as sickening as did his political opponents forced to endure it for years.

'Well, you're a gentleman. Or enough of one for me to be seen with in the club. Your clothes ain't *too* swell, and you've a neat watch – if there is one on the end of that gold chain.'

I wore a silk-braided swallow-tailed coat with pepper-and-salt trousers adhering to my legs, my white silk stock as smooth as a hard-boiled egg, my neck entirely disappeared in a high starched collar. I proudly drew a watch as slim as a coin from my canary waistcoat. 'My father's, sir.'

'I know your father died last summer in Spa. Not through disproving the curative powers of the waters, but through shooting himself over gaming debts. I also know that your charming mother enjoys life abroad, she having resided for some years in Geneva with Count Arezzo. Oh, the whole

3

Town's heard both scandals. So don't sit there looking like a housemaid who first feels a footman's hand up her skirts. We can talk better as one blunt Englishman to another. I know your line. You're a gossip gatherer, a muckraker for the newspapers. What's the point of disguising yourself as a man about Town?'

'Raking at *my* level, sir, demands dressing to match the company which provides the muck.'

'Are you sly? Avaricious?'

'Neither, but I enjoy tasty food, smooth drink and lively women, to all three of which my pen is my doorkey. The verses in the Virgillian style which I composed at Rugby School and Cambridge did not strike me as commercially promising.'

He seemed to respect this frankness from another blunt Englishman. 'You deserve a whipping, but the press is becoming as sacred as the Church of England, and for the same sentimental reasons. Do you know a lady called Miss Florence Nightingale?'

I shook my head. 'It's a pretty name.'

'You think so? It could have been Miss Pisa Shore,' he said mysteriously. 'Her father left the font William Edward Shore, but when he came of age, which was the year we beat the French, he changed his colours. He inherited a fortune from his mother's uncle, Peter Nightingale, a hard-drinking, hard-riding, hard-betting man, a mad Croesus known all over Derbyshire.' He scowled. 'Peter Nightingale was my own father's great-uncle.'

Wakley-Barlow spoke bitterly of bad blood in the family, of William Edward Shore already itching with money like a tinker with lice, of a contested will, a disputed lead mine among the spiky hills of Derbyshire. His malicious strokes drew newly-dubbed William Nightingale as idle, sulky and snobbish, rubbing into his skinny body enough learning from the stones of Trinity College Cambridge to face the sadness of a life empty of everything but pleasure.

'Money married money. Gold's a magnetic metal. WEN – that's what everyone calls Nightingale – took unto himself Fanny Smith, daughter of old Will Smith, an

MP for nigh on fifty years, who championed as many lost causes as your father backed rotten horses.'

Wakley-Barlow was becoming roughly affable. We were eating *côtelettes Reform*, a creation of the incomparable, lost Soyer. Wine is an abrasive of the quarrelsome, but food an infallible poultice.

'The Nightingales spread themselves across Hampshire at Embley House. They're well connected, the Palmerstons, Bonham Carters, powerful families. They do the rounds of the country houses, the London season, half a floor at the Carlton Hotel in Regent Street, opera, concerts, daughters presented at Court, you know the style. It's not mine. Always travelling abroad, in proper fashion, six servants and a carriage specially built. They winter in the Place Vendôme. How comfortable. How respectable. How deadly dull.'

I perceived him pricked by the imp of jealousy. 'But why a daughter named after the City of Flowers?'

'I'll tell you. After WEN married, he took his bride off to Italy, which was *à la mode* once we'd got Boney safely out of the way, for anyone who thought England not quite good enough for them. Fanny had a daughter in Naples, so they called the child Parthenope, which is Naples in Greek. Next year she had another in Florence. It could have been Venice. Or Leghorn. That daughter's an odd fish. She has an unhealthy preoccupation with the sick.'

'As many young ladies in society. It's like a longing to wash Christ's feet or lick a beggar's sores.'

'But Miss Nightingale's near thirty-four, and should have grown out of such fancies. Marriage usually cures 'em, as it cures much else of female feebleness. Perhaps she's inherited it from her grandfather, with his fondness for stroking the underdog. She's not content with sick villagers. She tried to nurse the poor at Salisbury Infirmary, which caused a scandal in the county and almost killed her family. Now Miss Nightingale is superintendent of something called the Establishment for Gentlewomen during Illness, in Harley Street. Which is under the wing of Lady Canning. The Postmistress-General.' He alluded with a wink to her

5

husband's official position. 'I want the egregious place derided, disgraced, shut down, Miss Nightingale jeered back to the oblivion from which she poked her sharp nose.'

Puzzled, I enquired why.

It emerged that Wakley-Barlow had laid out a fortune with suppliers of the Army and Navy. One of his contractors also supplied the gentlewomen's nursing home, and Miss Nightingale had set him about the ears. The woman was cracked, a fanatic, he declared. But she was intimate with Lady Canning, with a husband in the Government, and there was no knowing where rumours might end.

'I'm cautious. I saw enough men run down in the City by George Hudson's railways. Well, Mr Darling. I only heard your name by chance. What newspaper do you scribble for?'

He snorted when I said, 'The *Penny Pioneer*.' It was radical and crusading, popular among the poor for exposing among the rich the wickedness which its readers could not afford.

'Dig me a scandal to start a public outcry. I've pulled the trick before,' he reflected proudly. 'When some Bedlamite doctor near-bankrupted the Soho Water Company, with his moonstruck notion that the cholera was spread from its public pumps.'

His silk handkerchief was on the table. My fingers slipped three gold pieces from underneath. We were bound in a transaction as swift as an adder's bite.

2

I WAS LEFT on the Reform's front steps, between its huge pair of gas globes, the smell of sour cooking rising from the area. I had nothing immediately to do. I tipped forward my hat, strolled past the next-door Travellers' and Athenaeum Clubs, stopped a hansom at the bottom of Regent Street and gave an address in Brompton.

In a short, uncobbled street off the Brompton Road, stood a house no bigger than a gamekeeper's cottage, so new that its plastered white walls still seemed to gleam with wetness. There was a pretty front door with a transom, three windows up, two down, all opaque with lace. The snug garden, walled all round higher than a man, exuded the secretiveness of a coach with drawn blinds at night. A tall gate of black ironwork led to a well raked gravel path between newly planted laurels, berberis and box, the sombre shrubs beloved in my youth. Dog roses shone like pink stars upon pale latticework, fresh against the house front. I banged the knocker, sure of unseen eyes upon me.

The door was opened instantly by the maid, fourteen years old and just out of the orphanage, blue eyes too big for her face, strawlike hair consumed by a mob cap, floor-sweeping black bombazine trailing apron strings from a child's waist. I called her Little Nell, having a lifelong horror for the incessant infant creations of Charles Dickens.

'Is Miss Harriet at home?' Bobbing repectfully, the girl denied it, and lawks-a-daisied as I pushed masterfully past her. 'Miss Harriet cannot spare herself the pleasure of receiving me, just because she has not completed her toilette by four in the afternoon, through reason of not

7

rising till after luncheon. I'll amuse myself at the piano in the parlour. She adores my playing.'

As I expected, Harriet was already descending the narrow stairs to the tiny hallway with its green-and-gold wallpaper and bamboo hatstand, beautiful in her delight and disarray. The maid vanished like the shadow of a bird.

'You mustn't stay, not a second,' she greeted me breathlessly.

'Why not? Old Lard Tub won't come this hour of the afternoon. He's too busy piling up sovereigns in Mincing Lane.'

'Mr Larderton has become most irregular in his habits of late.'

'I can always jump out of the back window, and don my clothes on the way to Kensington Gore.'

'You *must* appreciate my position.' Her voice was desperate, her clutch of me fierce.

'But I appreciate it perfectly. Old Lard Tub paying for your house, your victuals, this lovely pink tulle frock—' I crushed a handful in my fist. 'Is more than a convenience. He is an utter necessity for a man like myself, who has his fortune still to make.'

'But if Mr Larderton *did* find you here, I should be ruined! Don't you see, Tristram? Out in the street, without a rag or crust to call my own.'

'How much more exciting. A mere husband could do nothing more drastic than box your ears.'

She laughed, we were already in her bedroom, with its forget-me-not wallpaper, its view across a tiny conservatory of fluted ironwork and engraved glass upon a back lawn with croquet hoops. I wondered whether Mr Larderton found time to play.

Miss Harriet Catchpole was as lithe as a sapling, golden haired, milk skinned, grey eyed, budding bosomed, an enchantress as valuable to a young man low in money and social position as the fairy princess to the toad. She was the daughter of the steward to a nobleman's estate, with a quickness and mimickry which gave her the speech and manners of her betters, and a realistic appreciation of her

8

value to society given her by the nobleman's three sons. She was dancing at the newly-opened Canterbury Music Hall in Lambeth when she caught the eye of Mr Larderton, a spice merchant, infinitely rich. I had met her the previous month detached from her protector in a crowd, as I watched by way of business Mr Gully's Andover win the Derby.

My finger-nails were tugging at her stay-lace. 'Who tied this? Lard Tub?'

'The maid.'

I laughed. 'There's many a husband mystified by finding a bow at night where he's tied a knot in the morning.'

'You're drunk,' she said disconcertingly.

'What nonsense. I had to share a bottle or two with an ill-mannered bully in the Reform Club, that's all.'

'The Reform Club?' Like many easily aroused women, Harriet was easily distracted. The Reform Club was inaccessible even to Mr Larderton. 'What were they saying about the war? Weren't they pleased that the siege of Silistria was raised?'

'If they were, they gave no evidence of it.'

I was impatient. 'Don't give me a baby,' she murmured. She always did, like a magic spell. Perhaps it was. For casual lovers of the last century, there was nothing else.

Now that I own the *Penny Pioneer* – rechristened the *Daily Pioneer* – now that I am a Liberal peer and a past Minister of State, now that I am seventy-eight (four years younger than Gladstone when he was still Prime Minister, as I repeatedly tell my editors), I mischievously contemplate publishing my diaries of the 1850s in next week's paper. After H G Wells' *Ann Veronica* last year, surely frankness is all.

They would reopen no scars upon those I have loved and wounded – my first wife has been dead thirty years. But how the councils of colleges and hospitals where I sit, how the House of Lords, the very Cabinet itself, would blush like lobsters dropped into boiling water. The circulation would rocket. Among the British public, who have a sound sense of relative values, I should be more popular than George Robey. It would anyway make a pleasing diversion

9

from the Kaiser and the other problems of the twentieth century.

I cannot walk today among the lavender beds of our Elizabethan garden without a look in my eye which mystifies my present wife. Harriet's sheets, crisp out of the press, always smelt of lavender. She and I lay that afternoon staring at the whitewashed ceiling, sweaty, entwined, innocently replete like a pair of children gorged with cake. A wakening thunderstorm growled. The curtain-lace was so heavy, the little room was in twilight. I turned my glance to the ill-glazed, gingery, china monkey with a detachable head on the mantelpiece, which regularly amazed me with its ugliness. There was no portrait, no trace in the house, of my involuntary host. He existed only in the jealousy of my imagination, as white, fat, mannerless and lustful.

'Come to the new Crystal Palace tomorrow, out on Sydenham Hill,' I invited.

'Pooh.' Harriet wrinkled her nose. 'What a peculiar invitation to extend at this particular moment.'

I extended it because I had free tickets from the firm who resited the Great Exhibition from Hyde Park, who wanted a puff in the papers. And because Harriet was not a diverting conversationalist in any but the language of love.

'But it's a magnificent sight,' I told her forcefully, recalling the firm's circular. It had been opened the previous week by the Queen, with the Hundredth Psalm, the Hallelujah Chorus and 40,000 Londoners. 'The vaulted roof is tremendous – greater in area than St Paul's in London or St Peter's in Rome, or both combined, I can't for the moment remember. And the basement!' I waved my naked arm. 'A labyrinth of steam-pipes and boilers, never before seen to man. The gardens! Filled with fountains, waterfalls, lakes and grottoes, they throw Versailles into insignificance. Or so they say. Educational, too. Geological strata and plaster casts of extinct animals.'

'I do not think that I should care to be seen in Sydenham observing mammoths.'

There was a flash of lightning, the rain started falling

in leaden drops. I risked spoiling my best clothes. The gathering possibility of Mr Larderton's arrival was the certainty of my own departure. She never let me stay the night.

'I must go home. I'll find an omnibus in the Brompton Road.'

'I often dream, lovey, of living in your place, just the two of us,' said Harriet.

'I don't think you would reside very happily in a room above the stables at Paddington Basin, which is full of stinks from the towpath horses of the Grand Union Canal, full of shrieks from the trains at Paddington terminus, raided by rats and comfortably settled by bedbugs.'

'It doesn't seem right, when you mix with the finest in the land.'

'I mix with them as an urchin. Who must be petted, lest he scream out some truth which everybody knows but nobody mentions.'

'But you like it.'

'I hate it. My occupation disgusts me. I can at least be sure it will end, when my readers grow tired of me. For it to continue, until replaced by the infirmities and disillusionments of age, is a fate infinitely worse.'

She was not interested 'Lovey, give me a present.'

'Why should I? Old Lard Tub gives you everything.'

'Not a shilling for myself,' she said resentfully. 'You know that, love. It's his game. Just to keep me here.'

'But I don't want you to escape, no more than he does.'

'Please, lovey . . . just a little present,' she implored.

Naked, cross-legged on the bed, hand cupped, childlike, she was irresistible. From the pocket of my canary waistcoat I handed her the three sovereigns for which I had sold myself to Wakley-Barlow. I had redeemed myself from both of them by the harshest of judgements, the verdict of a man's own vices.

3

I HAD the mental picture of Miss Nightingale. Vinegary, governessy, churchy, self-important, gloriously self-satisfied, falling upon the poor to sermonize them, scold them and scrub them, that a committee of noble ladies, peering with pious disgust over her shoulder, might salve their conscience about the next five guineas for a box at the opera, or fifty for a new gown or 500 for a new necklace. My childhood had been largely motherless and often penniless, and left me much exposed to Miss Nightingales.

The Establishment for Gentlewomen during Illness I found at No 1 Harley Street, a modern, stone-faced, five-storey house on the corner. It was a morning towards the end of July. I had needed time to effect my introduction, and I had been busy during high season working flashing stones from London's social dirt.

I banged the knocker, and drew a beautifully engraved card from a delicate silver case, both essential tools of my trade. I started back, card jutting from finger-tips like a jib-sail. The door was opened by a lady, slender and graceful, jet hair parted in the middle and curtaining a face of the reposeful beauty which the quattrocento lavished on its Madonnas. Her dress was startlingly plain, black cotton with lace collar and cuffs. Could *this* be Miss Nightingale? But she was my own age.

'Mr Darling? How kind of you to call. Sir Peregrine wrote from St George's Hospital.' My uncle was a surgeon there. 'I am Miss Bancroft, Miss Nightingale's secretary.' Her voice was quiet. For a young man of such lively imagination towards women, it threw a silken net of intimacy over us. 'Miss Nightingale will receive you in a few minutes. She is busy this moment at a deathbed.'

This chill greeting matched the hall, its bare boards polished like brown ice, its only furniture a hatstand without any hats. It reeked of washerwoman's soap and limewater. I felt the house and myself took an instant dislike to each other.

'I shall tell you about the nursing home. You have a pencil and paper? Good. Miss Nightingale takes notes of all conversations, and expects others to do likewise. You will want to know the number of patients in the house,' Miss Bancroft decided, ticking her fingers. 'Ten, of whom two are operation patients, three refractory skin diseases, two linger with consumption, two await their departure from this world and one is hysterical.' So ghoulish a catalogue uttered so calmly by so delicate a young woman, was an experience novel, shocking and exciting.

'Miss Nightingale does not approve of hysterical patients.' She folded long-fingered hands across her midriff. 'Miss Nightingale says that a hospital must house the seriously ill, or it becomes a mere lodgings, where the nervous are made more nervous, the foolish grow more foolish, the idle and selfish more selfish and idle. If no higher interest exists, illness becomes a woman's amusement and luxury. Miss Nightingale says that if she has nothing to occupy her except her meals and her mucous membranes, a woman's sole object will be to breakfast in bed and be pitied. We have guinea patients and half-guinea patients.'

Mucous membranes! No girl had ever conversed with me more intimately in a drawing-room than on chilblains.

'The Ladies' Committee take Miss Nightingale's opinion on any subject extremely seriously, particularly since she reduced the daily expenditure for each patient from one-and-tenpence to a shilling,' said Miss Bancroft. Then her hands fluttered, her hazel eyes glittered, she became a delightfully animated Madonna. On the dark-stained stairs I saw a tall, upright, sharp-nosed female in a frock like the secretary's, her waist looped with a chatelaine, a close fitting lace cap on brown hair parted in the middle and drawn into coiled plaits hiding her ears. She had a long neck, an oval face, grey eyes, excellent teeth and a delicate skin not lined too spitefully by her thirty-four years. She had no bosom, a deficiency I always thought in a woman like a bed without a pillow.

'I know all about Mr Wakley-Barlow,' Miss Nightingale greeted me pleasantly. 'I heard from Mrs Sidney Herbert, the wife of our Secretary at War, who is a member of my Ladies' Committee. You should know better, Mr Darling, than to share secrets with a man who drinks more than six bottles of claret a day.'

I stood like a delivery-boy caught stealing the cake by the housekeeper. The twin cowards of my eyes turned from Miss Nightingale to Miss Bancroft, but my glance ricochetted off.

'Please tell Mr Wakley-Barlow that I dismissed his contractor because the man sent me a bottle labelled "Spirits of Nitre" which contained ether. Had I not smelt it, I should certainly have administered it, and have faced an inquest.' Miss Nightingale sounded no more concerned than a hostess describing the social disasters of an unsuccessful dinner party. 'He also furnished the flue of a gas stove which came down the second time of using it. Had I not caught it, a patient would have been certainly killed by it. We were almost suffocated by gas,' she ended calmly, 'which went off in a series of partial explosions. One of the workmen sent to repair it got drunk, and fought the foreman.'

'I fear, Miss Nightingale, that I have no alternative but to leave instantly.'

'Do you? Well, you have troubled to make the journey, you might as well see the house. Has Miss Bancroft told you about my novel bells?'

'Bells?' I noticed that the way Miss Bancroft stood with hands clasped before her was exactly the attitude of her mistress. 'I don't think we spoke about bells.'

I was led to a panel on the first floor landing. It seemed that the valve of each bell stayed open until the patient was attended. This did not strike me of Mr Samuel Morse's telegraphic ingenuity. Miss Nightingale seemed proud of the arrangement, and I admired it heartily.

'Small detail is of mountainous importance to the sick.' The errant delivery boy was to be lectured by the house-keeper. 'The horror of a nurse who rustles!' A fat girl with a pink scrubbed look hurried past us with a faint swish of bombazine. 'The irritating fidget of silk and crinoline! I wish that people who wear crinoline would see the in-decency of their own dress as other people are obliged to. A respectable elderly woman stooping forward, invested in crinoline, exposes quite as much of her own person to a patient lying in the room as any opera dancer on the stage.'

I could not stifle a laugh at this image. 'I see you are well acquainted with the nether limbs of opera dancers, Mr Darling. Well, you may go home and write what libels you choose. They cannot impede the work God called me to. Did you know that God spoke to me on four occasions?' she asked prosaically. 'Calling me to His service. The first was on February 7 1837, at our home in Hampshire. I was sixteen. Why do you look surprised?'

'Only because none of my acquaintance has been ap-proached so directly. Even my other uncle, who is a bishop.'

She did not appear offended. I was never over-impressed with Miss Nightingale's voices. The word of God is often in the ear of young women who cocoon themselves in secret fantasies to escape from life's frustrations. It is a phantom, as the lovelorn hear their dear one sigh with the wind in the trees, or the timid the rapping of a skeleton from an unlatched door at midnight. I have an interest in human minds as a farmer in his chickens, because I scatter their feed every morning.

'I rely on God greatly.' Her sudden smile to Miss Bancroft had surprising tenderness. 'But I *must* remember that God is not my private secretary. With His help, I have succeeded with my work here *à merveille*. I arrived to an empty building, the nursing home was moving from Chandos Street round the corner. Notice the food lift, Mr Darling. Look at the hot water supply. The weary linen darned and patched. The carpets and curtains recut. I killed the mice, turned furniture covers into dishcloths, made our own jam at tuppence a pot, ordered the groceries in bulk from Fortnum and Mason's, reconstituted the diet, procured *The Times* and a library subscription from Mudie's, and saved £150 a year by dismissing the house-surgeon,' she ended proudly. 'And I instilled some discipline. Only this morning, I changed one nurse because of her love of dirt and clumsiness, and another nurse because of her love of gin and intimidation.'

After the Ladies' Committee got wind of Miss Nightingale's agitative talents, and had nervously debated whether gentlewomen might be nursed by a gentlewoman, she strode in like a captain boarding his first command, determined to have everything shipshape and Bristol fashion, and any of the crew daring to be indolent, insubordinate or inefficient promptly dumped ashore. She would have run with equal efficiency and alacrity a workhouse, asylum, orphanage, gaol and other places mankind ardently prefers to keep itself on the weather side of the door. On her daily and nightly rounds, later so familiar to me, Miss Nightingale heartened, commiserated, and organized, but the dirty work was done by the dirty nurses. She did not trouble to train the bad ones. It was easier to sack them, like the house-surgeon.

'Our patients are of all denominations,' she continued, conducting me into a first-floor room overlooking Harley Street. 'My Committee allow them to be visited by their respective priests and muftis, provided *I* will receive the obnoxious animal at the door.'

'Miss Nightingale believes schism to be the deceit of the Devil,' added Miss Bancroft.

'And may I give you a warning, Mr Darling?' The room was furnished with a plain desk bearing a pewter inkstand, a table with neat piles of documents, a scrap of carpet and two chairs which discouraged a long visit. 'I am afraid of no one. Though I find you quite harmless.'

'I fear it is I who have made a formidable enemy.'

'I hope not. I never make an enemy of any man. I am

never sure when I might need him again for my own ends. *De nos jours*, nothing is achieved or achievable except by men. It is fortunate for the world they should be so open for manipulation by any woman who combines a little logic with a little insight into the masculine nature. And Mrs Herbert tells me that all London society is calling you a clever little devil. But why become a tattler? You are of good family.'

'But of poor resources.'

'So you make a living through every man possessing an unknown vice, even a man who parades his wickedness. And every woman a secret more shocking than those which she whispers to her friends to appear more fascinating. Well, perhaps it is salutary. Now I must continue with the unending labour of my correspondence.'

She was already at her desk, metal nib in pewter inkstand. Miss Nightingale took much care with her letters. I have several hundred of them for posthumous publication. She drafted them first in a notebook, bestowing a telling phrase on many correspondents instead of wasting it on merely one, slicing up a good paragraph and buttering many pages with it. The unhurried days of conscientious, stylish, self-revealing correspondence have unhappily reached their brutal end in these busy ones, when men fly the Channel and motor everywhere, when there are 10,000 typewriter girls to click out the thoughts of London. I have also the manuscript of her novel, *Cassandra*. Like many other young women, she wrote it to relieve her mental turmoil. Like many other young women, she never finished it.

'Miss Bancroft will see you out,' said Miss Nightingale, not looking up.

I left the bare room crushed under the juggernaut of her personality. My humiliation was increased by noticing the delightful Miss Bancroft staring at Miss Nightingale with a look of adoration at her cleverness in defusing a dangerous young scoundrel. It was a look which held for me later much vexation and misery. Then it fired me with a suppressed desire, as she walked close beside me downstairs, to seize her, declare myself crazed with her, and that we must fly instantly to Paris, or Broadstairs, being more in reach of my purse, leaving Miss Nightingale to her deathbeds.

'The penny omnibus passes the corner,' she said, shutting the black front door and leaving me to retreat and remuster my routed thoughts.

4

'ARE YOU AWARE of an individual called Darwin?' asked my uncle Humphry, Bishop of Chelsea.

'Of course I'm aware of an individual called Darwin.' replied my elder uncle, Sir Peregrine Darling, Bart. Though lowly placed, I was highly connected. 'He's a Fellow of the Royal Society, like I am and like his father before him. He's a biologist. A retiring sort, not in good health. Once sailed round the world, and wrote a book about it.'

'He is masquerading as a country gentleman at Down, among the hop-poles of Kent, while concocting heresies to disprove the book of Genesis.'

'Now, the trouble with chloroform,' continued Sir Peregrine, deafened to the conversation of others by his own views stamping impatiently for expression, 'is its having ruined the art of surgery. Seven or eight years ago, when you had to fill 'em with rum and hold 'em down, the surgeon had to look sharp about his business. Bob Liston at the North London could relieve a man of his leg, wide awake, as quickly as a Seven Dials' pickpocket his watch, and near as painlessly. Made his students time his performance, like a prizefighter. Vain but deuced clever. Sorry he's gone. Aortic aneurism.'

'But is not chloroform the greatest of mankind's benefits?' I had been diverting myself watching Chelsea Reach, on a darkening mid-August evening busy with a hundred craft, each different from the rest. 'For which we should nightly bless our American cousins on our knees?'

'I didn't say anything about mankind,' replied Sir Peregrine shortly. He was white haired, crimson-faced, spring-heeled, a Berkshire squire who had taken to surgery in youth as naturally as to hunting, shooting and fishing, which he held to demand the same qualities of dexterity and judgement. He seemed to find operating the best sport available to a gentleman in Belgravia. 'I said that chloroform had taken the skill out of surgery. Any fumble-fingered dresser can turn himself into a surgeon, now he's got all day to scratch about the patient. Make his fortune at it, too.'

'Let us get back to Mr Darwin.' The bishop dabbed his full lower lip with a shiny napkin. We sat at a long black table in the long dark dining-room of his square, damp palace by Chelsea Physic Garden. It was a mausoleum for appetites. The meat was always tough, the potatoes overboiled and the butler's nose ran. It was a meal eaten once a year, to settle family business. Sir Peregrine was a childless widower, the bishop a bachelor, we were the only Darlings left. 'The world was created in 4004 BC, at 9 am on Sunday, October 23,' he said firmly. 'That was calculated in the last century by Archbishop Ussher and the vice-chancellor of Cambridge. The fact is printed in many editions of the Bible, and is incontestable.'

'It makes the Creation sound like a railway timetable,' objected Sir Peregrine. 'I've heard it disputed by the most respectable theologians after dinner. Sometimes so hotly that I fear for a taproom brawl. Mr Darwin won't make Canterbury Cathedral fall down.'

'But Mr Darwin is a man of science.' Uncle Humphry was sleek-haired, square jawed, peevish and unsmiling, as though resentful of the world's continued sinfulness despite his specific instructions to the contrary. Out and about, he wore an intimidating shovel hat, and indulged his pride with a spanking coach and pair, his arms glittering in gold on the black panels, like a nobleman's. 'The mob will listen to him. The mob believe that science is all-powerful, because it gives them steamships and gas lighting.'

'So the Church is afraid of Mr Darwin, because miracles are no longer the job of saints but of engineers?'

'Fear is unknown to the Church,' said uncle Humphry contemptuously. I was struggling to cut a piece of gristle. 'But Mr Darwin can do much mischief. The Church's authority rests on man's awareness of his own divinity. Once men suspect that they are not created in God's image, but are animals in hats and trousers, it will inevitably diminish. Once the authority of the Church goes—' He shook a finger at us. 'That of the State will follow, as surely as the crew will mutiny once the captain has fallen overboard and the mate cannot tell them what lies beyond the horizon.'

'Well, what are you going to do? Burn him at Smithfield? Or blackball him for the Athenaeum?'

'I'd like you to visit him.'

'I will certainly not play inquisitor to another Fellow of the Royal Society. Besides, I am far too busy, and the journey's damnably awkward.'

The bishop's sallow face coloured. He was getting into a temper, or as he would put it, a state of high moral indignation. 'Mr Darwin has assented to give me a glimpse of his arguments, that my good friend the Bishop of Oxford—'

Sir Peregrine snorted. 'Soapy Sam Wilberforce.'

'Might prepare some reply. I had arranged for my chaplain to go—' The bishop looked uncomfortable. 'But he was seized with a fear that he might have to inspect baboons in a state of dissection. He is a tender-hearted young man, and suffers from a delicate stomach.'

'I'll go, sir.' Uncle Humphry looked as though interrupted in the pulpit by a choirboy. 'You will not forget, sir, my facility for writing. My Virgilian verses.' Unlike Sir Peregrine, he was ignorant of my exact occupation. 'For a few guineas—'

'Guineas!' cried the bishop.

'Capital idea,' said uncle Peregrine. '*He* won't be frightened by a dead baboon.'

I left the bishop's palace after dinner in uncle Peregrine's coach. Night had fallen, the weather had turned dry, the cobbles stank of dung and refuse. We turned away from the river past Chelsea Cathedral, built by Henry VIII's Chancellor, Sir Thomas More, to be his own resting place – but as often mars such comfortable anticipations, Sir Thomas ended with his body buried in the Tower and his head on a spike at London Bridge.

'Well! What's the latest tittle-tattle in society?' my uncle asked at once.

'Little, sir, except that the round hat is the thing. Absolutely every lady in Town must wear the new bare-faced look.'

'And what did you make of Miss Nightingale?'

'She was most severe on me.'

'I've never met her. Only know her father, at the club. She has an owl. She calls it Athena, because she found it in the Parthenon while jaunting about Greece.' He added thoughtfully, 'Only a very strange woman would make a pet of an owl. She gives her father a lot of trouble, you know. I gather the whole Nightingale female establishment is far too excitable. Comes from giving birth in Italy, no doubt,' he ended obscurely. He suddenly thrust his head through the open carriage window. 'A scent! The cholera,' he explained. 'It often comes this time of the year, when the mercury's high and the water's low. I've a nose for it. Likely to be a sharp epidemic before it goes to ground, I fancy.' He sat back on the cushions, the springs creaking as we turned into the King's Road. 'Your uncle Humphry's wine is not fit to be offered Christians. Unless with the intention of turning them into abstemious Mahommedans.'

'Perhaps it is bottled specially for the Church, sir? It seems to make a man soberer the more he drinks of it.'

'Of course, he's frightened that his flock will turn into mules, if Mr Darwin conjures away Heaven and Hell in an afternoon. Who's going to give a fig then for canonicals and tithes? Once people don't have the choice of life eternal or eternal fire and brimstone, but don't go anywhere particular once they're dead? Not that I favour any doctrine which encourages public indiscipline,' he said, as though that were an affliction like the cholera. 'Look at the Reform Act. It snatched government from responsible hands and

22

thrust it into those of Tom, Dick and Harry, who have little stake in the country and less concern for its destinies. By the by, Mr Darwin lives at the bottom of a cart-track, he's a chronic invalid with ten children, seven surviving. Trying to prove his own theories, I suppose.'

The journey to Down *was* damnably awkward. In 1854 the railway companies had not spun their net across London to turn the descendants of Bob Cratchit into the forebears of Mr Pooter. Breeched and booted, I took the Brighton Company's line to Norwood, and hired a hack for ten miles on the white, ridged, powdery roads of the North Downs. The swallows and vivid butterflies were swooping and hovering over the hedgerows, the fat fields of Kent held lines of men scything the harvest, a thin finger from a cottage chimney announced a woman's concern with dinner. The village of Down had a church, a few clean flint cottages and the Queen's Head, where I restored myself at mid-afternoon with brandy-and-water. I asked for Mr Darwin's house. The landlord told me jocularly to follow the homing pigeons. The Fellow of the Royal Society was an enthusiastic fancier.

The house looked as though four had been chopped and cemented together by a drunken mason. A piano played vigorously from one window, a voice sang lustily a different tune from another, the front door breathed the ammoniacal miasma of small children. They scurried before me like mice, sucking their thumbs at me round doorways, grinning at me across the banisters like gargoyles. The big downstairs study had a long central table with sealed jars of biological specimens, labelled plants in pots and scientific instruments. Papers were everywhere, even surrounding the chimney-piece in clipped bundles, like bunches of honeysuckle an arbour.

Mr Darwin came in. Or reeled in, complaining of a disabling headache. He was forty-five, tall and bald, a round face and stubby nose set off by a ring of brown hair, thick whiskers and heavy eyebrows, resembling a pink china mask to which the packing materials adhered. He dressed as a farmer after a good harvest.

23

'For ten years I have not known for one day the health of ordinary men,' he said immediately. 'Thus I have become a Kentish hog. The noise, the movement, the eternal complications of London were too much for me. I took the fever, you know, when I was in South America with the *Beagle*. Please sit down.'

I took a chair well away from him, fearing it was catching. Though I later discovered that Mr Darwin suffered from nothing more contagious than disordered nerves.

He asked if I had read Lyell's *Principles of Geology*. I apologized for being a classicist. 'That book taught me how the present could be interpreted from the past, in animals and man as in rocks.' He reached for the table, holding up a speck in a chemist's vial filled with spirit. 'Take this creature, barely visible to the eye, a slug from the seaweed of the Falkland Islands. It has its place in the natural order of things. Though finding it could alone take two or three years, if my health permits it.'

He replaced the vial delicately. 'Pray tell the bishop, Mr Darling, that I stepped aboard the *Beagle* in 1831 with my belief unshaken that every word of the Bible was strictly and literally true. That belief remained unshaken when I stepped ashore at Falmouth five years later. Doubt crept over me slowly. Its spark was struck – though I did not glimpse it – in the Galapagos Islands. You know of the Galapagos Islands, Mr Darling?'

'I am as big a geographical dunce as Homer, sir.' I had notebook open on knee.

'They are on the Equator. Off Ecuador. We reached there from that confounded country, Tierra del Fuego. I was instructed by the finches.'

'Finches?'

I grasped from him that each of the Galapagos Islands had its variety of finch, which had adapted itself to local conditions. 'Any finch which did *not* adapt would be eliminated in favour of those which did.' He held his aching head. 'My theory is of natural selection, or survival of the fittest. A moment's thought must tell you, Mr Darling, that many more individuals are born than could

24

possibly survive. In any species, including man. To exist is therefore to struggle.'

We were interrupted by Mrs Emma Darwin – he had married his elder cousin – marshalling the servants with tea, muffins, seed-cake, sandwiches, boiled eggs in knitted cosies. The Kentish hog had a full trough.

'So it follows,' he picked up his argument, muffin in one hand, head in the other, 'that any animal varying from the rest of its species, in any manner, however so slight, but *profitable to itself* must have an advantage. It must have a better chance of surviving. You see?'

I nodded. 'It is much the same, sir, surviving in London society.'

He looked at me blankly. 'In short, the species continues through the preservation of differences in each individual which are favourable, and the destruction of those which are injurious. We survive because we are selected to do so, by the balance of Nature.'

So we sat across a Kentish fireside quietly demolishing Genesis after two and a half millennia, over seed-cake. In my callowness, I did not know I faced a genius, one of the handfuls of humans who could disturb the world in its sleep. Scientific theories were rising and bursting in London at the time like the bubbles in hot porridge. Another afternoon that August, I interviewed another savant, but more red-blooded. He had been tried for high treason in Cologne, acquitted but expelled from Prussia, as quickly ejected from France and received within our compassionate coasts, to be regarded with the same comfortable terror as the ladies of England saw Garibaldi in 1864. The visit had an effect on my career indirect but immediate.

I called for the *Penny Pioneer* upon Mr Karl Marx in his poky upstairs rooms at No 16 Dean Street, Soho. They reeked of coffee and cigars, and in my mind of gunpowder, burning and blood. He was a revolutionary whose scratching pen at night caused wounds from workmen's knives in the morning. A Jew, slight, square headed, delicate fingered, with a cascade of beard, he dressed as respectably as a senior clerk in the City. He existed on political articles for the *New York Daily Tribune*. Now his books are hard to find, his political neck broken by the failure of his International Working Men's Association, his political notion that labour is the source of all wealth discredited by our prosperity won by adventurous financiers. He is safely buried like an Englishman in Highgate Cemetery.

I was shown out afterwards by a maid-of-all-work in a crumpled dress and dragging stockings. A blazing day had reached a sultry twilight. A familiar voice shouted at me from Dean Street.

'You, sir! Stay where you are. You thief and cheat. Angus! Draw 'em up,' Wakley-Barlow ordered from his carriage window to his coachman on the box.

5

I THOUGHT instantly of flight, as quickly rejected it as undignified. With my back against the blistered green paint of Mr Karl Marx's front door, Wakley-Barlow approached pointing his cane like a rapier. I raised my hat. 'Good evening, sir. I trust I see you well?'

'In better health than you shall be in a minute or two, if you don't return my three sovereigns.'

'I fear they are long spent, sir. As you will readily understand, from your earlier philosophizing on my miserable station in life.'

He demanded furiously, 'Why have you not done some lampoon on Miss Nightingale?'

'Literary work of my quality cannot be produced overnight. *Childe Harold*, which you mentioned at our last meeting, took Lord Byron almost ten years.'

His face was a foot away, his belly pressed the single button on my swallow-tailed coat. 'I should have known! You're a damned cowardly scoundrel like your father, and a faithless money-grubber like your whore of a mother.'

'Would not your language be a little exaggerated for a Parliamentarian, sir?' I enquired mildly. I had decided my action, which was to be exciting, against my nature and unique in my whole life.

'It's what you deserve,' he roared at me.

'And that, sir,' I said, punching him simultaneously in stomach and face, 'is what you do.'

Wakley-Barlow fell into the filth, crying, 'Angus!' His coachman had already thrown the reins to a boy, who was regarding the incident with screeching amusement. He jumped from the box with his whip. The notion of flight reappeared in my mind, in a far more favourable light.

I ran into Soho Square, remembering with panic that at Rugby I came last in the Crick. Angus was large, young and red-faced, crying in broad Scots, 'Stop thief!', which luckily in Soho had no more effect than a shout of 'Fire!' in Hell. I dodged into Frith Street. I slipped on something rotten, and ran headlong into a lady, to whom I breathlessly made apologies.

'Mr Darling—!'

'Miss Bancroft—!'

'You would seem in a hurry.'

'I am being pursued by a man with a horsewhip.'

'Surely not unusual for a gentleman in your profession? Come with me.'

She took my hand, as though I were a child.

The houses in Frith Street are well-to-do. We slipped between a pair of them, and I found myself in a crooked alley, barely wide enough for two abreast. Miss Bancroft said nothing. She wore the same black dress, with a shawl and a plain black bonnet tied under her chin. The alley led into a narrow street which ran between the main thoroughfares of Soho. I doubted if the respectable residents of Frith Street ever braved it, or even admitted its existence. Miss Bancroft had led me into the slums.

'He won't follow you here,' she assured me.

The houses were half brick, half wood, all looking ready to collapse with a shove at one end of the row. They were human rookeries. Men and women sat in every doorway, leant from every window, lolled against every wall. The roadway had lost much of its cobbles, to become rutted and garnished with excrement which was not exclusively animal. There was a dead cat, a living donkey. A shattered pitcher, a holed bucket, a broken patten. No shred of old clothes, no dry crust, no strayed lump of coal, all being too valuable for the inhabitants. The chimney pots pointed from the huddled roofs in several directions, like the frenzied fingers of a madman trying to tear from his suffocating cell.

'What's the name of this place?'

28

'Cholera Court. Well, that's Miss Nightingale's name for it. It furnishes us with one or two cases a day.'

In an open doorway, a human bundle lay enveloped in a ragged blanket. A man leant smoking his short clay pipe from the window above. Outside, children were laughing as happily, and playing as ingeniously, as those in Berkeley Square. I shivered.

'You too would be on nodding terms with death if you lived here, Mr Darling.'

'You venture into so dangerous a place alone?' My concern over Angus was replaced by the likelihood of the bystanders turning upon our fine clothes and having us run an unpleasant gauntlet.

'Oh, I'm perfectly safe. I'm known as the cholera lady. In my company, they'll take you for a medical man.'

'Everyone knows there is cholera in London. But I didn't know that people were dying of it under the eaves of gentlefolk.'

'The slums are of little interest to the readers of newspapers. Surely you know that, Mr Darling?'

'Where do you take the sufferers? The nursing home?'

'Oh, that would never do. They are hardly gentlewomen. The Ladies' Committee would overrule even Miss Nightingale. We have asked leave of absence to nurse them at the Middlesex Hospital. Why not come with me now, to call upon Miss Nightingale? Yes, you must,' she said, as decisively as her mistress. 'It isn't far. Last time you came to us with unkindness in your heart. Now you can see what Miss Nightingale is doing for these poor wretches. You will be moved, I'm sure of it.'

I never wished to meet Miss Nightingale again in my life. But I relished half a mile's company of Miss Bancroft, my feelings were already stirred by the poor humans round me, I was curious to see what became of them.

We emerged suddenly into Oxford Street, busy with hansoms, carriages and omnibuses, the world going home to sup or out to dine. I flicked a farthing to the ragged-trousered boy with the crossing-sweeper's broom. The Middlesex Hospital was a pleasant building, two wings embracing a court, set in a small garden behind railings. Miss Bancroft walked through the front entrance with a brisk step. I followed, for the second time that evening affected with fear. I had never been before into a cholera ward, nor a ward of any hospital.

I found myself in a room the size of a church in a prosperous parish. The ceiling was whitewashed, the walls covered with umber distemper, a dozen windows down each side were open to the airless twilight, with which conspired a low fire beneath kettle and cauldron in the grate. It held thirty sturdy beds with canopies and curtains at their heads, above each a shelf for bottles of medicine, mug, metal plate and spittoon, under each a chamberpot. The floorboards were bare and stained, the furniture rough tables and benches, the upholstered chair was a single luxury and the decorations framed notices of the hospital regulations.

Every bed was occupied by one or two women and children, white and pinch-faced against the blankets. More were laid on the floor between and down the central aisle, some were on palliasses, some on the boards. Some were moaning, some writhing, some dribbling, some vomiting, some were still, some were open-mouthed and expressionless, all reeked of sweat, excreta, sickness and death.

In the middle was Miss Nightingale, as though welcoming me to her drawing-room.

'Well, Mr Darling! Have you come to mock us again?'

She wore the same black dress and lace cap, hands clasped reposefully before her. Behind her conversed two young men, one in a fustian waistcoat with flashy buttons, the other with loud plaid trousers, both smoking cigars, who from their lack of affliction by or concern with the surrounding misery I assumed to be medical students.

'If I succeeded here,' I told her feelingly, 'you could salute me as a second Alexander Pope.'

The gentlewomen's nursing home, with its smell of soap and limewater, its polished boards and patent bells and unrustling nurses, I had found amusingly genteel, petty and sentimental. This parade of poverty, dirt and illness changed cholera from a comfortably remote abstraction to shocking reality. There is an immense difference between hearing of a battle and seeing a man freshly wounded in it – as I was to find with unexpected dispatch.

I jerked round, at a screech from the doorway. A bedraggled woman, her tawdry gown torn and muddied round the hem, her dyed hair lank, face chalky under the paint and dirt, age uncertain, was being half-carried in by a hospital porter.

'Take your hands away! I'm a lady, I'll have you know.' She had grotesque grandeur. 'But a week ago, I was in silk and satins. In silk and satins! Dancing at Woolwich.' She looked down at herself, voice fading. 'For all I am so dirty, I am draped in silks and satins sometimes, real French silks and satins.' Her eyes met Miss Nightingale. 'I am a nurse, ma'am, like you, earning my five guineas a week, nursing ladies. But it goes. . . .'

Her legs slowly crumpled, either through her disease or the spirits she had taken to relieve it. I was struck by the creature's fight to preserve *herself*, an individual of rags, paint, dirt and vice, but a human being different from every other on earth, even in sight of impartial death.

'These are nearly all women of the unfortunate class,' Miss Nightingale told me in her matter-of-fact way, as two of the broad-aproned, big-bonneted hospital nurses caught the new arrival and searched for a place among the crammed humans. 'From Soho, Seven Dials, Drury Lane. At night, they come in every half hour, staggering off their beat. All filthy, often drunken, always frightened. The hospital has had to empty itself of usual patients to receive them.'

'What can you do for the wretches?' I asked, appalled.

'We put them to bed and wash them. We apply our turpentine stupes. Sometimes they recover, more often they are dead of the cholera within hours, dry as a stick, their stomach and bowels unable to hold even a mouthful of water.'

I frowned half in mystification, half in anger. 'But what causes this dreadful illness?'

'Overcrowding and accumulated filth. *Not* contagion.

31

That is an invention of some London doctors, which I equate with witchcraft and superstition. The contagion theory of spreading disease,' she said forthrightly, 'is disproved by good sanitation, which stops the outbreaks of fever whenever it is introduced.'

Miss Nightingale had a passionate disbelief in germs, and a lasting one. I heard that in her seventies she revoked a legacy for a professorial chair of statistics, lest the money be blown by the breeze of modern ideas 'to endow some bacillus or microbe'. She did not believe in specific diseases, only in unhealthy conditions. Her panacea was sanitation.

'So if you provide better sanitation for the slums, you would provide their denizens with half a lifetime?' I suggested.

'You might as well talk of providing them with £100 apiece. Where's the money coming from?'

'Some politician might be persuaded to prick the public conscience.' The only one of my acquaintance being Mr Wakley-Barlow, the plan seemed unpromising. Then it struck me that I could translate his own plot from evil to good. 'I could raise an outcry by writing of this room for the *Penny Pioneer*, in such a way that its readers would eat their breakfast with an uneasy conscience, if they could face it at all.'

'What? Are you changing from a gossip to a scold? You'll be for the ducking-stool next. Well, I should readily enlist you in the service of sanitation, Mr Darling. As I remarked, you are a clever little devil.'

A woman in the bed beside us, eyes staring at the ceiling, made a low moaning noise as though blowing bubbles deep in her throat.

'There is no point in hiding your light under a bushel, Miss Nightingale, if the bushel doesn't burst into flames. Nobody in Town knows your name. But unlike other philanthropists, you risk both your health and your susceptibilities. No other ladies but yourself and Miss Bancroft could face these horrors.'

'The sick are *not* horrible,' she told me sharply. 'They must be nursed. And they must rely too often on such women as you have just seen received. Women who have lost their characters, who you would find in the beds of the male patients, who are subject to liberties by the surgeons and dressers, and who are nourished mainly by spirits. Of course, there are nuns. I could have turned nun, to nurse with social impunity. But Roman Catholicism does not appeal to me. I distrust its easy enchantments, its self-discipline is for me unnecessary. Not that I am much impressed by the Church of England, either. It has for men bishoprics, archbishoprics and a little work. For women, it has what?'

She gave the impression of readiness to reorganize either religion on sound practical principles, if given its topmost job. Then she turned abruptly to the moaning woman, who now lay quiet, bright yellow fluid dribbling from the corner of her mouth. With a shock, I saw that she was no more. For the first time, I had heard the death-rattle.

6

THE COLD WIND first blew from the Crimea on October 12
1854.

It was a lunatic war, madder than our antics in South
Africa – an insanity made clear to readers of the *Daily
Pioneer*, particularly those who were incited to burn it in
public. The Russians and the Turks had fought regularly,
every twenty years for two centuries, hurting no one but
themselves. We went to war because the British Army
had gone without a battle since 1815, and having beaten
Napoleon must be usefully invincible. Wellington's cannonade still deafened military ears, and was about to kill 16,334
unwounded British soldiers.

There was a squabble over the Holy Places at Bethlehem –
the Turkish police shot a Russian monk or two – pain-
stakingly aggravated by our cleverly devious ambassador,
Lord Stratford de Redcliffe, and the cleverly bombastic
French one, the Marquis de la Valette. Czar Nicholas I
had just dropped his famous sigh over Turkey, 'We have
on our hands a sick man – a very sick man,' and Lord
Aberdeen's Coalition took fright that the Czar might
dismember the corpse before the invalid obliged by dying.
That would never do, the Czar in Constantinople, astride
the route to India. Even if he proposed to let us grab
unmolested Rhodes, Crete and Egypt as compensation.

Then the Russian fleet sank a Turkish flotilla off Sinope
on the north Turkish coast, their new Paixhans naval shells
splintering old wooden walls like garden fencing, dis-
gracefully disregarding the Royal Navy anchored in
minatory majesty in the Bosphorus. Palmerston resigned

34

in disgust, within a month howled back to office. The mediating Prince Albert found himself vilified as a Russian catspaw. John Bull shook his daily newspaper in his clenched fist and roared for war. John Bright shook his head and told the House of Commons the enduring truth, 'If war be not itself a crime, it is the inevitable parent of innumerable crimes'.

Our allies were the French. They had a brand new Emperor, happy to stimulate his subjects with a little war, and to smudge a map of Europe newly drawn on his uncle's departure to St Helena. The Russians' allies were the Austrians, but their brand new Emperor Franz-Josef had the sense to wriggle out. The war should anyway have been fought in the Baltic, not the Black Sea. The Crimea was a sideshow which grew like a deadly fungus.

While Admiral Sir Charles Napier was banging about ineffectively off St Petersburg, our troops which started as an 'Army of Observation' at Malta in spring, and in summer sailed to Bulgaria, were landing on the west coast of 'Crim Tartary', the Crimean peninsula. Our plan was to guillotine the Crimea, with its fortress, arsenal and dockyard of Sebastopol, at its neck with Russia. But we discovered on the spot a sea too shallow to bear a ship within sight of shore. Our commander was Lord Raglan, veteran of another Peninsula. He was so wedded to his experience as Wellington's aide-de-camp, that he generally referred to his present enemy as 'the French'.

The bloody little battle of the Alma river was fought on September 20, a victory acclaimed and expected. For the well-nourished middle class at home, the war pinched only as an official excuse for postponing the abolition of income-tax, an innovation which has occurred to no British Government since.

On that October Thursday, I had gone as usual about eleven in the morning to the *Penny Pioneer* offices in Salisbury Square off Fleet Street. They were only a couple of rooms with plain deal walls, scampering with messenger boys. Copy and proofs were strewn everywhere, impaled on spikes, or on nails between the batteries of brass speaking tubes. At inky desks with green-shaded gas-lamps, liberally scattered with bottles and tankards, men in their hats and their shirtsleeves worked amid the pots of paste and scissors on chains, closely and sometimes frenziedly together like sailors below decks, an impression emphasized by the regular thud of the steam presses next door, as unending as the engines at sea.

I picked from the floor a copy of that morning's *Times*. It carried a dispatch from 'Our Special Correspondent', dated Constantinople, September 30. That was Mr William Howard Russell, whom I had often seen in the Cheshire Cheese opposite. He was a short, thick-set man with a florid face richly decorated with black hair and whiskers, lavish in his consumption of brandy-and-water and cigars, particularly at someone's expense. It was hard to escape his brogue telling his ring of admirers stories which, like any Irishman's, were always ludicrous and always too long. Sometimes he burst into song. I had taken a dislike to him on sight, which can be as persistent and often as illogical as one painfully developed by acquaintance.

It is with feelings of surprise and anger that the public will learn that no sufficient preparations have been made for the proper care of the wounded, Russell wrote.

Not only are there not sufficient surgeons – that, it might be urged, was unavoidable; not only are there no dressers and nurses – that might be a defect of system for which no one is to blame; but what will be said when it is known that there is not even linen to make bandages for the wounded? The greatest commiseration prevails for the sufferings of the unhappy inmates of Scutari, and every family is giving sheets and old garments to supply their want. But why could not this clearly foreseen want have been supplied? Can it be said that the Battle of the Alma has been an event to take the world by surprise? Has not the expedition to the Crimea been the talk of the last four months?

I was interrupted by the copy-boy poking my ribs, bringing a galley-proof of my own article for our next morning's edition. I could not take my eyes from Russell's work. Mine was about Miss Nightingale and the cholera,

36

written to put the British public off its breakfast. Russell's would have soured the milk and rotted the eggs.

And when the Turks gave up to our use the vast barracks to form a hospital and depot, was it not on the ground that the loss of the English troops was sure to be considerable when engaged in so dangerous an enterprise? continued Mr John Delane's man at the war.

And yet, after the troops have been six months in the country, there is no preparation for the commonest surgical operations! Not only are the men kept, in some cases, for a week without the hand of a medical man coming near their wounds; not only are they left to expire in agony, unheeded and shaken off, though catching desperately at the surgeon whenever he makes his rounds through the fetid ship; but now, when they are placed in the spacious building, where we were led to believe that everything was ready which could ease their pain or facilitate their recovery, it was found that the commonest appliances of a workhouse sick-ward were wanting, and that the men must die through the medical staff of the British army having forgotten that old rags are necessary for the dressing of wounds.

How feeble, how ill-disciplined my own attack, I thought. I glanced regretfully at the proof in my hand. I had discovered some terrible facts. The cholera had killed 10,000 Londoners over the summer, 500 in an area of Soho barely 250 yards across. But I could find no phrase more pungent than labelling the Chairman of the Westminster vestrymen, who was responsible for the drains, 'Defender of the Filth'. I finished Russell's dispatch.

The manner in which the sick and wounded are treated is worthy only of the savages of Dahomy. The worn-out pensioners who were brought as an ambulance corps are totally useless. There are no dressers or nurses to carry out the surgeon's directions, and to attend to the sick during the intervals between his visits. Here the French are greatly our superiors. Their medical arrangements are extremely good, their surgeons more numerous, and they have the help of 50 Sisters of Charity who have accompanied the expedition. Why have we no Sisters of Charity? There are numbers of able-bodied and tender-hearted English women who would joyfully and with alacrity go out to devote themselves to nursing the sick and wounded, if only they could be associated for that purpose, and placed under proper protection.

That picture of the Scutari hospitals, across the Bosphorus from Constantinople, aroused immediately in the country resentment and its spouse anger, bearing their child, pity. So much was to be read in the faces of men going to work, heard in the voices of women at the washtub. Seldom have I seen such national indignation fired by a newspaper, to be expressed as hotly inside a penny omnibus as inside the Reform Club. (I must admit sometimes trying to engineer it, and sometimes successfully, though most regrettably from political expedience or simply to increase circulation.)

But nobody was much interested in my cholera. It was the Charon of the Thames, but it plied not for the hire of decent persons who kept clean houses. That Miss Nightingale should invade the wards of the Middlesex Hospital was seen by the gentry as perverse, disgusting behaviour for a lady.

Its best effect was bringing me nearer to Miss Bancroft in the writing. I do not believe that I was in love with her, a condition which inflicts more widespread misery among young people than poor dentition. I was too full of innocently conceited *joie de vivre* readily to share myself with another. But I had overheard her name as Jane, and I was piqued at seeing no chance of advancing my intimacy with a pretty woman unadhesive from Miss Nightingale.

Meanwhile, I had Harriet. That same Thursday afternoon, I lay on the lavender-scented bed amid the forget-me-not wallpaper in Brompton, when a loud double-knock sounded at the front door.

Harriet sat up with a shriek. 'Mr Larderton!'

'What nonsense. It's the butcher's boy or the muffin man.'

'My God! I'm done for.'

She was scrambling into her drawers. I lay on the bed, unclothed and unconcerned. Last time, it had been the rag-and-bone man.

'Tristram! The window – you always said you would.'

'I should break the roof of the conservatory.'

'Oh! Go, go! Please, please go!' She was trying to clasp her stays, laces flying like whips. I was amused at the pretty frenzy of her response to a false alarm. The bedroom door opened, and Mr Larderton came in.

He did not in the slightest match his image. He was skinny and short, with thin gingery hair and meagre whiskers edging a peaky face. He resembled a jockey in a frock-coat and black cravat for a funeral.

'Why aren't you in Newmarket?' demanded Harriet furiously.

'My horse was scratched.'

His glance transfixed me. I was already off the bed and into my trousers. 'This is too much,' he said quietly.

'The gentleman is my cousin.'

'I don't think that makes any difference.'

I was scrambling into my shirt. I was incapable of thought, my fright shameful. My youthful amours had been too hesitant, too clumsy or too scorned to lead me such a naked dance before. I expected Mr Larderton to draw a pistol and shoot me. Instead, he sat on a wicker chair and cupped his forehead in his hands.

He said sorrowfully, 'Harriet, you promised there would be no more.'

'But lovey-dovey! There *are* no others. 'Pon my honour.'

'I don't believe you,' he responded more forcefully. 'How did you meet this man?'

'He is a gentleman who made himself agreeable to me, when you abandoned me for your betting and champagne drinking at Epsom.' Harriet tried to sound dignified, as her stays slipped unheeded from breasts still warm with my attentions.

I paused, collar half secured. 'Harriet—! Do I understand there have been others? Here?' I glanced sympathetically at Mr Larderton, as he drew his handkerchief and started to weep. 'You have not been faithful to either of us,' I complained.

'Shut up,' said Harriet.

I took heart. I was no single enemy of Mr Larderton's but one of a platoon. To satisfy his honour, he would need not a duelling pistol but a Colt revolver. 'As the cause of your present distress, I must apologize, sir. But may I ask you to share my point of view? Such beauty as you have chosen for your own is clearly too tempting for many a hot-blooded young man.'

'Who are you?' he asked bleakly.

'A literary gentleman, sir.'

'I should have thought as much.'

Harriet began to cry, as piercingly as an ass at the full moon. She collapsed on the silk coverlet, head in hands, elbows on bare thighs, golden hair curtaining perfect shoulders, heaving with violent sobs. Only I seemed to have escaped the contagion of misery. I continued tying my white cravat in her dressing-table mirror.

'You're acquainted with the others, I suppose?' he asked me, looking at Harriet severely. 'Harry, Billy, Andy, I don't know.'

'I am as ignorant of them, sir, as you were of me.'

'You will quit this house immediately.'

'That was entirely my intention.'

Harriet shrieked. 'Don't leave me!'

'But surely another protector will shortly be along, with the regularity of the penny omnibus?' I asked. I was more furious than Mr Larderton with my temptress. She was nothing but a Haymarket whore. That at least spared me the moral obligation of averting her beating, or sharing it.

'Tristram, my only love—!' She crammed both sets of knuckles between her teeth, sobbing like a bellows at damp coals.

'Sir, may I offer you my hand?' I extended it to Mr Larderton. 'We are brothers in misfortune—'

'Go, go, damme, and don't talk so much,' he shouted.

Little Nell was clutching the banisters at the foot of the stairs, eyes like oyster-shells. 'Oh, lawks, sir! Is she dead?'

'Mr Larderton is too sensitive a person to take away Miss Harriet's life. Or even her living, I suspect.'

'Are you hurt, sir?' She was searching me for blood.

'You never mentioned the others to me,' I said accusingly.

'It wasn't my place, sir. Besides, I never mentioned you to them.'

'Were there many?'

'I shouldn't like to say, sir.' I handed her a silver coin. Turning crimson, she told me, 'Yes, many, sir. And some not so young.'

'No wonder the nights were denied me,' I sighed.

Little Nell bobbed, showing me out. I heard more sobs from upstairs. If Mr Larderton flushed Harriet from the nest, she had a comfortable supply of bird-seed.

7

ABOUT ELEVEN O'CLOCK the following night I left the *Penny Pioneer* office after handing my evening's work to the editor. He was a fat, red-faced man called Horncastle, with the peculiarity of wearing country clothes in Town, giving him the excuse when necessary of carrying a riding-crop for solicitors' clerks with writs. My copy was my customary gossip, gathered impartially from ballrooms and backdoors, fops and footmen, peeresses and parlourmaids. People are always free with malice about others, if sufficiently indebted to them.

I crossed Salisbury Square as usual to Daley's Rooms, part chop-house and part tavern, sawdust-floored with high-backed stalls, smoky gas and disagreeable waiters. My finery would have provoked in similar places ribaldry or a cheese-rind through the air, but Fleet Street even then was an area of quips and cranks, where anything passed.

As I left after eating, a small man I had noticed staring in my direction, in poor clothing and with the look of a short-tempered ferret, rose, followed me, and laid a hand on my arm. 'Guv'nor, I've a small proposition,' he said in a hoarse Cockney voice.

Propositions from the lower classes were my bread and butter. I asked his name, but he replied predictably, 'Never you mind.' He jerked his head. I followed him towards an alley guarded by a gas-lamp, which tumbled downhill to the blackness and stink of the river.

'What's it about?'

'About a Member of Parliament.' He led me into the dark. 'Listen, Guv'nor—'

He stopped, looked furtively up and down the empty

alley, and it was too late, the knife was already in his hand.

I instinctively kicked, but he jumped back on his toes like a pugilist. For a second which lasted to eternity, I felt the fear of death. My life would certainly have ended that night, were not a window thrown open above and the contents of a chamberpot, destined for the gutter, emptied on our heads.

I ran headlong for the gaslight, faster than from Angus and his whip. Breathless I found a cab, arrived home still shaking, to spend a trembling night empty of sleep. Who was my thwarted assassin? A common footpad after a dandy's watch? The paid executioner of Mr Larderton? He could easily have forced my name from the shattered Harriet. Or of Mr Wakley-Barlow? That seemed most likely, from the man's careless reference to an MP. Or someone else I had hurt with my pen? My occupation grew enemies like a wheatfield tares, though it was not one worth the life of a harvest mouse.

The timorous hour of dawn saw my decision to abandon the life of a tattler. My existence had been spared for something more worthy. But what? My uncle Peregrine had long offered the post of steward to his Berkshire estate, but there I should die only more lingeringly of boredom. More immediately, I must buy new clothes. I could hardly attend Lady Canning's *soirée* that same Saturday evening smelling of piss. I knew that Miss Nightingale would be there, and – I particularly hoped after losing Harriet – Miss Bancroft.

That day felt the first dank breath of autumn. The slates ran damp, and by evening the mist was clinging round the chimney-pots with the promise of lodging there, and in the lungs of Londoners, till next Easter. A fire leapt at both ends of the Cannings' cream and gold reception-room. It was already full when I arrived, gas glittering on diamonds and orders, three pale musicians in the corner intruding Chopin diffidently upon such splendid company. I had only few invitations to such great houses, generally from politicians seeking a puff, like the Crystal Palace removers with their free tickets. I was received as a gentle-man, which I was, if not acting as one. From practice, my eye first sought the liberality of the supper-table, then the footman with the champagne. It met next that of my uncle Humphry, in full episcopal fig.

He was staring at me in amazement, past a man holding him in conversation, who was about sixty, with a Roman nose, a strong chin, short curly grey hair retreating from a noble brow and an air of importance.

I could not fly. I did not wish to. It was going to be amusing. I listened to their talk, out of habit. My uncle's companion seemed a friend of Sir Peregrine.

'I was taken to St George's Hospital to see the chloro-form tried,' he was saying. 'A boy two years old was cut by Sir Peregrine for a stone. The stone was so large, and the bladder so contracted, he could not get hold of it, and the operation lasted above twenty minutes. Being performed under chloroform, it was exactly the same as operating on a dead body. A curious example was then shown of what is called the *étiquette* of the medical profession,' he continued in a comfortably amused voice. 'Sir Peregrine could not extract the stone, so handed the instrument to Keate, who is the finest operator possible, and he got hold of it.'

He did not appear to notice having lost his hearer's attention. 'Sir Peregrine begged to have the forceps back that he might draw it out, but he let go of it, the whole thing had to be done over again, not of course without increasing the local inflammation and endangering the life of the child. I later asked Keate why. He said that Sir Peregrine's 'dignity' would have been hurt, if he had not been allowed to complete what he had begun.'

He laughed. The bishop frowned. He had been entirely distracted by the mystery of sharing the same nobleman's reception-room as myself.

'All the great discoveries of science sink into insignifi-cance compared with chloroform,' the surgical onlooker ended floridly. 'Wonderful as are the powers and feats of the steam engine and the electric telegraph, the chloroform far transcends them all in its beneficent and consolatory

44

operations. Sir?' he added sharply and disconcertingly, fixing my intrusive face with a resentful glare.

The bishop had no choice but introduce his nephew. He indicated to me grudgingly, 'Mr Charles Greville, Clerk of the Privy Council.'

I had heard of Mr Greville. I knew that he was connected with the Cannings. He was connected with all the most powerful families in the land, which combined sadly with his comparatively lowly official post, but happily with his avidity for talking about everyone behind their backs. A useful man for me to know. But I could not. I was too far below him in both social standing and his own estimation.

He went to sow anecdotes in other ears, leaving the bishop staring at me blankly. I observed politely, 'I suppose it was inevitable, sir, that you and I should meet some time in society?'

'Inevitable? Why?'

'By the by, I hope you found my notes on Mr Darwin's conversation adequate?'

'What? Oh, yes. Quite adequate.' He continued to frown. 'I am reassured that he is about to attack the Book of Genesis with nothing more savage than a pair of Equatorial finches.'

The next instant, the bishop could have been in the Galapagos Islands himself. I was facing Miss Bancroft.

'Mr Darling! Great things are happening tonight. Mr Sidney Herbert is coming—' She stopped, aware of her impetuous impoliteness. I rapidly introduced His Lordship the Bishop of Chelsea. She bobbed. 'Mr Darling's pen has been at the disposal of Miss Nightingale, my Lord,' she explained.

My uncle looked even more puzzled. 'It is good to hear of a young poet so much in demand.'

'Poet, my Lord? Oh, but you must read the *Penny Pioneer*—'

'I certainly shall not!'

'Mr Darling is the newspaper's clever gossip writer. Everyone in society knows that, and is frightened to death of him,' she said smilingly.

'Tristram! Is this right?'

'Miss Bancroft is incapable of uttering untruths, sir, as I am sure you can tell from her angelic expression.'

The bishop's face worked. I was condemned to Hell, if Mr Darwin left it intact. 'I suspected that you were up to some such knavery. Will you kindly take note, sir, that I always thought your pretensions to be a literary gentleman were as false as the metre of your Virgilian verses. Good evening.'

Miss Bancroft was amazed. 'Why is he so cross?'

'He is my uncle.'

She put her hand to her mouth, blushed, but after a second laughed. '*J'ai fait un faux pas,*' she apologized, sharing Miss Nightingale's weakness for a French phrase.

'He will never ask me to dine again,' I said cheerfully. 'Which is delightful, because his wine is as vinegary as his opinions.'

We each took a glass of champagne from the footman's silver tray. The band respectfully ventured a polka.

'I know your christian name is Jane. May I use it?'

'No, Mr Darling. You may not.'

'We are surely too young to wear formality like the old wear rouge and whiskers? Do you still think me a monster?'

'No, only a midge, which can cause exaggerated irritation from a tiny bite.'

'Shall I buzz away?'

'A midge can keep you amused on a dull summer's day.' I saw Miss Nightingale across the room, in a green silk gown which I felt sure to be incapable of rustle. Miss Bancroft's was brown, hardly more showy than her working uniform. 'But I have more serious work to do than encouraging a young man's gallantry.'

'There is no more serious work for any woman.'

'Only for women so self-satisfied with their sex as you obviously are with yours.'

The room abruptly fell quiet. Mr Sidney Herbert had hurried in.

He was tall, brown-haired, handsome, with long straight brows and long soft mouth, clean-shaven, gracefully

46

patrician, just turned forty-four and immensely rich. He wore dark day clothes with a high collar and black stock, and like all Government ministers the bustling air of tearing himself from momentous duties to which he must impatiently return. His fine eyes were saucered in shadows. I thought even then that he looked ill.

He was Secretary at War in Lord Aberdeen's Cabinet. Secretary *at* occupied a different kennel among our dogs of war than Secretary *of*, who was the Duke of Newcastle. The Duke did the fighting, Mr Herbert balanced the ledgers. He was a senior accounting official, like several score others buried under the candle ends and cheeseparings of Whitehall.

I had heard something whispered about Sidney Herbert. He was related to the enemy. His mother was the daughter of a Czar's former ambassador to the Court of St James's. There was a link of stranger metal. In the Crimea, the Worontzoff Road which ran across the Chersonese Peninsula, and in the autumn of 1854 was coming into the fighting and London conversation, led to the palace of his uncle. This road was shortly to edge the most concentrated disaster in British military stupidity.

The room parted instinctively, as he made directly for Miss Nightingale.

'You know how much Mr Herbert has ventured beyond his official responsibilities?' Miss Bancroft said to me, face flushed with eagerness. 'He has taken charge himself of the military hospitals.'

'Then he is an angel who has rushed in where fools fear to tread. The whole Town is after his blood, since Mr Russell's dispatches in this week's *Times*.'

'He has always had a philanthropic interest in the sick. And of course, he is well acquainted with Miss Nightingale, since they met in Rome five or more years back.'

I edged away. I should have revelled in an evening chatting to Miss Bancroft, but my instinct for news was more compelling than a foxhound's nose.

Miss Nightingale met him with a delighted smile. 'Did you have my letter?'

I *had* to overhear what was said.

'No. Had you mine? Then they must be crossing this moment in the post. That's a promising coincidence.'

'Should I believe *The Times*?' she asked bluntly.

'Not wholly. Medical stores have been sent out East in profusion, I assure you. Lint by the ton weight, fifteen thousand pairs of sheets, medicine, wine, arrowroot, all comforts for the sick, in the same proportion. The only way of accounting for the deficiency at Scutari – if it exists – is that the mass of stores went to Varna in Bulgaria, and were not sent back when the army left there for the Crimea.'

A silent, curious room recovered its manners and resumed chattering brightly, though I noticed that few listened to another. Even the band had meekly stopped.

'But four days would have remedied this,' Herbert continued in his brisk way. 'Meanwhile, fresh stores are arriving daily. And thirty more surgeons, though the medical officers with the army stand already at one for every ninety-five men. Which is nearly double what we have ever had before.'

He ended the rapid catalogue of self-justification with, 'But there is a great deficiency – female nurses. As you must see, it is impossible to carry a staff of female nurses with the army in the field. But at Scutari, no military reason exists against their introduction. I have already received numbers of offers of ladies to go out.'

'But these are ladies who have no conception of what a hospital is.'

'Exactly. They would either recoil from the work, or be entirely useless, or what is worse entirely in the way.'

'Mr Herbert, Lady Maria Forster has sent me £200 to organize a small private expedition of five nurses. I have already seen Dr Andrew Smith of the Army Medical Department who would authorize us to go – if we feed and lodge ourselves there, and be no expense whatever to the country.'

'My dear Miss Nightingale!' he said ardently. 'There is but one person in England I know who would be capable of organizing and superintending such a scheme. I have several times been on the point of asking you hypothetically if you would. But we need forty nurses, not five,' he continued. 'Our new idea must be pushed on an impressive scale.'

'Forty? Then the selection will be difficult.'

'Of course the difficulty will be great,' he said candidly. 'Finding women equal to a task, after all, full of horrors. And requiring, besides knowledge and goodwill, immense energy and courage. The task of ruling them and introducing system among them will be great. And not least will be the difficulty of making the whole work smoothly with the medical and military authorities out there.' The footman with champagne stood impassive and unnoticed. 'I do not say one word to press you. But . . . your personal qualities, your knowledge and power of administration, and among greater things your rank and position in society, give you advantages in such work which no other person possesses.'

Miss Nightingale stood calmly, hands as usual clasped before her. Miss Bancroft was at my side. 'I chafe from three restraints.'

'Tell them,' he demanded.

'My Ladies' Committee at Harley Street—'

'Mrs Herbert has already released you,' he told her impatiently.

'And *Mr* Herbert—' She smiled. 'Would he give me advice, letters of recommendation? The medical staff at Scutari will be more frightened than amused at being bombarded by a parcel of women. You must say of me, "This is not a lady, but a real hospital nurse".'

'Miss Nightingale, deriving authority from the Government, your position would secure the respect and consideration of everyone. Especially in a service where official rank carries so much weight. This would secure to you every attention and comfort on your way there, and when you are there, together with complete submission to your orders. I know these things are a matter of indifference to you,' he ended flatteringly, 'except so far as they may further the great objects you have in view. But they are of every importance to those who have a right to take an interest in your personal position and comfort.'

Miss Nightingale nodded contentedly. I wondered if he had noticed in his eagerness her extraction from him of precise assurances about her position in the world of war. As I grew to know Miss Nightingale better, I recognized this characteristic of clear-headedness and caution, her sharp eye which could see a detail like an ant upon a landscape, combined with long sight for complications and consequences, and an ability for getting what she wanted out of human beings as stealthily as a pickpocket.

'What is your third impediment?'

'I must have the consent of my parents.'

He looked startled. 'But the request proceeds from the Government. Who represent the nation.'

She inclined her head graciously. 'Thus shall I put it to them. Are there stores you would advise us to take out? Dr Smith says that nothing is needed.'

'You may rely on Dr Smith's assurance about everything to do with Scutari. As Director-General of the Army Medical Department, he is responsible only to myself.'

I began sidling towards the door. I should miss my supper – silver dishes pebbled with scarlet lobsters, great golden raised pies caught my eye – but I had my tale and I must bear it at once to the steam-presses. The *Penny Pioneer* would publish a special edition for Sunday morning. Mr Horncastle would be delighted, and express it in sovereigns.

Miss Nightingale's voice lassoed me. I turned.

'Mr Darling, I know perfectly well that you have overheard all passing between Mr Herbert and myself, and that you are about to leave *sans mot dire* to write it all down for your newspaper. But I need your help.'

'Who's that?' demanded Herbert, looking as though I were the sweep's boy just appeared down the chimney.

'The gentleman who wrote the article about the cholera, which I admired and felt to be spirited and brave,' said Miss Nightingale generously.

'Cholera? What paper?'

'The *Penny Pioneer*,' she told him.

This caused Herbert to look at me as though I were the sweep's boy with spotty evidence of infective disease.

'Pen an advertisement tonight for forty nurses, ready to embark for Scutari,' Miss Nightingale directed. 'Where should they report?'

'My house, No 49 Belgrave Square. Any time of day,' said Herbert, addressing her, not myself.

'All shades of religious opinion may apply. Say that they are to work together in a common brotherhood of love to God and man,' Miss Nightingale continued in a business-like way. 'As for describing the work itself . . . well, they must know already what it entails and demands, any that do not, I shan't have them. Place it in the editorial matter, Mr Darling. Then there will be no charge incurred.'

'When can you leave?' Herbert asked her.

'Saturday.'

'*Next* Saturday?' he asked, amazed.

'Why not? A longer delay would only increase our importance here and diminish our usefulness there.'

'How shall you go?'

'To Paris, then take the steamer from Marseilles.'

'If you obtain your recruits,' he warned.

'And if I obtain my parents' permission.' She turned to me. 'Mr Darling, kindly be at Waterloo Station by four o'clock on Monday afternoon. I shall be leaving to visit my parents in Hampshire, and the journey will be my first chance of putting certain plans to you.'

'But Miss Nightingale! I have engagements in Town –'

'Oh, you need not stay in Hampshire. There is another train almost immediately back to London. Mr Herbert, will you take me on to see Mrs Herbert now in Belgrave Square? There are a thousand things to settle before morning. Miss Bancroft, kindly accompany us.'

They left me in the middle of the room, without another word. I had learned that a person once used by Miss Nightingale was discarded until again necessary to be taken in hand, like a golfer with his clubs.

51

8

'SO I WENT to Kaiserwerth to learn the prax. You know of Kaiserwerth, Mr Darling?'

'Is it not on the Rhine? Near Cologne?'

'Yes, it is an institute founded by Pastor Theodor Fliedner – a good and vigorous man. It is part asylum, school, teachers' college, penitentiary and hospital of a hundred beds. All conducted, of course, on the most advanced principles. I was four months there. Three years ago, while my dear mama and sister were taking the waters at Carlsbad. At Kaiserwerth, we were deaconesses. We wore blue print dresses and little white caps, we rose at five in the morning and worked till seven at night, with three breaks for gruel and broth. In the evening, we sat together in the great hall for Bible classes.'

She gave the impression of not enjoying it very much.

'The scenery was very fine. In its way. That broad mass of water, you know, flowing like the slow, calm, earnest, meditative German character. Pastor Fliedner's solemn and reverential teaching of the sad events of hospital life was something I have never heard in England.'

Miss Nightingale stared outside, as though searching for that metaphysical river flowing through an English countryside grey with twilight and drizzle, half obscured by the soot running with the rain down our carriage window. I sat opposite, comfortable on the buttoned horsehair of an empty first-class carriage, at Miss Nightingale's expense. She had provided the rugs, comforters, mittens, *Punch*, sandwiches – organizing a journey to Romsey Junction was trivial to one marshalling forty unknown and even unimaginable women for Scutari. Miss Bancroft had disappointingly been left in Harley Street.

'The nursing there was nil, the hygiene horrible. But it was the only training I had. A good nurse must be *well trained*. Do you know, I saw a poor woman die before my eyes in the village this summer, because there was none but fools to sit up with her. They poisoned her, as much as if they had given her arsenic. I saw an operation in Kaiserwerth. An amputation. But I dared not mention it to my dear sister, who would see no more in my interest in it than the pleasure dirty boys have, playing in the puddles about a butcher's shop. You will know, Mr Darling,' she confessed, 'because all London knows it, that my dear mother and sister, though loving and entertaining the highest ambitions for me socially, are obstinate and resentful over my chosen work. Which they do not understand, and treat as if I had come home from committing a crime.'

She had been talking as vivaciously since we had first puffed away from the Thames among the clean little villas of New Wandsworth. I never claimed I stood close to Miss Nightingale's heart. That would have been an exaggeration for any man, like a traveller feeling himself close to Pharaoh's tomb on the rugged outside of the massive pyramid. She spoke to me more freely than others because I was a professional listener who lived on intimacies. Or perhaps she was afraid of me, as society feared their urchin. Miss Nightingale knew from the start that I saw her secret. She had an intelligence which bit and a wit that stung, but the Pharaoh's tomb was empty. She was an impressive monument who had no heart.

'My family do not understand how women can suffer intensely from unused nervous energy, which makes them feel, every night when they go to bed, as if they were going mad.'

'But a nurse,' I objected, 'has no more social standing than a chambermaid who must every morning empty her master's slop bucket.'

'Hospital nurses are much abused. They have their faults, but most are due to want of proper treatment. They are lectured by committees, preached at by chaplains, scowled on by treasurers and stewards, scolded by matrons, sworn at by surgeons, bullied by students, grumbled at and abused by patients, insulted if old and ill-favoured, talked flippantly to if middle-aged and good humoured, tempted and seduced if young and well looking. They are what any woman might be under these circumstances.'

'So Sarah Gamp is as much a caricature as Mr Pecksniff?'

'Dickens! That incorrigible sentimentalist!'

'How I agree! He wells tears in the eyes of tradesmen's wives, like raw onions.'

There was a bond between us.

'Listen, Mr Darling. Salisbury Infirmary has been seeking "young, strong, *respectable* women who would be taught to look after sick people", since the end of the last century. Though when *I* intended to nurse there, it occasioned a vast consumption of sal volatile in my family. Admittedly, the poor are unsavoury to handle. Admittedly, I might have found myself touching men. Admittedly, there are *those things* heard about the surgeons and the nurses.' The brakes began to screech for Basingstoke. 'But the poor must go somewhere, having no homes to be sick in, amid the familiar attentions of their families, like the rest of us. Well, Mr Darling, our journey will be over before we reach our business. Will you come to Scutari?'

Such unexpected, such unbelievable an offer left me unable to speak. We began clanking into the station. Luckily, the normal shouting, slamming, whistling and waving of our stop at Basingstoke made no reply immediately necessary. I sat staring unseeingly through the window. Miss Nightingale sat frowning over *Punch*. When the London and South Western resumed their responsibilities towards us, Miss Nightingale explained her need for some deft pen to help with her correspondence, her reports, questions from the newspapers and dispatches to them.

'And you are indeed a clever little devil,' she informed me amiably. 'Besides, a man will counterbalance an

54

expedition weighted with femininity. You would be my secretary, to work with Miss Bancroft.'

An attractive prospect. But I objected, 'I am not the military type.'

'Am I?'

'I should soon be forgotten by the salons of Mayfair.'

'Is not that your very wish? Come, Mr Darling. Yours is better metal than need glitter in the light of ballroom chandeliers.'

I should exchange the unknown dangers of campaigning for those experienced of Wakley-Barlow's fury. I should stop Miss Bancroft coming home wed to a Cavalry officer with gorgeous mustachios and irresistible japanned boots. I would have regular dispatches commissioned by Mr Horncastle, for good fees. But all would be massively overshadowed by William Howard Russell of *The Times*. I begged time for thought.

'Till Saturday. If you like, join us unannounced at London Bridge Station.'

We arrived at Romsey Junction. I expected the yellow lamps of my return express already appearing through the mist. But disaster! A landslip in the Southampton cutting, blocking the up line. There was no train till morning.

'You shall stay the night in Embley Park,' Miss Nightingale decided. I could use dear papa's shaving things.

I hated the country. It was far too quiet for sleep, when an owl shrieks like a steam-whistle and you can almost hear the worms turn. Gloomy and sullen I sat in the trap, whipped along inky, wet lanes by the groom. I relished one night among dull strangers less than an indefinite number among the wounded at Scutari. There would be nothing to do except whist, and nothing to talk about except partridges, rents and trout.

Worse, I was superfluous in a house boiling with excitement over Miss Nightingale's new prospects. I stood in their drawing-room amid the kissing, clutching and sobbing, as unnoticed as a footman at a banquet. This gave a chance to observe my conscripted hosts.

Father Nightingale – 'WEN' – was much as etched in

the Reform Club by the powerful acid of Wakley-Barlow, who I made an urgent mental note not to mention as a mutual acquaintance. WEN was abnormally tall, skinny, bearded, with a tendency to lean against walls and furniture rather than angle himself into the chairs of normal humans. He was dressed in skirted frock coat, high collar and black stock, more like the county magistrate he had become than the country gentleman his wife wished him to be.

Mother Nightingale – Fanny – still showed the strong-featured beauty of the vivacious, extravagant, well-connected Miss Smith of Mayfair, before she had exchanged an indulgent father for a lazy and easygoing husband. Her clear complexion, her full lower lip, she had given to her daughters. Sister Nightingale – Parthe – bore a strong resemblance to Florence, though her nose was less sharp, her mouth smaller, her face fatter, her manner livelier. She wore her brown hair braided, and her dark eyes reflected frequent impatience at a remark or a characteristic.

There was a cold supper. I was clearly a mysterious species, regarded as Mr Darwin his Galapagos finches. They were itching for a family conference. I considerately pleaded utter exhaustion, and took my candle in the steps of the butler, a young Hampshire man, red-faced and raw handed, his fair hair cut as roughly as a soldier's, who for a small coin brought to my bedroom fireside an evening's supply of brandy and hot water.

I read a pile of *Blackwood's* till sleepy. Next morning, I wondered how the family conference had gone. Entering the dining-room for breakfast, I sensed immediately.

The four sat round the table in aggressive silence. WEN was reading *The Times*. Fanny was busy with the spirit lamp of the silver kettle. Parthe in yellow silk was solemnly decapitating an egg. Miss Nightingale wore a brown silk dress with a gold cross in a mother-of-pearl ring round her neck, and sat staring straight ahead. Their greeting was surprised. They had clearly overlooked my existence.

I helped myself silently at the sideboard to bacon,

chop and devilled kidney. The drizzle had been blown into a bright morning. Through leaded and mullioned windows I glimpsed part of the brick and stone house, which had three storeys, sixteen gables and thirty chimneys, and had been modernized by WEN from Elizabethan to Georgian. He was an enthusiastic architect, a friend of Sir Joshua Jebb, who designed the new model prison at Pentonville. But he grew bored with his plans, as with everything else, before the scaffolding was up. For thirty years, Embley's acres of oaks and beeches, thickets of laurels and rhododendrons, reposeful grassland, screened pathways, seclusive terraces and sensuous flowerbeds had insulated the Nightingales from the world.

I sat without speaking. WEN suddenly started reading from his *Times*.

'"In this war the Russians have hitherto exhibited a great inferiority in their conduct to that which they displayed in their campaigns from 1807 to 1812, when they fought the battles of Eylau and Borodino against Napoleon,"' he declaimed tonelessly. '"The position of Alma must have been much stronger than that of Borodino, yet how much more stoutly the latter was defended than the former. Their having allowed the allies to land without molestation is inconceivable—" Parthe, you are not listening.'

'I have a bad egg, Papa.'

'Reasonable competition for the war, I suppose.' He had a detached, gentle way with the exasperations of his family.

'To be read aloud to is the most miserable exercise of the human intellect,' the other Miss Nightingale burst out. It was plain all three females were in a raging temper. 'It is like lying on one's back with one's hands tied, and having liquid poured down one's throat. Worse than that, because suffocation would immediately ensue, and put a stop to the operation. But no suffocation stops the other.'

'*I* have no objection to papa reading all morning,' said Parthe sharply.

'Oh, it's all right for you, who go on with your drawing.

57

For me, who has no such cover, the thing is boring to desperation.'

'Caleb, another egg for Miss Parthenope,' WEN said mildly to the raw-handed butler in the doorway. 'So I have tormented my daughters? Well, the devil is either my Unitarian enthusiasm for the intellectual education of women, or my dislike of nothing in the world more than lack of occupation.'

'Lack of occupation!' exclaimed Florence. She could be as severe on her parents as upon everyone else. 'When I see you eating your breakfast every morning, Papa, as though the destinies of a nation depended on your getting done, I think you would be better employed as superintendent of a factory with at least 300 hands.'

Fanny joined the attack on the poor man. 'You could stand for Parliament again.'

'After twenty years?' WEN was then sixty-one, Fanny sixty-seven. She was to die at ninety-two, he at eighty, hurrying upstairs for a forgotten watch during another breakfast. 'I failed to win Andover only because I failed to bribe sufficient voters. The election was perfectly repugnant to me. I am still a Whig. I still hate the Tories, who became mighty only by beer, brandy and money. But I am too old to seek new causes for my old cudgel.'

'You mean, too righteous,' said Fanny.

'You mean, too indolent,' said Florence.

I observed to them that it was a pleasant morning.

Florence turned to me sharply. 'Very pleasant, Mr Darling. On my walk before breakfast, the voice of the birds was like the very angels calling me with their songs. The fleecy clouds looked like the white walls of Heaven. But when I looked at our rows of windows, do you know what I thought? How I should turn the place into a hospital, and how I should put the beds.'

'I had *such* ambitions for *both* my daughters,' Fanny complained tragically. 'Particularly you, Flo. You have such gifts as an artist, such beautiful letters you write, such charm you bring to everyone! How can you disappoint me by immuring yourself in a hospital in *Turkey*? I never understood how you tolerated even London out of the season, with absolutely nobody there.'

'I am determined to study nursing, to devote my life to that profession,' Florence replied obstinately, 'and there is nowhere in the world more valuable to practise it at the moment than Scutari. Do you think it is such a dreadful thing? I think it is a very good thing.'

'Nurse! How I hate that oft-repeated name,' objected Fanny. 'What a picture it brings to the mind! A woman sodden with gin, lascivious and lurid-tongued, as familiar with degrading sights and deeds as the very Devil with fire and brimstone. You know full well there are physically revolting parts of a hospital which no gentlewoman should see.'

I unwisely sought Florence's rescue by murmuring that a nurse offered the qualities of devotion and obedience. All I earned from Miss Nightingale was, 'That definition would do just as well for a porter, Mr Darling. It might even do for a horse. It seems a common idea among men, and even among women, that it requires nothing but a disappointment in love, or incapacity in other things, to turn a woman into a good nurse.'

'Flo, you know how I adore you and admire you, but you *do* take such strange paths to fulfil yourself,' complained Parthe.

Florence spread her large hands on the cloth. 'It disgusts you, does it? That these soft fingers born to embroidery, to flowers, to those of their dancing partners, should be soiled with vomit and excreta?'

Mother and sister paled at the words. I was completely forgotten. No fight is so intensely absorbing as seeks to spill the same blood. I continued with my kidneys, which were excellent. I wondered if I should be back in London with the tremendous news that Miss Nightingale was shirking Scutari.

'If only you had accepted Mr Monkton Milnes,' said Fanny in a painful voice. 'He was so devoted to you, Flo.'

'He asked only once,' said Florence. 'You know how I

wanted to find him lodging to give me another opportunity. I was miserable.'

'You were miserable because he became engaged to Annabel Crewe six weeks later,' said Parthe. 'Oh, Flo! You know how mama and I only desire your happiness. I am plainer than you, Flo. I am not so clever. I know that you despise me, that you try to dominate me—'

'Speaking as a county magistrate—' The women stopped, and stared at WEN. 'I am naturally concerned with administration of the county's hospitals and asylums.' He dipped a sliver of buttered bread into his boiled egg. 'I can understand Flo's interest in these institutions, which are so full of human misery, which can be so easily increased with unthinking administration or meddling.' He gave an incredulous smile, as though a thought had just struck him. 'Flo *is* rather masterful. Despotism is not the English way of governing things, you know. But I am proud of Flo's success in Harley Street,' her father ended, sounding deeply ashamed of it.

'You've always been thicker with Flo,' Parthe said resentfully, 'because she's quicker witted than me.'

'And less possessive, and less jealous,' Florence supplemented.

'Flo!' exclaimed Fanny. 'You'll make your sister ill again. She'll have to go to bed for a week, just like the time when you walked out of the house for Harley Street.'

'Oh, I've discussed my career with Parthe a thousand times. If she wishes to preserve her health, she should stop interfering in her sister's affairs and stay here at Embley with her books and country occupations.' She was angry, but as politicians are, calculating the best means of using it for her own way. 'I do not intend dangling about my mother's drawing-room all my life as an eternal *fille à marier*. You must think of me as a son, Mama. And a vagabond son at that. I am sorry if you are both jealous of my ambitions.'

'Ambitions, ambitions!' Parthe was sobbing, choking, pouring out her words. 'You have little or none of what is called charity or philanthropy, only ambition. You want to go East because you would like to regenerate the world with a grand *coup de main*, or some fine institute, and take the credit. You have a circle of admirers who take everything you do or say as Gospel, but I certainly do not believe in the wisdom of all you say simply because *you* say it.' She snatched impulsively at her wrist. 'I'm even wearing your bracelets – you shall have them back. There!'

She hurled them across the table, flying past Florence's neck and rattling against the skirting. I went on sipping my coffee. I always maintained that breakfast was not a social meal.

'It's only the intellectual part which interests you, not the manual,' Parthe continued wildly. 'Don't you understand yourself? You have no *esprit de conduite* in the practical sense. Oh, I know when you've nursed me while I've been ill, everything which intellect and kind attention could do was done. But you are a *shocking nurse*. Shocking!' she shouted. 'You've nothing but an insatiable curiosity in getting into a variety of minds, and an insatiable longing to influence them. And once you've got inside, they generally cease to have the slightest interest to you.'

'It seems that I cannot open my mouth here without vexing you beyond toleration,' said Florence quietly.

'Yes. You are the only murderer of my happiness.'

'I am a murderer only because I will not be satisfied with the life which satisfies you. You lie when you say you desire my happiness. You never think of it. My life here is but suicide. To get through every day here, to talk through every day here, leaves not a night that I lie down on my bed wishing that I may leave it no more.'

'We are ducks,' exclaimed Fanny tearfully, 'who have hatched a wild swan.'

Parthe gave a cry. 'I feel faint.'

'Quick!' cried Fanny, 'The sal volatile.'

WEN rose, with his *Times*. 'I am retiring to the library.' He often did at Embley. Sometimes he contemplated the books. Others, he just contemplated. The family revolved in a solar system beyond which only Florence directed an astronomical telescope. They were carelessly arrogant, unthinkingly conceited, inescapably snobbish, and all four a little mad. They enjoyed their fights. These provided a catharsis more refreshing than senna-pods, and occupied the dull days in the country.

Florence rose too, staring through the window, hands clasped in her usual way, lips moving either in prayer or calculating the number of sheets she would be taking to Scutari. She would go to the war, whatever the family said. No one could withstand the steel of her determination, with its edge of invective heated in her coals of rage. Fanny was slumped in her chair, sniffing vigorously from a dark bottle. Parthe was in tears, scarlet face against the cloth, beating the table with her fist. Caleb the Hampshire butler came in, noticed the bracelets on the floor, gathered them up, and stepping across to their wearer said cheerfully, 'Here's your egg, Miss Parthenope, and cook says it's straight out of the hen.'

9

FLORENCE NIGHTINGALE became a national heroine in an afternoon.

First, it seemed that her journey into the rosy clouds of self-sacrifice would be cancelled as unceremoniously as an excursion train. Sebastopol had fallen. It was in all the newspapers the next Wednesday morning, led by columns of the *Morning Chronicle* and *The Times* headed with colossal type. It was a 'shave', as the soldiers called false tales, though one founded on national confidence. The month before, Palmerston and his Foreign Secretary the Earl of Clarendon were preoccupied deciding if the Crimea might be restored to Turkey after victory, or occupied with our ally Napoleon III. The month after, Clarendon was admitting no chance of winning until another spring the war which he had lightly started during the last one.

On Thursday morning the Cabinet met. Without dissent they appointed Miss Nightingale 'Superintendent of the Female Nursing Establishment of the English General Hospitals in Turkey'. It was an innovation as startling for Englishmen as finding themselves seventeen years before suddenly ruled by a Queen. Everybody in Town was talking excitedly and expectantly about Miss Nightingale. I had an appointment with her late that evening, at Sidney Herbert's house in Belgrave Square.

No 49 stood on the corner of Grosvenor Crescent, across from my uncle Peregrine's St George's Hospital. It was huge, four-storied, its architecture untidy, as though the remnants of the elegant square had been stuck together by builders anxious to be off. There was an ostentatious glassed-in portico, a pretty little octagonal lobby, a hall with a massive staircase. The dining-room beyond had delicately embossed walls of Cambridge blue, windows round three sides, a handsome marble chimneypiece, an ugly central chandelier. I found Miss Nightingale at the head of the long dining-table, which was bare save for an open leatherbound ledger. She was in her lace-edged black, alone with Mrs Elizabeth Herbert, who was standing against a great gilded mirror, dark-haired, smooth skinned, deep bosomed, in coffee-coloured embroidered silk, serene, beautiful and pious. I had never before seen her. She was later to be my instrument for unlatching the door and releasing a stabled Miss Nightingale into the Elysian fields of her ultimate ambitions.

'I thought you might be a candidate,' said Miss Nightingale, as I was shown in.

'Has there been a rush?'

'There has not been a single one.'

She introduced me to Mrs Herbert, who said gently, 'The inducements are compelling enough. After all, the pay is *double* a London nurse's. Twelve shillings a week is generous, rising to sixteen if she can behave herself for three months.'

'And £1 if she manages to for a year,' said Miss Nightingale, shutting the blank book.

The terms were in all the newspapers. The nurse would be given uniform, but must provide her own underclothes, nightcaps and umbrella. Coloured ribbons were banned, and so was straying outside the hospital without three companions. She would get a pint of porter at dinner, at supper a glass of Marsala or an ounce of brandy. She might drink her own gin, in moderation. There was no moderation about intimacy with the troops, which was punishable instantly by sending home third class on salt pork and ship's biscuit.

'We have had to dispatch ladies hurriedly to caches of nurses all over London,' Mrs Herbert explained with disappointment.

'We have dug out five Roman Catholic sisters each from

64

the convents of Bermondsey and Northwood, eight from Miss Sellon's Home, which is Protestant, and six from St John's House,' Miss Nightingale enumerated.

'Which is Tractarian,' murmured Mrs Herbert.

'That still leaves sixteen,' said Miss Nightingale dourly. 'The sisters are anyhow more fit for Heaven than a hospital. They will flit about like angels without hands, and soothe the patients' souls while they leave their bodies dirty and neglected. They are eager for self-mortification. I am going to Scutari not to mortify my nurses, but to nurse my wounded.'

One of the Herberts' footmen entered with a letter on a salver.

'I only apply one test to a nurse,' she continued, opening the envelope. 'Is she a good woman, and does she know her business? By "good" I do not mean religious or noble, which are not in themselves sufficient. I am glad to include Romanist sisters in my party because they are vowed, so I shall not risk losing them from marriage to the soldiers.'

She was deeply religious because it was fashionable among well-born young women at the time, but she dealt with God exactly as she dealt with everyone else from the Cabinet to the supplier of the Harley Street flue pipe.

The letter raised her spirits. 'That's pleasing.' She handed it to Mrs Herbert. 'It's from my father, at his club. He came back to Town suddenly with Mr Darling and myself.'

In the Athenaeum, so quiet, so impregnable, so woman-less, between those chaste walls picked sombrely in black and gold, among those slim white columns haunted with inspirational dryads, amid that conventional taciturnity, in that crucible of consequential thought, WEN could sit gloomily over his chop and claret deciding his attitude towards his younger daughter.

'Mr Nightingale has settled £500 a year on me.' Florence was in peril of looking smug. 'And my dear mother and sister have telegraphed their congratulations. Instead of telling me that I suffer from *nostalgie de la boue*, they will soon be telling the whole country of its good fortune, that they encouraged me all my life to nose my way into hospitals. Look at that postscript,' she said with amusement to Mrs Herbert. '"Better write to me at the Athenaeum so as not to excite enquiry." I expect there are many men who are thankful that their club stands beyond the length of their wives' paper-knife.'

Mrs Herbert shortly left us. I showed Miss Nightingale the galley-proof of my article for next morning's *Penny Pioneer*. It was the first by which I stamped her image on the malleable metal of the public mind.

'Why do you begin, *Who is Miss Nightingale?*'

'Because *The Times* always calls you *Mrs* Nightingale.'

I read once more, over her shoulder, *She is young, graceful, feminine, rich and popular, yet she has forsaken the palpable and heartfelt attractions of her home, the assemblies, lectures, concerts, exhibitions and all the entertainments for taste and intellect with which the London season abounds, to sit beside the sick and dying. Now, at the risk of her own life, and the pang of separation from her friends and family, at the certainty of encountering hardships, dangers, toils and the constantly renewing scene of human suffering, she is setting out for the horrors of war. Miss Nightingale shrank not. A sage few will no doubt condemn, sneer or pity an enthusiasm which will to them seems eccentric, or at best misplaced, But to the true heart of the country, not one of England's proudest and purest daughters at this moment stands on so high a pinnacle as Florence Nightingale.*

'What do you think of it?' I asked proudly.

'Overblown.' She handed back the proof. 'Are you coming to Scutari, Mr Darling?'

'Might I not be more use in London?'

'No. But I will put no pressure on you to go. None was put on me,' she said crushingly.

I shortly left for home. I walked, a hansom being expensive, the omnibuses infrequent and anyway the vehicles of most Londoners in those days were their feet. It was foggy, the gaslamps orange, horses materializing suddenly from empty darkness, some muffled men indicated by

66

lanterns, others nothing but passing coughs. Hands in pockets, I strode by St George's Hospital towards Hyde Park Corner. My heart turned colder than the night. I was being followed.

I went faster. A cry came close behind me. I stopped, turned, prepared to struggle with an envoy of Wakley-Barlow come to slit my nose or my heart. It was Harriet.

'Tristram! Oh, lovey! I am finished.'

She fell upon me, grasped me tightly and started to cry.

'How did you find me?' I asked angrily.

'They told me at your newspaper.'

'Why are you out alone at this hour?' I demanded in the same tone.

'Because I've nowhere else to go,' she told me miserably.

'So Lard Tub's chucked you?' She was dressed for a summer afternoon, not an October night, in the same pink frock and a straw bonnet with pink ribbons. 'Well, you can't blame him, can you?'

'Oh, lovey—!' She looked up, cheeks streaming tears. The fog had turned our patch of pavement into a private apartment in which we could enjoy a *tête à tête*. 'I've not a penny. Nothing! Naught but what I stand up in.'

'You're lying. What about my sovereigns? What about the sovereigns of all the others?'

She gave a huge sob. 'He found them. My savings, my little hoard, my independence.'

I was curious. 'Where?'

'The monkey.'

I laughed. 'I *wondered* why you tolerated an object so ill-manneredly ugly.'

'You must support me.' she cried disconcertingly.

'You've not a bellyful of marrow-pudding, have you?' I asked in panic. 'You've a fine variety of fathers to pick and choose from.'

She shook her head fiercely. 'My angel, my love, it's you, it's only you I adore. Oh God, pity me.' She was suddenly a few frail bones wrapped in pink tulle. 'No, you'll not care to believe me. You'll not even care to re-member me. But it *was* only you, Tristram. The rest were

67

nothing, no more than Mr Larderton, who I abominated from the first second he breathed into my face.'

Her cheek pressed my cravat. Two young swells, hats tipped and canes atwirl, intruded into our walls of fog and guffawed loudly as they passed.

'Do you know why I gave myself for money? It wasn't greed. It was so I might escape, to live all alone with you, lovey. You'd never have known of the others. I'd have said it was a legacy or something. You're so poor,' she said sadly.

'But you took sovereigns from me too, sometimes,' I objected.

'I couldn't be sure of myself, I suppose,' she said artlessly. 'It was a big step, leaving the only roof to cover me in the world.'

I could never gauge if Harriet was as simple and misused as Bill Sikes' Nancy, or as subtle and mischievous as Becky Sharp. I was still undecided on the day of her death.

'Can I come back to your place, Tristram?'

'No.'

'Only for tonight,' she wheedled, fingers at my cheek. She asked pathetically, 'Don't you love me a little speck?'

I dropped into her hand all the gold that I had in my pocket, and in the world. Then I tore myself from her, and hurried round the corner of the hospital. I heard a gasp behind me. Whether of amazement, relief or triumph I did not trouble to decide.

Perhaps she would pursue me another night. Perhaps she really loved me. I had ill-used her as conveniently as had Mr Larderton. My conscience lodged some responsibility for fending her from destitution and degradation. But I should escape my conscience. I should go to war at Scutari, not through bravery but through moral cowardice.

Early the following morning, I found my uncle Peregrine at home in Savile Row. He sat reading the paper in his library of rosewood cabinets filled with embossed leatherbound books on surgery and science, the gentle, learned face of his profession which opposed the savage, bloody visage of the operating theatre. I had stood more than once, teeth clenched, in the bleak, cold, smelly, sawdust-floored amphitheatre where uncle Peregrine, cuffs turned back on an operating coat stiff with blood and pus, within a railed-off area like a boxing-ring, slit a man's leg off with an amputation knife pointed like an assassin's dagger. I had feared nothing in life more than the thud as the severed limb dropped into the tub of sawdust, which waited with the awful convenience of the basket on the guillotine.

I told him that I was leaving the following evening for Turkey.

'What? You will meet your end on the tip of a Cossack's lance?' He looked shocked. 'What a terrible thing it is, having young blood. Like walking about with your veins full of brandy.'

'The only Cossacks I shall encounter will be harmlessly wounded or already dead. But that's preferable to a ruffian's dagger in a London alley.'

As a man confessing on his death bed, I told him of both Mr Larderton and Mr Wakley-Barlow. He laughed at the one, grew concerned with the other. 'I know of Wakley-Barlow. A man of bad reputation, suspected of blood on his hands before now. He should be in a house of correction, not the House of Commons.' Uncle Peregrine was unlocking his escritoire. He produced a washleather bag full of sovereigns, which he poured into my hands. My stumbling thanks were shooed away. 'A few fees collected yesterday, the stone mostly, though a limb or two.'

He told me to buy a warm greatcoat from his tailor round the corner in Cork Street, stout boots from Lobb's, a waterproof hat from Lock's, some hampers from Fortnum and Mason's and claret from Berry Brothers of St James's. 'War is unpleasant enough in itself,' he cautioned me. 'And you, my boy, hate discomfort more than anything, even celibacy.'

As I still pressed thanks, he interrupted, 'I'd better warn you of the medical big-wigs out there. Dr John Hall is the Great Mogul. Plumed hat, you know, *et hoc genus omne*. Qualified at St Andrew's. Did well in the Kaffir

War, he was called from India for this business. Sailed straight for the Crimea, never came home. A man of about sixty, I suppose. Said to be possessed of a highly cultivated intellect. On the occasions I've met him in Town, the cultivation seemed blighted. Oh, you knew Bob Newbolt at St George's?' I shook my head. 'He's a staff-surgeon, one of my old students. Look out for him – it won't be difficult, you'll be living in each other's pockets.' He ended by advising, 'I shouldn't associate yourself with the name of Miss Nightingale more than you must.'

I was puzzled. 'But everyone applauds her as a worthy and unselfish lady.'

'That is nothing without a scientific training, which she does not possess. She does not believe in, nor understand the contagion theory. There is no glory in nursing the dying when they should never have fallen sick in the first place. Knocking off a Soho pump handle would do more to stop an epidemic of the cholera than a flock of Nightingales. Her reputation's on the gaming-table,' he warned me cheerfully, 'and I'm certain that she's going to lose it, as did the crafty Viennese inventor of mesmerism when chloroform came along. Now I must look into St George's for an abscess. And don't forget a thundermug, my boy, for under the bed.'

Another farewell was obligatory that afternoon.

'I read in the *Daily News* this morning that Miss Nightingale has recruited her nurses from High Church and Romanish establishments,' complained my uncle Humphry peevishly in his palace study, crossing his gaitered legs and stirring his tea, which matched his wine in thinness. 'The editorial opinion was strong, but mine is stronger.'

He disliked the Tractarians as ferociously as he had hated the Chartists, as treacherous underminers of Church, State and the order of things. He would have been pleasantly diverted by Dr Henry Newman and Dr Edward Pusey burning like a couple of candles at Oxford.

'Take little notice of journalists' indignation,' I told him patronizingly. 'It is as flimsy as the paper, and as mechanically contrived as the typesetting.'

70

'And what is Miss Nightingale's sect, pray?' he asked severely.

'The Good Samaritans. Which is, unfortunately, a very rare one. Almost half her party have no religion at all, unless you include among the religions of the world the worship of Bacchus. It is at least more universal than any of the others.'

'I see that you have finished your tea,' he said, rising.

That night, the nurses gathered at No 49 Belgrave Square. Miss Nightingale had finally impressed a motley crew of thirty-nine. The Roman Catholic sisters and Protestant deaconesses were serene in habits, the rest looked a sorry flock, penned in the dining-room in their hastily-concocted uniform. This was a lumpy grey tweed dress, a shapeless worsted jacket, a white mob cap, a grey woollen cloak and a brown linen band worn across the shoulders like an officer's pouch-belt, embroidered in red *Scutari Hospitals*. Entirely different from the 800 trained women of Queen Alexandra's Imperial Military Nursing Service, who sailed with the South African Expedition forty-five years later. But the Queen Alexandras' scarlet-caped 'gown of silver grey, bright steel chain, and chignon's elegant array', was modelled on the mawkish rig before my eyes that night. Miss Nightingale wanted them ugly. Then there would be less trouble from the men.

Sidney Herbert appeared, with his air of momentous preoccupation. The younger nurses looked at him like bemused kitchenmaids brought above stairs for the Christmas treat. He told them sternly that Miss Nightingale's authority was absolute and limitless, as unquestionable as Lord Raglan's over the troops. The nurses must mess together, sleep where she told them, go where she told them, do what she told them. The nuns would take their orders from Miss Nightingale, not from their Mother Superior. This struck me as an unthinkable effrontery to the Roman Catholic Church, but it being necessary effrontery Miss Nightingale would think of it. 'If any desire to turn back, now is the time of decision,' he ended chillingly.

I was looking at Miss Bancroft, who stood as reposeful

as ever against the far wall. I had plans for her in Scutari. A letter by the late post was passed to Miss Nightingale, beside her. 'From my sister at Embley,' she said to Mr Herbert, asking permission to open it. She gasped. We stared anxiously. Some desperate family news had crashed upon her like lightning. 'My owl!' she exclaimed. 'My owl Athena. In the excitement, my family forgot to feed it. My owl is dead. Poor little beastie, it is odd how much I loved you.'

With awesome steadiness, two tears crossed her cheeks and splashed upon the writing-paper. I later saw her at a hundred deathbeds, walking through cavernous wards washed with the tide of moans, watching men painfully survive to be broken beyond use, writing countless letters to distant widows, but I never saw her cry again. Perhaps she was tired.

The next evening, Saturday October 21 1854, my hansom set me down in the forecourt of London Bridge Station, with my trunks, hampers, boxes, bedding, brand-new greatcoat with fur collar and new travelling cap of military look. Miss Nightingale was on the platform, dressed like a Quakeress, nurses and nuns clustered round her like chicks in a barn. Few had come to see us off. I recognized only Mrs Herbert, bristling with furs. Miss Nightingale and Miss Bancroft were addressing a fair, balding man about thirty-five of grave ecclesiastical look, vaguely familiar to me. 'Mr Arthur Clough,' Miss Nightingale introduced him. 'My cousin. He has come to see us off.'

'You were at Rugby,' I remembered. 'I've seen your picture in School House.'

'I was there under Dr Arnold,' he said gloomily.

'Mr Darling is a literary man, Arthur, and will be familiar with your poetry.'

My embarrassment at complete ignorance of this Education Office functionary's verse was swiftly overwhelmed by another. A screech, quickly stifled, came from behind Miss Nightingale. I saw Harriet, hideous in nurse's uniform.

'You know Miss Catchpole?' Miss Nightingale was

surprised and pleased. 'She completed our numbers at the last minute.'

'Who are *you* seeing off?' Harriet asked angrily.

I stood open-mouthed. 'I'm coming too.'

'Oh, lawks!' she cried.

'But what . . . what in the world made you go to Scutari?' I demanded as furiously as she.

'*You* did. I read your article in the *Penny Pioneer*, that's why.'

'Miss Nightingale, a word—' A man who lives on his wits can no more afford to let them idle than a master his servants. I drew our Lady Superintendent a few steps down the platform. 'Miss Catchpole is an actress,' I muttered.

'Well?' I shrugged significantly. Miss Nightingale said, 'She bore an excellent reference from an official at the Foreign Office.' Someone else who has been to the discreet little house in Brompton, I thought crossly. 'If she is a frailer vessel, the nuns will provide moral ballast.'

'I think she should be left behind.'

'Why? She is the most intelligent in the whole party.'

'I got to know some scandal about Miss Catchpole, in the course of my work.'

'Then you will not repeat it. You are now engaged on an exploit more serious than London gossip. May I remind you, Mr Darling, that like the rest you come under my orders?' She turned back to Harriet. 'You still wish to accompany us?'

'Oh, yes, Miss Nightingale.' She had recovered from my materialization more expertly than from Mr Larderton's.

'You understand that it is not going to be a pastime of smoothing sheets and serving cordials?'

'Oh, yes, Miss Nightingale, I do,' said Harriet eagerly. 'My only wish is that we shall journey with no delays, and get straight to nursing the poor fellows.'

'Good,' said Miss Nightingale crisply. 'I appreciate determination. You're the one who'll be first at the wash-tub.'

We sailed as a cargo of feminine gentility, the British

press puffing our sails. The country then imagined, the world does now, that she crusaded with ladies who shared her high birth, social position, intelligence and altruism. But Miss Nightingale commanded as mixed a company as Captain Fluellen at Agincourt. They were an uneasy alliance of brave nuns and a timorous, gin-soaked rag-bag of young women raw to nursing, old women worn out by it, scullerymaids discharged without a character and the recent inmates of hospitals and jails, their motives no higher than their skirt pocket.

Tenniel's cartoon in that week's *Punch* had a female as ugly as his *Alice in Wonderland* Duchess, with poke-bonnet, baggy umbrella and pattens, on deck amid tin trunk, camp stool and carpet bag with extrusive gin-bottle, aboard a paddle-steamer bound East, captioned *How to Get Rid of an Old Woman*.

As often, *Punch* was nearer the mark.

74

10

THE WIND which was shrieking into our faces through the Bosphorus blew a hole in the clouds, and the sun lit like a flash of gunfire the clustered domes, forests of minarets and crammed roofs of Constantinople. It was seven o'clock on the Friday morning of November 3 1854. I had come on deck as the Peninsular and Orient steamship *Vectis*, yellow quarantine flag quivering at the foremast, dropped anchor off Seraglio Point at the mouth of the Golden Horn, a slaty, choppy pathway of sea into the heart of the city.

The Mediterranean had tormented us wickedly. Our groaning decks had run wet since Marseilles, the rigging was in flails, the spars splintered, the deck cargo and galley washed overboard, the cabins below damp or even awash, the cannons fitted to save us from the enemy cast overboard to save us from capsizing. It was no compensation that St Paul suffered similarly in the same waters. I stood in my fur-collared greatcoat, drawing my first breath of the East, which I knew only as a puzzling region of *tchibouques*, dragomans, sickled swords and sweet coffee. Though exciting with the potent sorcery of novelty, that morning it resembled a bad daguerrotype washed out. Miss Nightingale was still stretched on the horsehair bunk in her cabin, where she had passed the whole voyage. *Mal de mer* is a fearsome leveller.

I turned my eyes opposite to the Asian shore, to the suburb of Scutari, the 'Silver City', spiked with cypresses. It was dominated by the square, squatting, ochre building with a red-tiled roof, three storeys high and almost two furlongs in each direction, a pinnacle at each corner like a vast upturned billiards-table. This was the *Selinie Quicklaci*, the Turkish barracks for 15,000 troops which had become the British Barrack Hospital and our destination. I heard a gentle, regular thumping against the paddle-box under my feet. Curious, I leant over the bent iron rail. Both bloated, both with limbs askew, both with tongue stuck from gaping mouth, were a dead horse and a dead man.

We had started as heroes. We arrived in the morning at Boulogne to find a crowd at the docks, the fishwives in starched white caps seizing the boxes of *les bonnes soeurs*, and my own considerable luggage, for carriage on their backs to the railway terminus. The hotel proprietor laid his menu at our disposal without charging a *sou*, and *par miracle* I observed a French waiter refuse a tip. We ran immediately into rough social country. Miss Bancroft and Miss Catchpole were ladies. Could they sit and eat with nurses? Where did the nuns eat? What about me? Miss Nightingale dissolved the fastidiousness by making everyone sit together and serving us with her own hands. At the Gare du Nord, we were greeted by cries of *Vivent les soeurs!* I much enjoyed it.

We stayed for two nights at the hotel near the station.

'You see, I am never *désoeuvrée*,' Miss Nightingale greeted me cheerfully in her bedroom, which I felt no more impropriety at entering than a colonel's tent. She sat in her black dress, the bed covered with ledgers, notebooks, letters, tradesmen's bills and telegrams (as we were beginning to contract 'telegraphic dispatch' to the fury of the Greek scholars, who wanted to call it a 'telegrapheme').

'I have to organize one day and plan the next, decide which stores are important to buy, which persons are important to importune or assuage, and keep up the good spirits of forty women who have mostly travelled no further before than the Great Exhibition at Sydenham, and who have inherited a national terror of all things French. I have been trying without success to extract some nurses from the convent of St Vincent de Paul, and I must buy bonnets for the ones I have – it is horrid rushing after frivolities when one hears the news from the Crimea.'

'It seems that Sebastopol, which fell so easily for the newspapers, is impregnable for the army.'

We were interrupted by the *valet de chambre's* knock and the explosive entry of an extraordinary female. I thought at first she was a child. She had a child's height and figure, enormous childish eyes, her features were so delicate they appeared in danger of chipping like a Coalport tea service, her hair resembled the top-knot of a Yorkshire terrier.

'Clarkey!' screamed Miss Nightingale, leaping up and kissing her fervently. 'This is Madame Mohl,' explained Miss Nightingale, introducing me, 'whom I have known since we were nineteen.'

'Despite the "Madame", I am English, not French.' 'Clarkey' bubbled at me. 'No, I am neither, I was Miss Mary Clarke, who was half-Irish and half-Scottish, and Monsieur Julius Mohl was born German but became French while waiting eighteen years for me to make up my mind about marrying him. There! My whole history in one breath. I'm just one poor exile married to another.'

'Madame Mohl holds the most intelligent *salon* in Paris,' Miss Nightingale corrected her friend with pride, clasping her tiny waist tightly. 'You see, Mr Darling, how she is so full of *esprit* and *espièglerie*. To me, Paris is Clarkey,' she declared, provoking from the visitor a smile as loving as her own.

I made hurried excuses to leave, the two ladies seeming eager for an intimate gossip. I did not like Clarkey. I dislike all hoydens who rompingly trespass against the delicacy of their sex. Though perhaps I was simply distressed by the hair. I had never heard of her before. I never saw her again. But she shone upon my life an influence as distant and as powerful as an evil star.

The stimulation of my journey was marred by the one travelling companion whom I admired and knew little of, and the other of whom I was ashamed and knew far too much about me. I was determined to send Harriet home. She could not drown my reputation in the Mediterranean because her own was lashed to it, like a *mariage républicain* during the terrible noyades of Nantes. But I was troubled because she was going, through a mixture of my indifference and my exhortation, to where she would be both miserable and useless.

During our three days in Marseilles, the nurses were taken to view the basilica of Notre-Dame-de-la-Garde, under the chaperonage of the British consul's wife. I detached Harriet.

'You want to get rid of me because of Miss Bancroft,' she at once countered my dissuasion. We were in the open by the church, the morning cold and blustery.

'I have never been alone in the same room as Miss Bancroft. Even fully clothed.'

'If you want to remind me of my foolishness and humiliation, why must you be so coarse?' she asked crossly.

I apologized. 'I'm inviting you to take the express back to Paris, because you are running unnecessarily into danger and discomfort, to both of which you are unsuited.'

'What if you turned back now yourself? What would everyone think of you in London? Why should you give me the same shame?'

'Nobody expects a pretty woman to be a heroine, no more than a swallow to play the hawk. Anyway, you'd never make a nurse in a thousand years.'

'Why?' she said sharply.

'You're too selfish.'

'You are telling me that I can't acquit myself as well as those gin-soaked harridans and dimwitted nuns? You forget, my friend, I've had to make my way in the world. I'm nimble and adaptable.'

'But don't you see? It's only the gin or the veil which steels them to face a hospital's horrors.'

She smiled. 'Then perhaps I shall adopt one or the other. Why shouldn't I be with you, Tristram?' she asked with her old sweetness. 'I've no one else of my own in the world.'

'There'll be no love-making under Miss Nightingale's rule,' I told her severely.

'We'll see,' said Harriet.

We sailed on Friday, October 27. The morning brought

78

news of a battle along the Worontzoff Road, bloody and indecisive, perhaps a defeat, hundreds of men wounded and likely to be arriving in Scutari the same moment as their unpractised nurses. I hoped it was another shave. We steamed to Malta, with the mail. The island was full of troops in transit, loafing, bored, curious, ribald, drunken. It was our first whiff of the war.

That morning at Constantinople, the yellow jack was hauled down, we were open to visitors and porters screaming for our baggage. I stared fascinated at the officials, turbaned and petticoated, their vests of brilliant and varied colours, their waists ringed like everyone in Turkey with weapons – long pistols, daggers, the *yataghan* like a sailor's cutlass, many inlaid with silver, all brightly shining in honourable contrast to the wear and dirtiness of their garments.

Lord Stratford de Redcliffe – 'The Great Elchi' to the Turks – sent the Embassy First Secretary, who went below to Miss Nightingale. Miss Bancroft shortly appeared with my instructions to go on ahead and report myself to Major Sillery, Military Commandant of the Barrack Hospital. She brought chilling news. It was no shave about the battle. It had been fought outside Sebastopol, in a valley north of Balaclava, with 500 men killed and 500 horses lost of Lord Cardigan's Light Cavalry Brigade. The wounded were aboard the transports, and expected any hour.

I ordered a *caique*, the Turkish skiff which plied the Bosphorus as the gondola the canals of Venice, varnished and painted, a floating piece of furniture more than a boat, to which I committed with distrust myself and my baggage. I distrusted even more the *caidjees* pulling the oars, both dressed in voluminous pantaloons and turbans, with long drooping moustaches, lean faces and sharp eyes expressing smouldering disdain for their lowly occupation, as if they would prefer to be cutting my throat with one of the bright-handled daggers tucked into their belts of rolled shawl.

It took an hour to cross. The distance was a mile, the current flowed from the Black Sea at ten knots. The water was foam-speckled and full of jelly-fish. Above wheeled and mewed the wild Bosphorus gulls, which Byron called the ghosts of the Houris. *Glanced many a light caique along the foam*, I remembered from *Childe Harold*, the favourite work of Mr Wakley-Barlow. Once under the shelter of the high Scutari banks and out of the current, the water smoothed and the *caidjees* in a violent perspiration paused for breath. I noticed the jetty, which seemed made of matchwood.

Inspecting my arrival with demoralizing apathy were a group of Turks and a few dozen British soldiers. I had my first shock. The army to myself and all Britons was a column of gorgeously attired pink-faced men marching behind a military band. These looked like beggars from the London kerbstones, ragged, dirty, bent, some with crutches, some lacking arms and legs. Another feature caught my eye. The shore which in the distance seemed picturesque grassland thick with bending and waving cypresses was a huge cemetery. It had three miles of tombs, jammed together like the houses of the London poor, some elaborate marble boxes, some like kerb-posts, the ground between rough and unkempt. The corpses arrived regularly from Constantinople by *caique*. I later discovered that its most beautiful monument marked the grave of a Sultan's favourite horse.

One man waiting was different. Tall, broad, impassive, separated from the rest, in a dark blue officer's cloak, with short cape and high collar held by a chain, its scarlet lining flashing in the wind, on his head a dark blue forage cap with shiny peak and chinstrap. He watched without changing position or expression my scramble to the jetty, over-assisted by Turks, my shouting in English to the uncomprehending *caidjees* about my luggage. After some minutes, he stirred himself.

'Darling?' He was pink faced, in his thirties, gingery moustache drooping over the angles of his mouth, a scrub of beard edging cheeks and chin, his grey eyes looking at me perplexedly. He gave a casual salute, 'I'm Newbolt.' He jerked his head across the Bosphorus where the distant

Vectis glinted in the pale sunshine, now peaceful as a basking shark. 'I hear you've brought us reinforcements?'

'Yes, forty nurses.'

'Well, the women are becoming as scarce and as broken down as everything else in Scutari. What the devil are you doing in that galley? Sir Peregrine wrote that you were a literary gentleman.'

I explained that I was Miss Nightingale's secretary. I had expected from my uncle the man to greet me like a brother. Instead, he had clearly taken a dislike to me on sight. He inspected my fur-collared greatcoat, my military-looking cap, my growing pile of luggage with a glance which sneered.

'Bono Johnny will take your traps up.' His curt nod indicated the Turks. There was no baggage cart, no vehicle. I had left the borders of Europe which went on wheels, for Asia which lumbered on litters. The only horse in sight was a dead one, surrounded by a pack of dogs like wolves, who snarled and bit at the corpse and each other. 'They'll probably steal something for their pains. The soldiers aren't strong enough to lift a candlestick. How are your boots?'

He lit a cigar, not offering me one.

The massive hospital was half a mile from the sea, two hundred feet above us, up a steep slope of scrubby heathland, now rutted wet mud broken by a few bare trees straining in the wind. Long pennants streamed from two of the towers. The landing-stage led into a village, their two or three winding lanes like cracks between walls blank of windows, everywhere the wet charred remains of fires, or rubbish which appeared established for years. Long-beaked, long-legged birds looked down at me from the roofs, their wings seeming hunched against the cold. A few turbaned faces stared at me impassively, as though the British were blown there as inevitably and inexplicably as the foul weather.

'You'd a good berth, Darling. Forty dollies to yourself, all the way from London.'

'Dollies! Over half were nuns, the rest not fit company for a gentleman.'

'Scutari fits a gentleman for any company.' He nodded shortly to a group of half dozen women beside the village. They were undeniably my compatriots, tattered, bemudded, shawls drawn close over dresses brightly coloured, even spangled. 'I sometimes wonder if I'm working in a hospital or a whorehouse. There's two or three hundred camp-followers in the basements. Old wives and new widows, out from home on the army transports, allowed on colonel's discretion, you know. Their only occupations are giving birth, getting drunk and hiring themselves out.'

'It's hardly a holiday resort.' Every step seemed to bring a new surprise.

'There's nowhere else,' he said in his surly manner. 'There's been no general depot for the army since Waterloo. If the regiments didn't feed them, they'd be dying in Chatham, as their men are in the Crimea.'

We started squelching up the track. 'I heard news of the battle.'

'A terrible business. There's bad blood between Lord Raglan and Lord Lucan, who commands the cavalry division. The whole army knows that. There's worse between Lucan and Lord Cardigan of the Light Brigade. It doesn't make for the easy transmission of orders. The story is, the ADC brought a message to attack a few Russian guns. Instead, the Light Brigade charged in the wrong direction and attacked the entire Russian army. I don't know who's going to do for us first, the generals or the cholera. But you wouldn't know about the cholera,' he said condescendingly. 'Men went down with it like flies at Varna, because of the low-lying camp. Marching into battle at Alma, they were dying on the grass before they got there.'

'On the contrary, I know a deal about the cholera,' I corrected him. 'I wrote of Miss Nightingale among its victims in London.'

'Miss Nightingale!' His anger flamed out. 'Why all this fuss? Why is Miss Nightingale sailing among us? Why this female package? Why you yourself, whatever you're supposed to be doing decorating it? That blackguard in

The Times, I suppose. All Russell did was to exaggerate and comfort the enemy. They can read English in St Petersburg, you know. Things aren't perfect here, but we do our duty. In the Peninsula, at Waterloo, the wounded were left to die, at best thrown in a cart, or given their chance with the amputation knife on a farmhouse floor. For the first time in human history, we're taking proper care of our sick and wounded. No wonder the system creaks a bit. So did the *Great Britain* on her maiden voyage.'

I refused a reply. I was angry myself. Admittedly, nobody cares for criticism, and it was intolerable seeing it embodied in forty females. But we had been advertised as the 'Angel Band' of saviours, and it was equally intolerable being told to go to Hell.

We reached in silence the long esplanade fronting the hospital, followed by a curious band of soldiers, Turks and children. I stopped to admire the rainswept view. The hospital was on a point, the Sea of Marmara on one side, the headland hiding the humps of the Princess Islands, the windy funnel of the Bosphorus and Constantinople on the other. 'I hope your ladies have brought their water colours,' said Newbolt.

There were slim-pillared kiosks, and a huddle of primitive huts from wood and canvas thrown roughly together, like English cowhouses. Newbolt explained in his taciturn way that they were sly-grog shops and stews. 'Your soldier is an animal who can do without neither a drink nor a woman, sick or well. Your Greek or Jew appear to provide them, as surely as the lice in the soldiers' shirts. About a third of the army has the clap or the syph. Some of the men would put their prick where I wouldn't stick the ferrule of my umbrella. This is called the "Main Guard",' Newbolt explained as we approached the huge barrack gate, muddied to the knees. 'The place isn't a hospital. It's a sizeable village joined together. Parts I haven't visited, nor with luck ever expect to. You're messing with me, by the by. It won't be what you're used to, none of the muffins and bohea of your literary salons.'

'You don't care for literary persons?'

'I'm not acquainted with any. It's just that I imagine them all effeminate, conceited, quarrelsome and sickly.'

We were interrupted by the appearance through the Main Guard of a clergyman in billowing surplice, followed by a coffin under a flapping pall upon the shoulders of four military bearers, then a dozen marching soldiers and a handful of hat-holding civilians. The discouraging procession turned towards the cemetery, just beyond a row of huts guy-roped against the wind, and a verandahed house or two flying the Union Jack, suitable for nabobs.

'A sight you'll soon no more notice than the milkman's cart at home,' Newbolt told me. 'There's more dead than living in Scutari.' In the gateway, wider and deeper than Trinity at Cambridge, the smell was so offensive I instinctively held my nose. It was the stench of Cholera Court, into which the whole British army had been marched, even the London swells of Guards officers, who would as little enter a slum as be seen carrying a parcel in Bond Street. My gesture afforded Newbolt satisfaction. 'The sewers run just under the floors, and most are blocked. The prevailing wind blows air up the open privies, which are scattered about everywhere – Turkish fashion, crouch to it. Ladylike nostrils must get used to our perfume.'

Inside the gate stood Major Sillery, fat and red-faced, in dark blue undress uniform and forage cap. 'So, the Female Nursing Establishment has arrived,' he exclaimed as Newbolt introduced me. 'All preparations have been made for your reception, and I assure you that everything is perfectly in order.'

He had a voice of plushy respect edged sharply with self-justification, like a Jermyn Street grocer defending an over-ripe cheese. I shortly discovered that Major Sillery had been promoted from the ranks, and in moments of emotion dropped his 'h's'.

'Though I must confess, Mr Darling, I have no notion why you should be sent out here at all. I had nothing to do with the medical stores left at Varna,' he continued mysteriously. 'My responsibilities lie within these four walls, which are enough to test the talents of a simple soldier.'

'I don't think that Miss Nightingale is concerned with Varna, sir. Only the immediate problems here.'

'I had *nothing to do* with Varna,' he said vigorously. 'It all appertained to the *Bombay*. She should have brought two thousand beds and other items back to Scutari, but the lighters were needed to embark the Heavy Cavalry for the Crimea, then the weather turned stormy and the captain had to sail without our stores. So you see, Mr Darling, no one's really to blame, no one at all.'

Newbolt lit another cigar, looking bored. I enquired about Miss Nightingale's accommodation. 'I've lodged the whole party in the north-west tower,' Major Sillery explained with satisfaction. 'There's a large kitchen, with several rooms above. I'm sure the ladies will be well suited. I am a simple soldier, who can but do his best. They shouldn't have come at all, you know,' he repeated plaintively. 'They'll only be in the way.'

Newbolt asked for a pair of field-glasses from a nearby officer. 'Two *caiques* have arrived at the landing-stage,' he announced. 'Both loaded with femininity.'

Within an hour, Miss Nightingale and Miss Bancroft had struggled up the muddy track, heading the first half-dozen nurses in their laughable uniforms, bedaubed, frightened, huddling together like ugly ducklings. We were led to the north-west tower by Major Sillery. The kitchen was five yards square, half a dozen windows through walls a yard and a half thick overlooking the Sea of Marmara and the Bosphorus, facing the dome and minarets of the Selemye mosque. In the middle was the body of the white-whiskered Russian General Chekanoff, who died in Scutari seven days after falling prisoner with three bayonet thrusts and two musket balls in his sixty-five year old body.

II

'A WHET-CUP, a *coup d'avant*,' said Newbolt, relish lightening his usual dourness. 'A custom stolen from our enemies, as spoils of war. The Russian understandably needs a strong glass of aquavite before stomaching his oily fish.' He thrust two anonymous bottles at me. 'Raki? A sort of Turkish absinthe, which smells like perfumed gin. Or Turkish brandy, whose composition confounds chemical analysis?'

'Brandy.'

He poured half a tumblerful. I gulped it down. It tasted like an essence of burnt logs, and had the effect of a shell exploding in a horse. Newbolt looked at me with more respect.

'It's not the hock and soda water you literary gentlemen are used to.'

'This elaborate display of scorn is growing tedious. The only writing I do is scandal for the *Penny Pioneer*. I cadge it off housemaids for a shilling, and from their mistresses by indulging their jealousy. Its greatest reward is the perfectly agreeable one of eating lobsters and champagne at someone's expense.'

It was five o'clock the same afternoon, nearing dinner time. I was in the opposite tower of the barracks, sharing with three doctors the accommodation enjoyed by the forty-two women. Our kitchen was used only as a mess-room. The walls were whitewashed brick, the floors, like all in the barracks, of cracked tiles and greasy boards, perforated with stopped-up rat holes. The door was invisible under engravings of society ladies from the *Illustrated London News*, which lay in worn copies on the floor.

86

There were two hard chairs and a pair of upturned packing-cases, whose cheering contents from home were scattered about the long, rough table – stone jars and tins of food, chocolate, tea, tobacco, pairs of thick woollen gloves, straw everywhere. Three greasy tin plates and a bare ham-bone were piled upon Guthrie's *Commentaries on Surgery*, which was issued to all medical officers as the only text on military surgery written in English – fifty years ago, during the Peninsular War.

Like everywhere else in the hospital, the mess smelt of sewage. The one window was closed against the wind. I noticed that the cockroaches lived undisturbed, and doubtless kept company with bedbugs and lice.

'I don't know what to make of you, Darling,' Newbolt said despairingly, as though I were a patient with some mysterious but fatal illness. He had thrown off his cloak, and wore the dark blue undress frock coat, with plain blue trousers. He thrust more faggots into the square, iron stove, its angled pipe running through the window. Fuel was scarce, as Miss Nightingale shortly discovered, from learning the orderlies had chopped up the operating tables for firewood. Warm for the first time, I took off my fur-collared great-coat. 'Good God, do you always dress like that?' I had my usual silk-braided swallow-tailed coat, stiff collar and white stock. My pepper-and-salt trousers were stiff with mud, my boots split. 'Or are you to be married tonight?'

'I have nothing else.'

He grunted, poured himself a glass of brandy and drank it as quickly as myself. 'Listen, Darling – I'm a professional surgeon, like a professional soldier. I don't give a fiddlestick's end for the way I strike people. The only eyes I value upon my reputation are my own. I do my business here as best I can, setting and amputating limbs, suturing wounds, enucleating eyes, chopping off the tattered bits no more use to a man. Clearing out the dead as soon as they've chucked breathing to make room for more, seeing they go naked because we need the shirts. How do you expect me to welcome with open arms some well-bred young lady who chatters at society balls and's thick as thieves with Mr Herbert? Everyone knows that Miss Nightingale's a spy set on the army by the War Office.'

'Be patient. You'll see Miss Nightingale's as much a professional as you are.'

There was a knock, the door opened for a soldier in a stained red jacket and crumpled forage cap, his white moustached face like scratched parchment, his frail body bent with the burden of a bucket emitting steam and the smell of boiled meat.

'Kipping, the plates are dirty.'

The soldier took a rag from his pocket and began slowly wiping the grease from the tin platters. I observed that drink had added to his infirmities. 'The hospital's short of water,' Newbolt explained. 'You get a pint a day, and take your choice if you drink it, shave with it or wash your shirt in it. There're only three fountains, so Kipping spends most of the morning queueing up.' He lit a pair of candles in wax-encrusted bottles and asked conversationally, 'Kipping, is that dragoon dead?'

'Yes, sir. And buried.'

'The cholera.' Newbolt poured two more glasses of brandy. 'Without the cholera we could manage. But the cases flooded from the transports before we could better equip the barracks for a hospital than whitewashing the walls. Kipping, get this gentleman a bowl, or something to eat off. Steal it if you must. I hope you've brought a spoon?' he added to me, as the soldier shuffled out. 'There's no cutlery.'

We drank the spirits. Newbolt poured more.

'We've 2,000 patients here, and the likes of Kipping are each responsible for nursing a hundred of them, twenty-four hours a day. What colonel in the field would release a good, healthy man to the Army Medical Department, who are mere civilians? The army is in the Crimea to fight, not to nurse. Valiant stupidity! Whatever your friend Mr Russell says, you can't blame the Army Medical Department for giving the wounded short shrift, nor accuse us of creating more suffering than we're supposed to relieve.'

'Who is to blame, then?'

'Lord Raglan, of course. There's plenty of medical officers, each regiment has its pack-horse and panniers, dressings and instruments, enough medicines for six months. ten stretchers and hospital tent, 40,000 cholera belts, medical comforts – no army ever went to war so ready for its disasters. But Raglan had the hospital beds, the ambulance waggons, everything, left behind at Varna. The generals and admirals in charge of transport are just as guilty. At Scutari, we've also got the Turkish Military Hospital, half an hour's walk across the common, 1,000 beds. Just south, we've the General Hospital and the Sultan's Summer Palace, officers only. But what's the use of the finest hospital in the world, if you can't take the patients to it?'

The door burst open. My other two messmates were staring at me with astonishment and hostility.

With mocking ceremoniousness, Newbolt introduced me to Dr Horace Wiley, 'A citizen of President Franklin Pierce, come all the way from New England to perform the chloroformist's sleight-of-hand.'

The American was young, tall, sallow, with a short black beard. He wore white cavalry breeches, highly-polished top-boots with spurs, and a bright blue frock coat with velvet collar and bright buttons, a uniform I later discovered he had invented himself. 'Are you a medical gentleman, sir?' he asked solemnly.

'No, he's a nursemaid,' said the other, who was introduced as assistant staff surgeon Thomas Handshear, of Bartholomew's, young, plump, fair, with pink shining face, always grinning. He wore a shooting jacket, a bright check waistcoat and green velvet trousers. Off duty, officers could wear what they cared and retire to such comfort as they might. Once done with the defeat of his Light Brigade, Lord Cardigan sought the champagne, the French cook and semi-circular stern saloon of his four-bedroomed, two-galleyed yacht *Dryad* in Balaclava harbour.

'Oh, lor'! Boiled salt pork again,' complained Handshear,

sniffing the pail. 'They're feeding us hardly better than the men. Couldn't Kipping pick up anything in the bazaars?'

I offered a preserved ox tongue and claret from my luggage. Kipping, reappearing with my plate, was immediately sent for it.

'I heard a shave that Dr John Hall was paying us another visit.' Handshear poured two more drinks from the bottle. Wiley had a Puritanical outlook, except when it was inconvenient.

'I doubt it,' said Newbolt sourly. 'When he appeared after Alma, he told London the hospital "was as good as could possibly be expected". No man likes to see himself so flatly corrected.'

Handshear took one of Newbolt's cigars. 'By the by, old fellow, there's a damnable fuss at the end of the corridor. Big dragoon pouring blood like a steam-pump.'

Newbolt swore. 'Didn't you do anything?'

'But I'm off duty,' Handshear complained. 'Why should I miss my dinner?'

'I'll have to take the leg off,' said Newbolt, sounding irritated. 'Horace, can you double up as chloroformist and assistant on the artery?'

Wiley threw back the brandy. 'Right away.'

'I'll help,' I offered.

Newbolt scowled. Tucking a flat, polished wooden box under his arm. he said curtly, 'You'll do. Come on.'

The Barrack Hospital – to grow as familiar to every Briton that winter as his last slumber's nightmare – was a square round a huge parade ground. Only the western wing and half the southern could be used, the rest being damaged by fire and open to the weather. Our kitchen opened on to a first-floor landing converted into a surgery, leading directly to a corridor as wide as the nave of a church and as cold. The walls were stone, with windows looking from one side, on the other racks for the rifles of the Sultan's troops. The lath-and-plaster ceiling was supported every ten paces by a stout arch, from each dangling a square lamp with a candle. Along each side were the sick, packed closely, all lying on the floor.

There was a constant noise of groans, moans, coughs, gasps, swearing. 'Are you acquainted with Professor James Simpson, of Edinburgh?' Wiley asked me courteously as we strode behind Newbolt with his cigar, deaf to importations for succour.

I said that I regretted not.

'Professor Simpson gave the world chloroform. My friend Dr William Thomas Green Morton of Boston first of all gave the world ether. And precious little credit he got for it.'

Wiley said he was in Scutari at his own expense, from scientific curiosity over chloroform in war surgery, for which it was tried in the Mexican War. The Crimean was a war to which any man might apply his talents or inquisitiveness. These 'Travelling Gentlemen' – 'T Gs' – were officers' brothers and friends, or tourists camping beyond gunshot range. After the savage little brush in the fog at Inkerman, the day after our arrival, a party of merchants from Manchester inspecting the dead through their eye-glasses were angrily conscripted by a colonel to dig the graves for them. There were ladies, too. Mrs Duberly, later known to everyone for her *Journal Kept During the Russian War*, rode old battlefields with such relish that she was called by soldiers 'The Vulture'.

'Watch your step, Mr Darling,' said Wiley politely.

The corridor led into a long barrack-room, round the walls a Turkish divan – a wooden shelf, upon which more men were huddled under blankets, and below which I could hear rats scampering. I slipped. I was walking through an inch of watery excrement, spilling from the Turkish privy in the corner.

'It's the men's own fault,' said Newbolt. 'They stuff the drains with rubbish. The engineers would have to pull the walls down to find the pipes. They suggest closing all the latrines to install a flushing system, which is not particularly helpful when everyone has diarrhoea. If they don't arrive with it, they soon get it. You'll get it yourself, Darling, most likely.'

I set my teeth tight, trying not to retch.

'And only twenty chamber-pots in the hospital,' said Wiley gloomily.

'There's the tubs.' Newbolt nodded towards a stinking vessel in the corner. 'If we could get the orderlies to empty them.'

'You're unfair on Russell,' I said angrily. 'Things are worse than we could even imagine in London.'

Newbolt puffed his cigar. 'A soldier knows he's going to suffer when he takes the shilling. What are they? The scum of the earth enlisted for drink.'

'They wouldn't care to hear you call them that.'

'I never did. It was the Duke of Wellington.'

Two rats scampered ahead, between the patients. 'I've seen several men with rat-bites,' said Wiley thoughtfully. 'Too weak to move, I guess.'

Newbolt laughed. 'The rats may rid us of Miss Nightingale. Who's ever known a lady not frightened of mice?'

We clattered down some stone stairs. At the end of another corridor, we reached the patient.

He was a big man. He was white, trembling, moaning on the floor, covered with a greatcoat stiff with blood and mud acquired six weeks before at the Alma. He had a sheet, rough as a sail. It was bright red with fresh blood, which ran in a slow, thick rivulet across the tiles, channelling itself into the cracks. He had no pillow, no cup, no water bottle, no attendant. Half a dozen comrades looked on listlessly, only two with the strength to prop themselves on their elbows.

'Damn me,' muttered Newbolt. He ground cigar-butt under heel, and I noticed ash mingle with the gleaming blood. 'Horace, some light.'

The American drew from his side pocket a Turkish lamp I had never seen before, a compact candlestick with a concertina of parchment a foot high to spare the flame the draught, topped by a handle.

'You've got to lose your leg, old fellow,' said Newbolt.

The man's lips moved. After some seconds he said, 'I ain't afraid.'

92

'You won't feel a thing,' Wiley soothed him. 'You'll sleep like a babe.'

Newbolt produced some flax from his uniform pocket, thrusting the strands through the buttonhole of my swallow-tailed coat. 'Push your fist in the groin here, to stop the pulse of the femoral artery. You won't funk?'

'I've seen Sir Peregrine's house-surgeon do it.'

Newbolt grunted. 'But not holding a Turkish army lantern in his other hand.'

Out of his box came a knife with an ebony handle, edged and pointed like a bayonet, a short saw as from any carpenter's tool-bag, hooks, sponges stiff with dried blood. I grew aware of the sweet, sickly smell of chloroform, which Wiley was pouring in a thin stream from a small green bottle upon a triangle of handkerchief across the man's face.

Newbolt turned back his right cuff. I exclaimed, 'Aren't you going to screen the men from the sight?'

'What with?' His knife pierced the front of the thigh.

He made a triangular flap of skin and flesh, impaled the tip with a hook and drew it back from the front of the thigh-bone. Wiley leant casually across the man's body to take it. My spare hand held aloft our shrouded flickering candle, the other I struggled to keep tight in the groin. Newbolt showed his familiarity with operating on the floor by rolling the man over, and almost myself with him. He repeated his cut. I noticed that the blood had turned dark as port wine.

He snatched ligatures from my lapel to tie the big artery. I could stand up. Six sharp strokes of the saw severed the thigh-bone, glistening in the lamplight like a pipe-stem from a full-lipped mouth. The newly severed limb was slid impatiently away across the bloody tiles. Wiley looked up and said calmly, 'He's a dead 'un.'

Newbolt had begun to trim the edges of his flaps like a Piccadilly butcher fat from the joint. He stopped, straightened, glared down at his knife then at the soldier's bared face. 'Damn, damn,' he said. 'Good work wasted.' I swayed, almost fainting at a man dying under my hands.

'You've a good deal of blood on your beautiful coat, Darling.'

Newbolt threw the stained greatcoat across the corpse. A soldier barely three feet from our lamplit knot covered his face with his hands and began to weep. My weak voice asked, 'Why did he die?'

'I'll tell you why he died,' Newbolt said angrily. 'Because when Mr Sidney Herbert wanted this barracks as a hospital, he was asking for a miracle. A hospital from what? Where were we to find the beds, blankets, food, medicines, even the scrubbing brushes to shift the filth? Our supplies were rotting and rusting in Varna. We needed Bono Johnny by the hundred, and in Scutari most of the Turks are dead in the cemetery. Muddle, ignorance, laziness, stupidity! All the way down from Dr Andrew Smith, sitting in his little office at 13 St James's Place, caring for the whole army's health with twelve clerks and £1200 a year. It's Mr Gladstone at the Exchequer, and all the politicians before him who've made a deity of cheapness. They're part of a horrible conspiracy which ended this man's life in pain, lying on the floor. I told you Russell was lying in *The Times*, because I wouldn't see the hospital run down by some outsider who'd never walked among the blood and filth we're accustomed to, if we'll never be indifferent to. I told you we were overwhelmed by the cases when we'd done nothing but whitewash the walls. There was nothing else we could do. We had plenty of whitewash.'

He turned abruptly, and started putting back his instruments, still bloodstained. He ended in a low voice, 'Horace, get an orderly to sew him in his blanket. Don't forget to save his shirt.'

I walked back with Newbolt in silence. As we passed in the dim light, the men again called piteously for attention. Newbolt hunched his shoulders. His time would be wasted, scattered among so many in useless fragments. 'That wasn't bad, Darling. For a Fop.'

I have since been complimented by prime ministers and presidents, but never so richly, nor so needfully.

I was impatient to leave the melancholy wards and

corridors for our living quarters. There I discovered Handshear sitting on one side of the stove with the brandy bottle, roaring with laughter, Harriet in her nurse's uniform and Scutari sash on the other.

'What are *you* doing, prowling like a tabby cat?' I asked shortly, irritated by seeing her in the company of another man.

'She came with a message from The Bird,' Handshear answered for her. ' "The Bird" – good name for Miss Nightingale, eh?'

'Why wasn't she chaperoned?' asked Newbolt, refilling his tumbler.

'I had one of the smelly old nurses, but she went down to the basement once she heard about a canteen selling gin. Won't you introduce me to this gentleman?' Harriet asked primly.

'You must return to your quarters,' Newbolt ordered.

'Oh, don't pitch into us like that, Bob,' Handshear complained to his senior. 'Let Miss Catchpole stay awhile. We don't see dollies like her every afternoon. By the by, we've eaten the tongue,' he added to me. 'It was delicious.'

'Poo, what quarters!' Harriet wrinkled her nose. 'Fourteen of us nurses in one little room, ten nuns in another. Can you imagine it? Not even civilized beds, just those horrid hard divans. Only one little bowl between us to wash our faces in. I'm used to better things than that, I'll have everybody know,' she said grandly.

'Sleep here,' Handshear invited. 'That's what hospitals have nurses for, isn't it?'

'Shut your gob,' she told him sharply. He fell into disconcerted silence. Wiley entered, and went straight to the cold bucket of salt pork.

'What about our dinner?' he asked gloomily, tipping the last of the bottle of brandy into a glass.

'Tom's got a cheddar cheese,' said Newbolt. 'He's been eating it in his bedroom in secret.'

We gathered chocolate, Bath Olivers, a jar of mixed pickles and a tin of Donkin and Hall's stew, which we spooned up cold. It reminded me of illicit feasts in the

95

freezing dormitories of Rugby – which trained me admirably for Scutari. Harriet sat on Wiley's knee, with the excuse of never before meeting an American gentleman. We drank my claret and opened another bottle of brandy. She asked Wiley to give us a song from home. The New Englander intoned *I Come from Alabama* lugubriously and repeatedly.

Even Newbolt's sarcasm seemed to melt in the warmth of her vivacity. Towards midnight, he repeated that Harriet must return to the north-east tower and that he would escort her, as he mistrusted the three of us. She remembered 'The Bird's' message – I must report at ten in the morning. To Miss Bancroft, she told me archly, playing her fingers under my chin.

I went to bed in the dark, we were so short of candles. I was conscious of meeting a man too sensitive for his profession. Without his shell of hostility, Dr Newbolt would have appeared as freakish as a skinned tortoise.

I WOKE the next morning in the dimness, with a headache, wondering where I was. Kipping shortly appeared with half a cup of hot water for shaving. A tin bowl of tea with bread and jam made my breakfast. I was alone in the mess-room when Newbolt strode in.

'Look—' He took me by the shoulders and pushed me to the window. 'There's a cargo of trouble.'

He passed a pair of field-glasses. Two ships had anchored overnight off the point, one a paddle-boat, the other a screw steamer, both flying the white Ensign.

'The *Cambria* and the *Andes* with the remains of Balaclava,' said Newbolt. 'They're hospital ships. There'll be two or three transports under sail on their way. Say, 500 or more men aboard each? Having enjoyed a voyage of 300 miles in ten days, probably on deck, without drugs, doctors, dressings or even much to drink. That's the usual plan, ten dying a day, the sailors chucking the cholera corpses over the side like dead horses. We have to clean up the mess. Well, I'm a professional surgeon. If I couldn't contend with every variety of bodily disaster which mankind brings upon itself, I'd chuck it and take to religion.'

I could see through the glasses *caiques* nestling against both ships and rowing for the rickety jetty. I looked at my father's watch. It was barely eight. 'Can I lend you a hand?'

'Please yourself.'

'I should like to,' I insisted. 'I don't really think that I shall be utterly useless here, as Miss Nightingale's secretary. But you make me feel so.'

I donned my fur-collared greatcoat. Outside was a blustery morning, throwing rain into my face by the pailful. The first pair of *caiques* were already unloading below. Tattered, bloody, bandaged, some shawled in blankets, some tottering on sticks, helping one another where they could, the lucky ones carried on stretchers, or by armpits and knees between a pair of Turks, the luckless thrown screaming to the ground by their slithering bearers, the troops mounted the drenched and greasy track to the refuge they had craved since the instant of wounding.

The Barrack Hospital was a treacherous end of a terrible journey. The men had been first collected in farmhouses, their wounds dressed and operations done lying on straw. There were no operating tables with the army, Dr John Hall believing it a poor surgeon who could not extemporize his own. He had not noticed that the squatting Turks had no tables of any sort.

The wounded were then moved by pannier, or by the *araba* – the wicker-sided Turkish cart, loose planks on a pair of axles with four small wheels, drawn by a yoke of their scrawny oxen – or mostly on their feet. Some were strapped to seats on the backs of mules, and found sometimes sitting stone dead. They went down the hill to Balaclava, the fishing village aggrandized as the army's main port, its harbour crammed with craft like Boulter's Lock on Bank Holiday, their anchors liable to dredge up limbs amputated by the surgeons or bodies relinquished by the equally overworked gravediggers.

They boarded transports as overloaded as understaffed. The captains were furious at the degradation of ferrying the sick. One sought to avoid it by concealing his cargo of medical stores, which were found months later, looted and spoiled.

The extra patients could not strain the resources of the barrack hospital, because there were none. They had to be laid somewhere and they had to be seen by a surgeon, both ridiculously difficult under the cumbrous administration. They were collected within the massive arch of the Main Guard, a hundred or more men leaning against the walls, squatting and lying on the rough stones of the floor. Their eyes were closed, their mouths open, some showed life only by the thin stream of breath from their pinched lips into the frosty air. They were in rags, thighs and shoulders red from rubbing against the decks, some worn to raw flesh and bare bone. All were shivering, all emaciated, all stinking, all were lively with lice.

Handshear moved among them, collecting names for his Diet Roll, to be returned daily in duplicate to the Purveyor, Mr Ward— 'Poor Old Ward'. Several spoke to me cheerfully, with the British soldier's desperation to make the best of his plight. Upon one pale, quaking wretch I instinctively wrapped my greatcoat. A *beau geste*, but a foolish one, for I never saw it again and heard it was sold almost immediately for ten shillings.

Many were weak not from the ravages of the enemy but from those of dysentery, diarrhoea and cholera. Several were already dying. Once inside, they might rally, then sink suddenly, feet turning black from the collapse of their circulation. For the following month, we were burying forty-five a day.

I wondered where Miss Nightingale was.

The rushed preparations in London, the uncomfortable journey, our shock on arrival, the indifference of our greeting, were surely to be eradicated that morning by the awareness of our value. But there was no nurse in sight. When I reached the north-west tower, they appeared to be enjoying a sewing-bee. At one end of the crowded room the nuns sat on the floor, at the other the uniformed nurses, all busy with needle and thread. Miss Nightingale stood in the middle with Miss Bancroft, as calm as if in Harley Street with no problems more savage than the rustle of the nurses' dresses.

'Slings for stumps, slings for arms, bandages, shirts, dressings, all can luckily be improvized from materials we have brought for our own use, as you can see, Mr Darling. We should be scrubbing as well as stitching, because the quarters are filthy and the hairs of the general we found in occupation disturb my nurses. But there are neither brushes nor brooms, and household soap has become more valuable then blocks of gold.'

I followed her into a small room leading from the corner, with a single high window, in our quarters a store. She had a camp stool and her papers spread across a portmanteau.

'Why aren't you doing your proper work?' I asked at once.

'Because I haven't been invited. We must not show *trop de zèle.*'

I noticed the pewter inkstand from Harley Street. 'Invited? This is hardly a society ball.'

'Your memory is short.' She sat on the stool. 'You printed my official instructions from Sidney Herbert in your own newspaper. I was to place myself in communication with the Chief Army Medical Officer of the Hospital at Scutari. That is Dr Menzies, who apparently nobody sees, because he has so many duties he can manage to do none of them. I am under his orders completely. Everything relating to the distribution of the nurses, the hours of their attendance, their allotment to particular duties, is placed in my hands – *subject to the sanction and approval of the doctors.* Admirably concise. Would that Lord Raglan made his intentions as clear to Lord Cardigan.'

'But your nurses might as well be still sitting in Mrs Herbert's dining-room—'

'I will not move one nurse from this Black Hole of Calcutta until I receive Dr Menzies' summons. I must blazon my humble submission to the doctors. If I upset them, we shall be disregarded and despised, and might as well pack our bags to be homeward bound on the *Vectis.*'

'You're vain,' I said angrily. It was the first time I had dared disagree with her. To argue with Miss Nightingale was to grow closer to her, because she had to extend her intelligence in your direction. 'Men at this moment are literally screaming for your ministrations. But you won't give them until you are implored to, so that your qualities might be valued by others as you value them yourself.'

She replied only, 'Save your breath, Mr Darling. You may be needing it for moving the tubs which serve as night-stools.' She sat stiffly straight, hands folded on lap. 'You and not myself are speaking with your emotions. And emotions are as useless for getting things done as unconfined steam for working an engine. Pity is valueless for treating the sick – or treating with the officials who control their miseries. Pity as much as you like, but firstly plan. I am surprised at your naivety.'

'Why should I crumple under your opinions? I'm a camp follower, not a disciple.'

'You must accept my doctrines, or go home. If I stepped into the wards without instructions, I should be breaking regulations. And the heads of all officials here are so flattened between the boards of Army regulations they remain old children all their lives. But like children, they will come running to mother once they are frightened.'

She reached with her toe to crush a louse scampering over the floor. 'I can say with Queen Elizabeth, "I thank God I am endowed with such qualities that if I were turned out of the realm in my petticoat, I were able to live in any place in Christendom." Though Scutari is not Christendom in any respect. The Main Guard might well be inscribed, *Lasciate ogni speranza, voi ch'entrate*, but rather than give a dying man a drink unasked, I shall sit here all day. Tomorrow being Sunday, we shall go to church. The hospital chaplain I hear is an inspiring preacher.' She plucked pen from inkpot. 'Will you please find Dr Menzies, to say I have a limited supply of medical comforts – arrowroot, sago, jelly, eggs, port wine, there is an official list – which my nurses can make into portions for his disposal.'

I was determined to play Polonius rather than Rosencrantz in this grisly Elsinore. I found Dr Menzies in Major Sillery's office, on the landing above our own quarters, both at a trestle table covered with papers.

First-class Staff Surgeon Menzies was in command of the hospital's medical affairs. He was a gingery Scot who said little, and would have preferred to say nothing at all, for fear of committing or compromising himself. Major Sillery always said too much, for fear of not sufficiently justifying himself. It was their contrasting way of admitting a common failure. Both wore the blue undress uniform, in which officers worked at Scutari.

' 'Pon my soul, sir, you *do* take a simple view of army administration,' Sillery answered my request, red face glistening with sweat. Unlike the wards, his office enjoyed a roaring stove. 'There is an official way of doing things, which everyone must adhere to, or nobody has any notion where they stand. When Dr Menzies decides a man needs medical comforts, he instructs the Purveyor, Mr Ward—'

Menzies grunted. 'Poor old Ward! Sixty-eight, goes back to the Peninsula and the Walcheren expedition.'

'He is hard-pressed, with only two clerks. You can't expect the army to sit on a fat rump of purveyors and the like, Mr Darling. Your Parliamentary gentlemen would soon wax wrathful at the expense. Mr Ward indents the Commissariat, on the appropriate form—'

'Forms, dockets, receipts,' said Menzies gloomily, indicating the table with a sweep of his hand. 'Requisitions, reports, diet rolls. What time's left for me to see a sick man?'

'The Commissariat either supplies the articles, or returns the form marked "None in store".'

'What then?'

Sillery looked at me pityingly. 'Articles unavailable obviously cannot be supplied.'

'Does the Commissariat always trouble to look?'

The men exchanged an uncomfortable glance. 'Things are not right here, I cannot but 'umbly deny it,' said Sillery, wiping his face. 'But the situation will shortly be transformed, believe me, sir. *The Prince* is on her way via Balaclava, loaded with beds and bedding, medicines, clothing, all we could want. They'd be here now, but for the navy's infernal habit of marking medical stores "Not Urgent". 'Ave the goodness to inform Miss Nightingale.'

I smelt scandal reeking of blood and gunpowder, not the perfumes of London drawing-rooms. 'Why have the men no spare shirt, no dry socks, no extra blanket, when they come in?'

Sillery looked triumphant. 'Lord Raglan's orders. They were to march light, and Sebastopol was expected to fall easily, so they left their knapsacks before the Alma.'

'Two months ago? Couldn't they be retrieved?'

'Matters are not arranged as neatly on a campaign as you civilians expect.'

'Why are the privies so filthy?'

Menzies replied curtly, 'Privies are not my affair. If I got men to clean them, I should be accused of stepping on the Purveyor's toes.'

I had another question. 'Why is the army more frightened of using its initiative than facing the enemy?'

'Sir, you are getting above yourself,' growled Menzies.

'I have reason to,' I said importantly. 'I am charged with writing dispatches for the *Penny Pioneer*—' Sillery looked alarmed, Menzies contemptuous. 'Can I include the news that Miss Nightingale and her nurses have been promptly ordered to work in your wards?'

'Mr Darling, see reason.' Menzies was exasperated. 'We have 510 wounded coming ashore now, another 540 due from the *Andes*, two more vessels still loading in Bala- clava harbour. I have *four miles* of beds, you've seen for yourself. To let loose a party of delicate ladies upon this would be a cruelty to them, and cause the utmost con- fusion to a system in which they have no place.'

'If they do, Major Sillery can easily order them back to the boudoir which he has provided.'

They looked at each other again. *The Times* had done mischief enough, but it was the newspaper of a gentleman. The *Penny Pioneer* would hurl the equivalent of a Cockney's dead cat. Were they, too, frightened of the urchin?

'If that proviso is clearly understood,' said Menzies.

I rose. Within half an hour I was overseeing a pair of grumbling, clay-pipe smoking, elderly orderlies, hauling out the overflowing latrine-tubs to a distant cesspool.

13

IT WAS THE HOUR of the 'professionals', Newbolt, Handshear and Wiley. The wards were all blood and jagged bones, men with bloody rags in place of arm or leg, sometimes both, occasionally all four. Men pierced with musket balls, ripping with indifference through skin, flesh, bone, eyes, joints or throat. Hands and feet lay on the floors of the wards, amputated arms and legs, some in their sleeves and trousers. Shortly, a small, bloodstained room was established for operating, which many of the men preferred death to entering.

I won my release from the latrine-tubs through Wiley, who pressed me into service as an amateur chloroformist. We operated on a door or window-shutter across a pair of chairs if we could find them, on the ward floor if we could not, in view of succeeding candidates for the knife and handkerchief of Lethe. My first inexpert ministrations had men groaning and struggling beneath me, sometimes they half-slipped from the improvised table. I supported them with my spare hand while Newbolt or Handshear worked fast. I grew better. I proved that The Bird's little man had not a chicken's heart.

Amid this gory chaos walked Poor Old Ward, spare, frail, in the blue undress uniform of an apothecary, a sheaf of forms under his arm. His responsibilities in the hospital comprised cooking, washing and cleaning – though not of the wards, which was the doctors' duty – paying the staff wages, stopping part of the soldiers' for being there, writing their wills and arranging their funerals.

'Poor old Ward,' said Newbolt. 'Menzies hates him quite as savagely as The Bird. Last June, he tried to get rid of him by having a medical board pass him unfit. But Ward had chums in high places, who got Lord Raglan to quash the proceedings without setting eyes on him. That's how the army works. You can see Raglan's point of view. He's almost as old as Ward, and almost as inefficient.'

It was the evening of Wednesday, November 15. I had been in Scutari ten days, and a mental sextant was beginning to fix my position on the uncharted waters where strange tides had borne me from London. The war was 300 miles away to the north-east. After forcing the Alma river in September, Lord Raglan had found an attack on Sebastopol from the north blocked by a massive star-shaped fort on a commanding hill, and decided instead to march round the Russian flank, settling his army in a crescent of besieging trenches to the south.

His base was the small port of Balaclava, six miles south of the trenches. Lord Raglan's General Headquarters, and the Headquarters of the Medical Department, were a mile or two out of the town. There was nothing else between Lord Raglan and Army Headquarters at the Horse Guards in Whitehall, nor between Dr Hall and Dr Andrew Smith at No 13 St James's Street. Balaclava had a couple of small hospitals, and another being improvised from a church, but most of the sick and wounded were ferried across the Black Sea to the medical base at Scutari.

The *caiques* connected us with Constantinople, and Constantinople connected us with home, by the electric telegraph and by sea, through the Straits of Gibraltar or more speedily through Marseilles and the Straits of Dover. A favourable wind of circumstances could blow a letter from London to Scutari in a week. There was plenty of shipping – sail, paddle and screw – and there was never enough.

The weather had turned worse, as bitter and blustery as midwinter in the English Channel. Behind the picture-decked door which separated us from the cathedral of suffering, we were cosy enough. We had wood for the stove, if no coal, none being issued by the Commissariat because none had been issued during the Peninsular War.

We were waiting for Kipping from the officers' kitchen. We dined generally off preserved soup, Black Sea turbot, good value at five shillings, mutton, hash and pickled cabbage, dried fruit and rice pudding. Sometimes an officer shot quail for breakfast. We had plenty to drink, French wine, Turkish spirits, the rum ration, porter at three-ha'pence a pint, 'Zest' from home, and for a luxury, goat's milk.

Newbolt was cleaning his instruments, Wiley playing complicated patience with a ragged pack of cards, at which his New England conscience never allowed cheating.

'Ward's a ghost, anyway,' Newbolt squinted down the edge of his amputation knife, as an officer along his sword. 'The purveyors' department was killed by economic strangulation after Waterloo, but the purveyors somehow remain to haunt us. Neither the doctors nor anyone else has the slightest control over them, while they control absolutely everything we do.'

'Why shouldn't you be proper officers?'

He laughed. 'Can you see it? Those swells in the Guards and the Cavalry, fractioning their authority with medical men? At home, we call by the tradesmen's entrance, and they rate us lower than the veterinary. The great Baron Larrey survived comradely animosity only as Napoleon's pet.'

Wiley swore, sweeping up his display of cards. Handshear came in, picked up the bottle of raki, poured himself a drink and sat on a packing-case with a greasy *Illustrated London News*. 'Watched a flogging this afternoon,' he remarked casually.

I sat up, the horrifying being always compelling.

'Fifty lashes, which is the stiffest dose,' he continued in the same tone. 'One of the cavalry depot troops. They set up the triangles in the courtyard, and paraded the regiment to watch. I had to stand right up by the adjutant. He counts the farriers' strokes, and sees they pitch in properly. They do it in relays, you know. Can't have them getting weary.'

'What's the effect?' I asked, engrossed.

Handshear's eyes turned to his magazine. 'Oh, to start with the back goes black and blue, then it opens up. It's like taking a ripe plum and bursting it in your fingers. Afterwards, it just pours blood.'

'You were to see they didn't kill him?'

'That was the idea, I suppose. The army's a little sensitive since the case of Private White at Hounslow. About ten years ago, when they could purge them with 150 lashes. He died a month later, and the vicar wouldn't bury him.'

'Despite three army doctors certifying that death was not in the remotest connected with the punishment,' said Newbolt.

'They did a post mortem – chest full of fluid, back muscles pulp, coroner's verdict, death from flogging.'

Newbolt snapped shut his instrument case. 'And one of those three army doctors was—'

'Dr John Hall, who sits in authority over us all in Balaclava,' supplied Handshear. 'I wonder if the vicar did so well in the Church?'

'What did your poor fellow today do?' asked Wiley.

'Stole a blanket.'

Newbolt stood up, pouring raki for all four of us. 'How's that man whose nose I stuck back?' he asked Handshear.

'It's not sloughing. He'll go home an Adonis. You used Liston's method, didn't you?'

Always eager to join their professional talk, I said, 'Sir Peregrine had much admiration for Mr Robert Liston.'

'Liston was all cut and thrust,' said Newbolt disparagingly. He swallowed his drink and poured another. 'In his haste to remove one unlucky man's leg, he whipped away his testicles with it.'

'In another case,' said Handshear, 'Liston incidentally amputated the assistant's fingers and an onlooker's coat-tails. Like most of our surgical cases, the patient died later from hospital gangrene. So did the assistant. The party with the coat-tails dropped dead of fright that the knife had pierced his vitals. It was the only operation in history with a mortality of three hundred percent.'

'You gentlemen are not telling the truth,' said Wiley severely.

Kipping appeared with our cauldron of mutton stew.

After dinner, I had to visit Miss Nightingale in her tiny room. It was now furnished with an unpainted deal table, where she sat every evening and much of every night with her correspondence. The starkness was eased by a French clock and an oil-lamp. I noticed she used a Turkish *divin*, an ornamented brass pen-holder with a portable ink-well attached. The kitchen outside now had brown curtains with bobbles, and she had somehow collected some sticks of English furniture. I saw little of her. She was always about the hospital, up to twenty hours at a stretch, meeting the constant fresh detachments of sick and wounded, apportioning them quarters, supervising her nurses.

'There is a shave, Mr Darling,' she greeted me sombrely, 'of a terrible hurricane falling upon the army outside Sebastopol. I hope it proves as false as most others. It would be the last and bitterest pill for so many who contemplated a single summer's hard fighting, then home.' She picked up the copy I had written to the *Penny Pioneer*. 'As usual, you're overblown.'

It was a testament of praise to Miss Nightingale – flowery, sentimental, as our readers loved in their cottage parlours, city attics and kitchens below stairs.

'It is important to turn your finest face upon the public, and to deafen them with the sound of your own trumpet.'

'Why?' she asked bleakly.

'So they will be eager soldiers, should you need to lead the invincible army of public opinion.'

She changed the subject. 'I have a task for you, Mr Darling. Half the hospital lies empty, because it was damaged in the fire. The thought has occurred to nobody that a hundred Turkish labourers could start work tomorrow and repair it. As I have Mr Herbert's assurance of the Ambassador's help to the utmost of his powers, please send a diplomatic letter about this to Lord Stratford's palace—' She inclined her head towards Constantinople. 'While the British army continues bleeding to death under its windows.'

We were interrupted by Miss Bancroft leading in Major Sillery urgently. He was redder and shinier than ever in the candlelight. 'Miss Nightingale, an 'orrible disaster has befallen us,' he started agitatedly. '*The Prince* – sunk with all 'ands, with all our stores, there's a proper 'urricane blowing at sea. In the Crimea, the 'ospital tents are uprooted, the 'uts smashed, uniforms near blown from the men's backs. I don't know what we shall do, I honestly don't, Miss Nightingale.'

'It's no good wringing your hands,' she told him sharply. 'We lack the fundamental necessities of medicine, and even of furnishing. With the influx which Lord Raglan writes us to expect any morning, this will otherwise cease to be a hospital and become merely a shelter for the dying. Supplies must be bought in Constantinople.'

'Bought? What with?' he asked pathetically.

'*The Times*' Fund. I have £30,000 from the public at my unfettered disposal.'

'That would never do,' he cried in horror.

'Why?'

'The army, madam, cannot accept charity.'

The Times had been attacking the army. For an officer to take *The Times*' money was like taking the enemy's. 'Then suggest what we do instead.'

'Mr Ward may have more in his stores than he knows.'

'The constant confusion about stores requires the purveyors to keep their wits about them – which some of them have not,' she told him shortly. 'Mr Ward's realm should be split into three provinces – one providing food, another hospital equipment and clothing, a third keeping the daily routine going. This is a hospital of 4,000 beds. These beds should have the appropriate complement of equipment and clothing, without requisitions for separate items on countless dockets collecting the signatures and counter-signatures of busy surgeons. Let the patient shed his hospital clothing like a snake when he goes out, and receive from the quartermaster's store what is requisite for him to become a soldier again, while the next patient succeeds to his bed and equipment.'

'It can't be done,' said Sillery forthrightly.

'It *must* be done. It worked in Harley Street, didn't it, Miss Bancroft? And Scutari is but Harley Street writ large. But the matter of applying simple principles is never simple. I shall spare your feelings, Major Sillery. I shall scour the stores and request Lord Stratford to dispose of *The Times*' money for me.' He looked relieved. 'Otherwise, I shall offer the whole £30,000 as a prize.'

'For what, madam?'

'For the discovery of anyone in Scutari willing to take responsibility for anything.'

Two afternoons later, my diplomatic letter produced not Lord Stratford – who would be honestly baffled by an invitation to visit a soldiers' hospital – but Lady Stratford de Redcliffe. Handsome, haughty, attended by a military *attaché* in scarlet full dress and an official in speckless top hat and boots, she stepped from the brilliantly lacquered Embassy *caique* to a submissive greeting from Major Sillery and a sycophantic one from myself.

Our visitors reached the hospital with their feet like ploughboys'. Lady Stratford would not enter. Who might blame her, with the stink seeping beyond the walls? Our party passed through the Main Guard to the courtyard. She assured me that Turkish workmen could be found immediately, their wages paid by the Embassy. Then she felt sick, and left.

I found an interpreter. I found one hundred and twenty-five reasonably robust Turks in the village and shanties. I found Captain Gordon of the Engineers to take charge. After five days, the labour force struck for higher wages.

I pleaded. They said, 'Yok'. That meant 'no', decidedly. I resolved on Miss Nightingale's authority to confront Lord Stratford.

Our jetty being unusable two or three times a week at that time of year, I had an uncomfortable ride on a mile of almost impassable road in an *araba* to the harbour at Kadekoi. It was an overdue excuse to see Constantinople and to leave my melancholy military surroundings.

My eye took refreshment from rich Turks in costly furs and shawls, their slippers and saddle-cloths embroidered in gold, their ladies bundled in white linen and struggling along the muddy streets in two pairs of slippers, attended by their slave women. From doorways came whiffs of burning aloes or *patchouli* – the smell of the Ottoman, as those of seacoal and the washtub among Londoners. The only part of the ladies visible being dark eyes above the *yashmak*, I stared so hard in mannerless curiosity of what lay confined within their clothes, that one stopped, looked quickly to see no Mussulman was in our twist of the alley, and with the painted finger-tips which struggled against her enveloping drapery, for a second drew the *yashmak* aside. I had so startling a view of dark, mischievous, smiling beauty that I remember it today.

I had money in my pocket. I visited the bazaar, where the goods lay in front of the counter and the shopman sat upon it, smoking the ubiquitous *tchibouque*. I ate heartily and toothsomely in Giuseppini's Hotel. Then I went to see The Great Elchi.

The Embassy was across the Golden Horn in the district of Pera. I was struck by its incongruous resemblance to the Reform Club, and was later amused to discover they had the same architect. A fiercely-moustached dragoman led me through a central glass-roofed court full of fleshy green plants, to a dazzling staircase of many-coloured marble mosaic. After keeping me waiting sufficiently to indicate my miserable lowliness, a young English secretary in frock coat and black stock revealed an apartment the size of a ballroom, with five tall windows, two superb chandeliers and a pair of fireplaces under long mirrors, decorated by white columns each supporting a lion and dolphin embracing the Royal Arms. I walked the length of the floor eyed with increasing chilliness by our ambassador.

Lord Stratford was the most important person in Turkey, and by his own estimation in the whole world. He had been ambassador at the Porte, on and off, since Wagram and Napoleon's marriage. He was to have had St Petersburg, but Czar Nicholas would not have Lord Stratford. He was the cousin of Lord Canning. He was exactly the same age as Poor Old Ward.

He now looked at me in disbelief as I stood before his gilt-encrusted desk in a room which would have taken a hundred of our casualties, my clothes worn and grubby through their repeated sponging of British soldiers' blood, my collar frayed, my boots cracked. The Great Elchi himself sat in beautiful frock coat and glistening linen, tall, stooping, eyes set deep under heavy brows, thick grey hair carefully parted and brushed, a broad jaw and a mouth like a crack in the ice.

I respectfully implored his help in putting our labourers back to work.

'Workmen?' He was lost. 'But I am not concerned with workmen.'

I explained humbly Lady Stratford's initiative.

'I know nothing of such an unusual arrangement, nothing.' he said, puzzled and amazed. 'I fear that some misinterpretation or mistake has been made by those unconversant with the functions of diplomatists. But pray convey to Miss Nightingale my appreciation of her great accomplishments in the field of charity. I am convinced that much comfort may be derived by the sick and wounded from that attractive source. All those who lie in their hospital cots at Scutari will be uplifted by seeing passing among them a young lady presenting the refined manners and graciousness of London society. The privilege of these soldiers, to be ministered by Miss Nightingale, is indeed great. I hope that they express proper gratitude for such devotion by their betters, which is an expression of the patriotic spirit inspiring our nation to victory.'

Speech was crushed from me by the weight of his condescension. The sleek young Englishman entered noiselessly, dropped a paper on the desk gently, and left obsequiously.

'Your Excellency will know that Miss Nightingale has command of *The Times*' Fund.' I wished to make the most of my audience. 'Miss Nightingale would much like Your Excellency's help in its disposal.'

His quizzical expression vanished. I had touched his heart. 'I have given deep thought to the disbursement of this considerable sum,' he told me with satisfaction. 'This money was, of course, subscribed through public feeling being falsely aroused by *The Times*' own correspondent. He wrote without troubling to seek an interview with Lord Raglan, or any senior officer. Though I doubt if he would be acceptable to such gentlemen. General Pennefather has been forthright enough to declare that he would as soon see the Devil as Mr Russell. But this money would be impossible to return to its myriad donators. Nor need it be. Nothing is seriously lacking in the Scutari Hospitals, nothing at all – so I learn from Dr Hall. Please tell Miss Nightingale that the sum could be most worthily dispensed by building an English Protestant church in sight of the Golden Horn, in the district of Pera.'

'A *what*?' I exclaimed.

'That would be to me the culmination of my many hopes and much labour,' he continued with dreamy self-con-gratulation. 'A Protestant church! Here in Mohammedan Constantinople! What a signal indication of British pres-tige. It would be a monument to my mission. Miss Nightin-gale is, I know, sensitive to the service of God.'

'Yes, Your Excellency. And Miss Nightingale believes it to include the service of man.'

The Great Elchi's eyes, straying heavenwards in con-templation of this criminal misappropriation of funds, turned severely upon me. 'Exactly what position do you hold in Miss Nightingale's retinue, Mr Darling?'

'Firstly, to make a record of her work at Scutari. I am a literary gentleman, sir.'

The eyes softened. 'And I am a poet.'

I congratulated him.

'I have penned many verses, in such intervals I could snatch.' His hand was already in the deadly desk drawer. 'I shall read you some.'

'But sir! You must be unconscionably busy. Your humble

servant does not deserve such honour from Your Excellency's own lips.'

'Fortunately, I allotted an hour to your business,' he assured me.

I reported to Miss Nightingale that evening in the 'Sisters' Tower', as it was becoming known. Her response was characteristic.

'I have a golden rule in case of emergency. When I want a thing doing without delay, I do it myself. Mr Darling, you are to give the workmen what they ask, and engage another hundred – which will be simple with rumours of your generosity. *The Times*' Fund will pay, and luckily I have money of my own. With £30,000, I shall become not a saint but a shopkeeper. You shall buy wholesale in Constantinople, and I shall establish myself in our kitchen as a general dealer in socks, shirts, knives and forks, wooden spoons, tin baths, tables and forms, cabbage and carrots, operating tables, towels and soap, small tooth combs, precipitate for destroying lice, scissors, bedpans and stump pillows. *Je vais faire les choses grandement*. I shall distribute the comforts which Dr Menzies dismisses as superfluous, but are in fact essential for the lives of the patients.'

'On requisitions made by the surgeons, signed and counter-signed, according to regulations,' I reminded her, smiling.

'Groove-going men!' she dismissed the lot.

It was time for her night round. We left for the familiar stench of the restless wards, with their unexpected revelations of a man dying or dead. I could not pass through them unmoved, but Miss Nightingale was never stirred by sickness. She thought only of the best practical means to make a sufferer more comfortable, to take down a dying man's last wishes, to stop another's tears or screams. She was as cool as a competent gentleman's cook smelling the roast burning.

'I can truly say, like St Peter, "It is good for us to be here," ' she observed. 'Though I doubt whether, if St Peter had been here, he would have said so.'

114

The candles from the high ceiling were few, and gave a poor light. I took from my pocket a concertina Turkish lamp, like that Wiley had passed me for the amputation. I had bought it that afternoon in Constantinople. I fitted a candle, lit it, and handed it to her.

'Most useful,' she approved. 'As the gales continually blow the windows in, and occasionally the roof off, to leave us under water for the night.'

She raised the lamp, throwing her shadow, grotesquely huge, over the lines of men and the single, meek grey image of a slipshod night nurse. As we walked along, I remarked, 'There was a statue of the Virgin Mary which stood in the seventeenth century before the church on an island – I've forgotten its name – in the Tiber at Rome. She held a lamp, which was lit every night for the sailors. She was called "The Lady with a Lamp". It's a good phrase. It would catch the imagination of John Bull. May I transfer it to you, in my next dispatch to the *Penny Pioneer*?'

'I have abandoned any attempt to rein the charger of your imagination, Mr Darling.'

'Perhaps I should persevere with my poetry, Miss Nightingale?' I asked lightly. 'Compared with the steam-engine rhythms of Lord Stratford's stanzas this afternoon, my Virgilian verses float to the ear like thistledown.'

'You would be much better advised, Mr Darling, applying your talents to advertisements for soap.'

14

LIKE EVERY OTHER outpost, Scutari developed an idiosyncratic life of its own. Everyone assumed a function different from what they expected to be, or started to be. Characters brightened and dimmed. All at the Barrack Hospital knew Harriet. She was the best nurse, deft with a blood-soaked, pus-stiffened dressing, or with banter and seemly titillation. Nobody knew Miss Bancroft, who had faded to a soft shadow of the sun which shone over us with daily increasing fierceness.

Christmas was coming, however incongruously. Jostled by Turkish infidels, elbowed by death and misery, we should scrape a little celebration with the plum-pudding and custard from our tin bowls, as hungrily as any homesick Christians throughout the Empire.

Uncle Peregrine had written expressing the widespread dismay at there being so much of everything at home, and so piteously little at the war. There seemed some invisible rusted stop-cock between the flood of British prosperity and the destitution of her army. He followed his letter with a wooden chest three feet square, sent by the fast screw steamer *Himalaya* – as I write, still in the service of the P & O Line – and Messrs Grace & Co of Constantinople, the shipping agents who handled most of the regimental baggage for the Crimea. My other uncle sent a Bible.

I was unpacking my box in our mess-room just before luncheon one morning in mid-December, with Newbolt and Handshear enthusiastically helping me draw the potted partridges, tea, coffee, chocolate, candied fruits, beef essence and French brandy from their straw nest. Our picture-covered door flew open for Horace Wiley. He was usually a man closely self-controlled in emotions and speech. Now his eye was wild, his pale New Englander's cheeks as scarlet as a British guardsman's coat.

'Look at this, you fellows.' He threw a document among the tins and earthenware jars on the table. 'From Dr John Hall, Hippocrates of the British army.'

The American's indignant finger quivered at a printed memorandum from the Inspector-General, distant in Balaclava.

The Use of Chloroform, I read. *Medical officers to be cautious in the use of chloroform. This is not to be used in patients with severe shock from wounds, as few of such cases will survive its employment. Public opinion is admittedly against this course, but public opinion is founded on mistaken philanthropy. However barbarous it may appear, the smart of the knife is a powerful stimulant, and it is much better to hear a man bawl lustily, than to see him sink silently into his grave.*

'Bawl lustily! The smart of the knife!' Wiley said furiously. 'Mistaken philanthropy! I learned the art of chloroforming from the hands of Dr William Thomas Morton – greatest benefactor of his age – and I will not see any man go under the knife without it.'

'Oh, you'd never get a new idea into Hall's head without a trepan,' said Newbolt, pulling the cork of my cognac.

'I don't have to obey his orders,' Wiley consoled himself.

'You don't, and we can't. Hall's orders are incapable of fulfilment, because they depend on medical equipment which exists only in his imagination, and a medical system which exists in nobody's.'

'Enlist Miss Nightingale's support for chloroform, Horace.' Handshear stuck out a tin mug for brandy. 'She can do anything. The hospital's buzzing from end to end about "Nightingale Power". The Bird's taken a fancy to you, too.'

'To me!' Wiley looked alarmed. 'A London society lady?'

'Yes, because you're an American. Not one of the stiff-rumped British officers.'

A slow, pleased smile stirred his face. 'That's strange.

I sort of felt I'd made a hit with her. We had a long talk about Boston.'

'Follow it up,' Handshear suggested. 'Talk to her about Chicago, New York, Cincinnati, San Francisco. You're lucky, the United States is an extensive place.'

Wiley searched for a glass of my brandy. 'Do you really suppose she's taken a shine to me?'

'Write her a letter and find out,' Newbolt suggested.

'But what should I say?' asked Wiley despairingly.

'I'll hold your pen,' I offered.

He seemed eager to oblige. A space was cleared, he sat down with paper, a Perry's patent Birmingham pen and the brandy bottle. He read aloud with Puritanical solemnity the note I had concocted.

Dear Miss Nightingale,

These short weeks that you have graced our hospital, and softened our lives, have won you the admiration of every medical officer, save a few sour old curmudgeons. Your masterful will, your everlasting good sense, award you rightful dominion over the minds of men.

But there is one whose feelings have quickened beyond reverence towards a lady of such creditable character and refreshing personal characteristics. I beg leave, my dear Miss Nightingale, to correspond with you, as I believe we may draw solace from each other, in the hard exile which we both suffer at Scutari. I also offer the compliments of the season.

'Its point could not be missed by the shyest virgin of Miss Frances Buss' North London seminary,' declared Handshear.

'Women are as susceptible to flattery as to the chlorosis,' Newbolt added.

'And Miss Nightingale is a woman like any other,' I said. 'As were Cleopatra or Good Queen Bess.'

'A mighty fine *billet doux*,' said Wiley with satisfaction. 'Can't say I remember writing one in my life before.'

He signed it with a flourish, rapidly folded it and applied a wafer, and accepted my offer of delivery after luncheon.

The Sisters' Tower was now being called the Tower of

Babel. Every day it was full of Turks and Greeks, French and Italian officers' servants, chattering in their own languages as they jostled among the orderlies, soldiers, officers and civilians. Everyone knew the worth of waiting to see Miss Nightingale, whose nuns and nurses could supply anything from an india-rubber bed to a pot of shoe-blacking. She foraged every morning from Poor Old Ward's stores, Major Sillery and Dr Menzies aghast about the findings of some future Board of Survey on so dreadful an irregularity. But the army could not court-martial a woman. Miss Nightingale enjoyed having grand motives to break petty rules. She had initiative and she delighted in exerting it, as much as she luxuriated in self-conscious self-sacrifice. At Scutari she queened it, her power absolute.

'Nursing is the least of the functions into which Miss Nightingale has been forced,' said Miss Bancroft, taking my sealed letter. She indicated the crowded kitchen. 'She is Barrack Mistress rather than Hospital Matron, or perhaps she is Chief Washerwoman.'

The beds and blankets at Scutari had never been washed, at best sluiced with cold water, which never killed the lice. Miss Nightingale had persuaded Captain Gordon and his engineers to fix coppers and boilers in an outhouse. Charac-teristically, she killed two foul birds with one stone. Half the soldiers' wives in the basement were separated from the bottle with paid laundrywork, the rest issued with 200 scrubbing-brushes and set on the floors.

'You might say of Miss Nightingale's work at Scutari much as General Bosquet said of Lord Cardigan's at Balaclava – *C'est magnifique, mais ce n'est pas la guérison.*'

'Puns are the wit of the witless,' she said severely, making a poor one. 'Miss Nightingale has a new task for you, Mr Darling. She wishes you to make a proper record of the deaths and burials.'

I objected this was a most unChristmasy request.

'At present, three separate registers are kept.' She ticked her fingers, as she had listed her patients in the hall at Harley Street. 'First, the Adjutant's daily headroll of soldiers' burials, on which Miss Nightingale presumes no one is entered who is not buried, though it is possible that some are buried and not entered. Second, the Medical Officers' Return, of which Miss Nightingale is certain that hundreds of men were buried who never appeared on it. Third, a return made in the Orderly Room, which is only remarkable in giving a totally different account of the deaths from either of the others.'

I promised to resolve this posthumous muddle.

'Miss Nightingale also desires you to make arrangements for post-mortem examinations by the doctors in the dead-house, which Dr Menzies has agreed to. Miss Nightingale believes that the doctors unwittingly kill hundreds of men through their lack.'

I took away these sombre instructions in search of Harriet. I had seen her little since the night we arrived. I had certainly no chance of making love to her. Though such opportunities clearly existed in the hospital, because ten babes a month were born among the women in the basement.

I found her in the corner of a corridor lined with patients on palliasses, boiling up a bowl of tea on one of the portable stoves which Miss Nightingale had freed from the custody of Poor Old Ward. 'You know that Dr Hall has issued an order forbidding cooking in the wards,' I warned her.

'Poo to Dr Hall. When a man cries for a hot drink, I give him one. Dr Hall would sooner see twenty men die from neglect than the smallest infringement of military discipline.'

'In London,' I told her admiringly, 'I never imagined you had such spirit.'

'In London I was selfish. Here perhaps I am more so. I have discovered a woman's true pleasure is only caring for someone else.'

'Nor did I imagine that you would abide Miss Nightingale's regulations – if not Dr Hall's orders.'

'"All nurses will be required to rise early, to be punctual at meals,"' she quoted, startling in her mimicry of Miss Nightingale's voice. '"It having been found that some of the nurses have believed they were to be on equality with the ladies or sisters, it is necessary they should understand that they will remain *in exactly the same relative position as that in which they were in England.*"'

I contributed, '"Any nurse found intoxicated will at once be discharged, and her pay will immediately cease."'

'"Each nurse must engage *not* to receive presents of any kind from any patients, rich or poor."' Harriet giggled and looked round like the Ottoman lady with her *yashmak* in Constantinople. By a thread round her neck she pulled under her ugly grey dress a man's heavy gold ring set with three diamonds. '"Nurses are never to wear flowers in their bonnet-caps, or ribbons." Does this signify?'

'Who gave you that?' I asked severely.

'A soldier.'

I was angry with her. 'Which one?'

'Shan't tell.'

The ring was slightly familiar. 'Harriet!' I exclaimed. 'Not Major Sillery!'

'Well, he was no more clumsy than Mr Larderton.'

'Oh, Harriet!' I complained sorrowfully. 'How could you?'

'Listen, lovey.' She patted my chin. 'How do you suppose he keeps in such a sweet temper towards Miss Nightingale? It's a miracle. She provokes him worse than a fishwife. He can't send us all packing, but he can ask to pack up himself. *Then* who would Dr Hall send us? Some regular martinet. That's as sure as the Devil's in London. See what a service I'm doing everyone?'

I could say nothing. I had to accept such high motives. Though I suspected that she was more concerned in replenishing her capital before returning home.

The next morning, I was breakfasting off a shilling loaf, cold pork with mixed pickles and a tin bowl of tea, when Handshear came into the mess hurriedly.

'Confound these patients. They always die at the most inconvenient hours,' he complained. 'I'm ravenous.' He cut himself a thick slice of pork. 'Darling, the Bird is cawing for you. She came along to watch my patient croak, an event which usually puts her in a good humour. Isn't she a petticoated Valkyrie? If I were a patient and saw her approaching with her gentle smile, I'd die of fright. But her feathers are ruffled this morning, it seems.'

'For any reason?'

'Wiley's love letter, my boy. The Bird recognized your style, obviously. It must be as distinctive as Wordsworth's.'

With the feeling of approaching the Levée's room at Rugby for a flogging, I went up to Miss Nightingale's cubbyhole office. It was now protected from the noisy kitchen by a heavy curtain. She sat at her plain table, Miss Bancroft standing beside her. Handshear had been right. Two scarlet florins on her cheeks marked the price of her anger.

'Mr Darling, I am resigning.'

I looked at Miss Bancroft. Her eyes were two vials of anxiety and fright. I should be first with the news to the world. A splendid chance to make my fortune.

'My object here is unobtainable, if the nurses will not accept the discipline which maintains us as a body amid our privations.'

I thought of Harriet's dalliance with Major Sillery. But Miss Nightingale threw across the table a cutting from *The Times*. They had printed a letter which Sister Wheeler, one of the nuns, sent home to her family. She was a nurse who thought that patients should be fattened like geese, always carping against Miss Nightingale's cunning care to give nothing without the doctor's written order. Sister Wheeler was emotional. She had written excitably of callous doctors and bungled surgery, and managed to make the wards appear filthier, bloodier and more mortal than the ones we struggled with.

'That foolish woman has shattered the twin keystones of my arch here,' said Miss Nightingale bitterly. 'The complete obedience of myself to the doctors, and the complete obedience of my nurses to me.'

'Oh, *The Times* only printed it as a stick to beat Lord Aberdeen. They're hot after him, for his general conduct of the war.'

'Miss Bancroft, Sister Wheeler must go to Kouali,' Miss Nightingale ordered. A hospital had just been opened in the Turkish cavalry barracks, five miles north up the coast. 'Pray remind her that I have already been forced to send six nurses home for levity. And this very morning, six more came declaring they wished to be married, followed by six sergeants and corporals asserting their claim to the brides.'

She glared, as though it were my fault. 'Last night came Mrs Lawfield. "I came out, ma'am, prepared to submit to everything, to be put upon in every way."' Miss Nightingale imitated her mincing voice. '"But there are some things, ma'am, one can't submit to. There is the caps, ma'am, that suits one face, and some that suits another. And if I'd known, ma'am, about the caps, great as was my desire to come out to nurse at Scutari, I wouldn't have come, ma'am." Caps and bonnets! More trivial than the fleas which jump all over us. Even the scarf, the cloth which the soldiers respect, which saves them from molestation, they call "frightful". My nurses are a hard team to drive. Finally, there is *this*.'

A letter followed *The Times*' cutting. 'Forty-seven more nurses are arriving by the *Egypt* steamer *tomorrow*, if you please. Under the superintendence of Miss Mary Stanley—'

Miss Bancroft gasped. 'But she's your friend!'

'Friend? I have no friends, it seems,' Miss Nightingale told her bleakly. 'Mr Herbert has consigned the party directly to Dr Hall.' She paused, to let the horror permeate through us. '*I* was to have sole charge of *all* the nurses here. Mr Herbert has sacrificed me. He has sacrificed his own written word. I am resigning.'

'Miss Nightingale,' Miss Bancroft implored, 'when we are tired and strained, we see enemies and feel stabs when both are phantoms.'

'Enemies? Among all the men here, is there *one* really anxious for the good of these hospitals?' she exclaimed. 'Is there *one* who is not an insincere animal at the bottom, who is not always thinking of getting on the winning side of all our necessary arguments? *I* am the only one who really cares for the patients. I sacrificed my own judgement and went out with forty females, well knowing that half that number would be more efficient and less trouble, and experience has justified my foreboding. I shall stay at my post only until I have provided in some measure for these poor wanderers,' she ended piteously, 'though how to house them, feed them, place them, care for them is not to be imagined.'

I was glad to be dismissed. The room was too small to contain such powerful emotions.

'But Mary Stanley!' exclaimed Miss Bancroft outside. 'The Bishop of Norwich's daughter, you know. Miss Nightingale and she spent a winter together in Rome. They absolutely adored one another.'

'Miss Nightingale is piqued like any woman with her nose out of joint.'

Miss Bancroft smiled. 'Perhaps it is wholesome for us to be reminded that Flo is still a mortal, which we were beginning to doubt,' she said with deep satisfaction.

15

THE FOLLOWING AFTERNOON brought a letter from my uncle Humphry. It must have arrived in Scutari by the same mail as Sidney Herbert's to Miss Nightingale, with news of her spurned reinforcements. But the baffling circuitousness of our administration could delay letters within the hospital longer than their ten days from London.

Dear Nephew, the bishop wrote.

War has broken out in England. It started in The Times, *with the customary furious letters signed 'Anti-Puseyite' and 'Bible Reader'. It spread to the 'religious' press, with all its emotional stridency (which I distrust intensely) and is now spluttering in many pulpits. Miss Nightingale has been accused of going to the East with no purpose save spreading Puseyism among British soldiers — though others accuse her equally of Unitarianism and Supralapsarianism.*

Congregations are being warned against raising money for sick soldiers which will pass through Popish hands. The fault is Miss Nightingale's own. As I indicated before your departure, Miss Nightingale sailed with too many Romanists and High Anglicans (Mr Sidney Herbert is of course a Puseyite).

I now learn from a canon of Canterbury, Dr Stanley, that his sister, Miss Mary Stanley, has already left with a party of nurses which includes fifteen nuns. This will raise the proportion of Romanists at Scutari, and the cry of 'No Popery!' from our more fanatical newspapers and vicarages.

I happen to know that Miss Stanley is about to be received into the Roman Catholic Church, if not already secretly within. I also know that behind Miss Stanley is our former Archdeacon of Chichester, now turned Papist, the persevering propagandist Dr Manning.

The nation's anger so blazes over Scutari, he wishes to use the heat to boil his own porridge. He is a man whose deficiencies of principles are balanced by his excrescences of ambition.

I confide in you because Miss Nightingale's name is on every lip in the land, and I beseech her to beware, or at least be aware, of these Popish plots. At best, Miss Nightingale should pack all Romanish and Puseyite nurses home forthwith. At worst, she must utterly forbid proselytizing by the nuns among the soldiers. I charge you with the solemn duty of making this clear to Miss Nightingale.

Send by an early post an accurate account of your sectarian difficulties in Scutari. I pray that you are conducting yourself as a Christian gentleman. Your uncle Peregrine never leaves me in doubt of the opportunities offered by hospitals for sinfulness.

I did not see why I should play my uncle's missionary. I had read the letter while walking the length of the hospital to the Sisters' Tower. I discovered the kitchen silent and tidied, the heavy curtain drawn aside, Miss Bancroft with Miss Nightingale, who sat at her table, sharp nose elevated in indignation.

'They have arrived.' Miss Nightingale had changed her forbidding uniform for a black merino dress trimmed with black velvet, with clean linen collar, cuffs and apron, and a white lace cap. She was looking pretty for her visitor. It was wholesome to find her not only mortal but feminine.

We received a party of three. Mary Stanley was pale, pretty, Miss Nightingale's age, a little too hollow of eye and cheek, beautifully dressed in wine-coloured silk. She clearly knew her welcome was amiss. Someone must have warned her aboard the *Egypt*.

'You look troubled, Mary,' said Miss Nightingale briskly.

'I . . . I actually found *something* on my gown. Actually *something*,' she confessed in horror.

'A flea?' asked Miss Nightingale casually. 'We have ceased to think about those things now. They are everywhere. The vermin here could carry off the four miles of beds on their backs, and march them into the War Office and Horse

Guards. You cannot expect the refinements of the Episcopal Palace at Norwich.'

Mary Stanley looked more shocked at the words than the fleas. One companion was a vast nun with a complexion like a slice of boiled silverside, Mother Bridgeman. The other a frock-coated, fair-haired, drooping, sweating, brow-mopping young man seemingly on the point of collapse, the Honourable Mr Jocelyne Percy. I imagined him overpowered physically by the hospital, but he was mentally by Miss Nightingale. 'I am here entirely at your service,' he said breathlessly, bowing deeply. 'To be your footman, your fag, I have abandoned entirely my life of ease, pleasure and luxury, that I might devote my enthusiasm to the commands of you, the Lady-in-Chief.'

Miss Nightingale said nothing. There was only one seat in the room, and she sat on it. I tried to squeeze away, but she said, 'Mr Darling, I need two witnesses. Our visitors will sign my notes of the conversation.'

'But why such formality, such coldness?' Mary Stanley exclaimed.

'To whom are your nurses responsible, Mary? To whom are you?'

'Why, they are responsible to me, and I to Dr Hall,'

'If I may say a word, now,' interrupted Mother Bridgeman, with an accent as thick as Irish stew, 'my sisters answer only to myself, and I answer only to my bishop. That's a matter I must make plain, right from the start. It is completely and absolutely inflexible.'

'I have toiled my way into the confidence of the medical men here,' said Miss Nightingale, her fury as cutting as Newbolt's busy amputation knife. 'I have, by incessant vigilance, day and night, introduced something like system into the disorderly operations of my nurses. And the plan may be said to have succeeded in some measure, *as it stands*. But to have all your women scampering about the wards of a military hospital all day long, which beyond the limits of my own discipline they certainly would do, would be as improper as absurd.'

'I do not *scamper*!' cried Mary Stanley.

'How do you intend to organize your nurses, pray?'

'Well, there are the ladies—'

'Ladies!'

'Who will not, of course, wear uniform. And there are the nurses. Whom one regards as . . . well, as one's maid-of-all-work.'

Miss Nightingale tore into her. 'By strict subordination to the authorities, by avoiding all individual action, I have introduced a number of arrangements. They are within the regulations of the service, useful on a large scale, but not interesting to individual *ladies*. I have diet kitchens for 700 of the worst cases, wash-tubs, bath-houses and night-stools. Which are not so amusing as pottering and messing about with little cookeries of individual beef teas for the poor sufferers personally. The "Lady Plan" of yours will end in nothing but spiritual flirtation between the ladies and the soldiers. It pets the particular man, it gets nothing done in general, The ladies will all quarrel among themselves. The medical men will laugh at their helplessness, but like to have them about for the sake of a little female society. Which is natural, but not our object at Scutari.'

'Dearest Florence—' A tearful meniscus rose at her lashes. 'If I have given you pain by coming here, I heartily ask your forgiveness. I never failed to do you justice at home, for what you have gone through. In my lonely hours since you left, I have felt all that you have been to me. I have so missed the words of sympathy that used to cheer me. Often did I sit thinking how and where you were resting on the great battlefield of life.' She sighed. The tears spilt. 'Would that I could have you up in my rooms as of old, and talk over the wondrous chapter of life which has passed over you this year.'

Flattery washed a rock bare of sympathy. 'I have no Mary Stanley.'

'Flo! But how you loved me—'

'Yes, and no one will ever love you more. To her whom I once thought my Mary Stanley, I have nothing to say,' Miss Nightingale pronounced. 'You have injured my work.

You have damned my courage, pursued me by treachery. Her whom I so loved and trusted!'

I could have felt no more uncomfortable than straying into a boudoir and discovering both ladies *déshabillées*. Miss Bancroft, hands folded as usual, bright eyed and pink-cheeked, smiled with satisfaction, as she had smiled in Harley Street at Miss Nightingale's spiking my pop-gun. Mr Jocelyne Percy was in a muck-sweat. Mother Bridgeman broke the tension by declaring loudly, 'The position of my sisters will not be of nurses, but of assistant ecclesiastics.'

'In years to come,' the Lady-in-Chief added, 'the world will have heard of Miss Florence Nightingale. Yet not one of Miss Mary Stanley.'

The Irish nun demanded irritably, 'Will you give attention, please, to Mother Bridgeman?'

'Mother Brickbat,' spat Miss Nightingale in her direction. Shortly the party broke up, to the variable relief of its members.

That afternoon, I suggested a compromise. Mary Stanley shortly took half her nurses and nuns to the Naval Hospital at Therapia. Mr Jocelyne Percy shortly took himself off to England. But Miss Nightingale was never the same. Always jealous about her work, she became like a passionate woman with a wayward lover. With the standard of a rival commander raised at Therapia, anyone who did not care to obey Miss Nightingale felt no longer the duty to do so. The despot was diminished. Her subjects disregarded her for empty squabbles over religious trifles.

Dear Uncle, I wrote to the Bishop's Palace at Chelsea the following Sunday.

Conditions have improved in the hospital during December. The men are reasonably clean and comfortable, have beds, enough food and even a few comforts. All this was achieved by the cool head and shrewd management of Miss Nightingale, who had the letter from Windsor, with which you will be familiar, read from ward to ward by the chaplains, ending with 'God Save the Queen!'

I assure you, sir, that Miss Nightingale is as adept a propagandist as Dr Manning, who I learn is disturbed not by the number of men dying, but in doing so without the Last Sacrament. Since the arrival of Miss Stanley's party, we seethe with theological rancour. The chaplains accused Miss Stanley's nurses of circulating improper books in the wards – not French novels, sir, which I sought for confiscation, but the Puseyite John Keble's verses The Christian Year *(which is Wordsworth and water).*

Miss Nightingale complains that she is caught between a Protestant howl and a Catholic storm, which distracts from her real work. Miss Nightingale would like some Presbyterians to keep the balance, but not over fourteen stone, three of such nurses being nearly swamped in a caique. *Would that a gentleman of your great qualities and authority were here to restore us to our senses!*

After I had applied my threepenny stamp – only the men's letters went free – and posted it, I had a sickly fear that my uncle might take my invitation seriously.

Then Harriet died.

On the morning of Christmas Eve, Handshear told me in his usual casual manner that she was ill. I found her with three sick nurses in a small square room at the base of the Sisters' Tower. She had the cholera. The disease had stuck to Scutari like a life-sucking leech, despite the cold of winter. She was ashen, thin as a stick, mouth loose, eyes fixed, deadly purple fingers caressing her cheeks, her hands, the foot which Miss Nightingale gently tucked into the blanket covering her palliasse on the floor.

She screamed, wrenched by the fearsome cramps. Then she moaned, moved her eyes, seemed not to recognize me, called me lovey. I took her cold fingers. One of the rats, which had come to regard themselves as rightful co-tenants of the building with humans, was staring at me just past Harriet's head. Miss Nightingale seized a club kept in the corner for these intruders, and split its skull before it could scamper beneath the wooden divan. She had brought her customary efficiency to rat-killing.

Florence nursed her own sick. With the men, she would swoop above the heads of nurses and orderlies to dress a wound, set a limb, or with her portable ink-pot take down precisely dying wishes. I now watched as she applied the stupe. She groped with tongs among the torn squares of old blanket in a tub of boiling water, wrung one dry in a canvas sleeve with sticks across each end, sprinkled it with chloroform and spread it on Harriet's hollow stomach, afterwards rubbing the heated skin with mustard and turpentine. The two other women were convalescent, and lay drinking tea, unconcerned. Death was our stock-in-trade.

The disease which felled the robust trunks of guardsmen in a day swept the leaf of Harriet's life from the world in a morning. I was there when she died. I left her a little bulge under a blanket on the floor.

'I think you knew her better than you cared to pretend, Mr Darling,' Miss Nightingale said on the landing outside.

'Yes, I knew her very well. She loved me. Perhaps she didn't, she only loved herself. It was impossible to tell. No, I didn't know her at all,' I contradicted myself.

'Would you write to her family, or shall I?' I was about to admit that I never knew her family, when Miss Nightingale drew from the pocket of her black dress a ring with three diamonds, looped on a thread. 'It's a man's ring.'

'It's her brother's. She kept it for luck. She was very attached to him.'

'A valuable object to wear as a charm?'

'I'll see he has it back.' I took the ring from her.

'Martyrs there must be in every cause.' Miss Nightingale sighed deeply. 'But it leaves me one pair of hands the less.'

Corpses were never left long at Scutari. Their space was needed, and the rats ate them. We buried Harriet at dusk on Christmas Eve in the British part of the cemetery at Kalyon, a mile distant, two furlongs from the sea. Her body was stitched in the blanket she died in, and lifted on an *araba* pulled by half a dozen soldiers. Miss Nightingale wrapped it with a white pall, emblem of youthful purity. Harriet went to the grave with us still sharing a joke.

There was the chaplain, Dr Menzies in scarlet and gold full dress and cocked hat, a dozen nurses, Miss Nightingale. It was a wild night, which strained the cypresses and drenched the mourners. Miss Nightingale's Turkish lantern kept blowing out, but the clergyman long ago had the burial service by heart. We slid her into a shallow grave in the brimming cemetery. The soldiers had buried a dozen that morning. I noticed a clawed hand and wrist sticking in lifeless supplication from loose earth. Carelessness always comes with Christmas.

The burial, even the memory, of Harriet were tidied away from the busy concourse of Miss Nightingale's mind. We went straight from the funeral to her office. She had more tasks for me. I would supervise the three hundred women amid the dirt and vermin in the basements, establish a lying-in hospital, see the thirty-six nursing mothers were properly fed, eradicate prostitution.

I was irritable, my emotions in fragments, angry at Miss Nightingale's inhuman detachment. I objected shortly that I was unsuitable for the last duty, having no morals.

'The causes of vice are not moral but physical,' she informed me, 'filth, overcrowding, drunkenness, ignorance and want of occupation. In civil life, you don't expect every workman who does not marry before thirty to become diseased. In military life, you do. Why? Because a workman has occupation and amusement, and consorts with honest women. People always say that a woman like me can't know anything about it, but because I know more about the actual workings of the thing than most men, I cannot hold my tongue.'

'I doubt, Miss Nightingale, the possibility of even a corps of sanitarians making the army a moral institution.'

She looked at me sharply, and reminded of something searched among her papers.

'Our work here makes either angels or devils of men, and women, too. The cubs you mess with are somewhat devilish.' She found Wiley's letter, and ripped it into shreds. 'I intended passing this to Dr Menzies. But I shall tolerate the unlicked cubs, in hope of their growing into good old bears.'

I went straight to Major Sillery's office. He had sent a detachment of six riflemen and a corporal to precede the funeral with reversed arms, but did not show his own beefy face. I threw the ring into the circle of lamplight on his table. He said nothing, his fleshy lips open, his fat cheeks sagging.

'I shouldn't wear it again,' I told him angrily. 'Miss Nightingale didn't recognize it, when she took it from Harriet's body. Though she was suspicious – perhaps she thought it was mine. But a lapse of Miss Nightingale's usual powers of observation cannot be relied upon to happen twice.'

He started to say something, but even unaspirated speech was beyond him. I stamped down to our mess-room. The three others were drinking champagne from tumblers and eating Christmas goose at the brightly candle-lit table, all in untidy civilian clothes.

'Hurrah! The Bird's chick,' cried Handshear, glass aloft. 'Just in time to join the fun and gobble the gosling. Horace! Fill a bumper of the Widow for the worthy Darling.'

'I don't want anything to eat or drink.' I sat on my uncle's packing case by the stove.

'Whoa! He's in love,' said Newbolt.

'I've just been to a funeral.'

'That's hardly unexpected,' Newbolt objected. 'It's easy to die in Scutari Spa.'

'You know who it was.'

'She was a pretty thing,' reflected Wiley seriously. 'Sure was a pretty thing.'

'It distressed me. Tremendously.' I was confessing as much to myself as to them. 'I'm not inured to death like you doctors. I'm not hardened to the blood and sickness, and all the dreadful deeds you must do. I join in, because otherwise I might as well be dancing in Mayfair ballrooms. You don't know the number of times I've had to fight back vomit. Or tears, which would be worse.'

'Aw, come on, drink up and forget it.' Wiley urged solemnly. 'Only thing, drown your sorrows.'

'I'll go to bed. I don't want to be the skeleton at your feast. Though I suppose to you a skeleton wouldn't signify much.'

They would have liked me to stay. They were good-natured men, sensitive to my distress but by their professional natures unable to share it, or even show it. It would not be fair to sit and spoil their dinner, goose and champagne not coming our way every day. 'By the by,' I said to Wiley, rising from the packing case. 'The Bird is furious with you about that love letter.'

'Not with me she ain't.'

'You can take my word for it. I've just watched her tear it to bits. It was touch and go whether she sent it to Menzies, with one of her vinegary little notes attached. If you'd been a British officer, you could have found yourself court-martialled.'

'No, she ain't mad with me, not one little bit,' said Wiley smugly. 'I'm no greenhorn. I signed it with the name of Thomas Handshear.'

'Why, you Yankee swine!' shouted Handshear.

In my cold, dark bedroom, I could hear them laughing. Our joke on Miss Nightingale was now less significant than the bug crushed under my foot. So was her resignation, of which no more was heard – exactly as I had expected.

16

AFTER CHRISTMAS, the hospital smelt better. Captain
Gordon and his engineers cleaned the sewers. They got
six hundred baskets of muck, two dead horses, a dozen dead
dogs, a mixed dozen of sheep, cats, rats, donkeys and two
men. The beds which the patients feared to take, next to
the privies and swiftly fatal, became no more perilous than
all the others.

The engineers built a narrow-gauge railway from the
jetty to the Main Guard, they boarded windows and holes
in the roof, the wind and snow no longer blew from the
Bosphorus across the patients, as though still exposed on the
deck of their transports – from which we unloaded several
with flesh and clothes frozen together, boots to be sliced
away piecemeal, each with its backing of flesh, sometimes
undressing them down to bare sinews and bare bones, one
or two lying close for warmth frozen inseparably to each
other.

The pale horse galloped unreined through the wards.

A British army of 10,000 men had been marooned on the
heights overlooking Sebastopol by Lord Raglan, as effec-
tively as if abandoned on those overlooking the North
Pole by Commander Peary. There was a bigger British
army of 12,000 men in the hospitals. The abandonment of
knapsacks in September, the hurricane which sank the
Prince in November and flattened their huts, left nothing
between the troops and bitterest cold than their linen suits
of summer. They supplemented their rags with sheepskins,
horse-hides, and cut-up blankets, pulled mess-tin covers
over their ears, grew long beards and moustaches which

sometimes froze so that they could not open their mouths. There was not a tree, not a twig for a fire, the ebony-hard vine roots hacked from the frozen ground were running short, sometimes they enjoyed a bag of charcoal in their ragged tent, and died of the fumes.

The army was only five miles up the road from Balaclava, but the road was single, narrow, and impassable. Great-coats, blankets, beds, tents, drugs, food, comforts were crammed into the Turkish Customs House at Constantinople, but of use only to the Turks who pilfered them. All awaited issue through the proper channels, which had long run dry. The Thin Red Line was so attenuated that Parliament stuffed it with German mercenaries at 2s a day, who aroused more disgust from the men than the enemy or their own generals. But the army's organization had broken down. Heroism was not enough.

On the first night of the New Year of 1855, I left the Sisters' Tower with Miss Nightingale on her night round. This had become my chance in her day for a talk. I was then writing weekly to the *Penny Pioneer*, and wanted to know more of the intimate correspondence she appeared to enjoy with the Queen. Miss Nightingale had implored Her Majesty that the ninepence a day, stopped from a sick soldier's pay for the delights of Scutari, should be reduced to the fourpence-ha'penny he paid if having the good fortune to be wounded instead. She petitioned also that the Scutari cemetery should be ceded by Turkey to Britain, Her Majesty's own subjects inside it steadily overtaking those of the Sultan.

She lit her Turkish lamp as we set off. 'Do you know, I am now clothing the British army, Mr Darling? Our convalescents must leave in their hospital dress or go naked, having arrived barely clothed and half shod. I have anyway substituted Turkish dressing gowns for hospital dresses, though three bales marked "Hospital Gowns" stand in the passage because nobody has the authority to open them.'

We went through a door into the avenue of sick. It was quieter than usual. All to be heard was the friction of our soles on the tiled floor, already worn into a groove between the rows of beds. 'I can believe the shave that there are not 2,000 sound men in the whole army, because I have received 3,400 sick since mid-December. And purveying is still nil – socks, drawers, coffee-pots, earthenware urine cups, everything, are monotonously docketed "None in store". Do you know the person I pray to have here?'

'The Prince Consort?' I suggested flatteringly.

'A good innkeeper. The principle of running a hotel and a hospital is exactly the same, it is a matter of cooking, bed-making and making people comfortable. We need soft bread instead of the eternal hard biscuit, because the men's gums are sore and their teeth gone from scurvy. Yet they have scurvy only through bad housekeeping. The navy has known for a hundred years that scurvy at sea could be cured by a ration of lime juice. There are 20,000 gallons of lime juice in the Commissary's stores, and there they remain, for the same reason that the Commissary's 3,000 pounds of tea stay unissued, while the troops in the Crimea get green, unroasted coffee beans to drink. Oh, for an inspired inn-keeper!'

We reached a fever ward. The doorway was choked with two grisly processions of stretchers in the candlelight, one carrying in the sick and the other carrying out the dead. We had a new epidemic. Miss Nightingale called it 'gaol fever', to most it was 'Crimean fever', Newbolt suspected it was connected with the rats and lice. Many of the patients developed a red rash, indicating the typhoid fever which was to carry away Prince Albert seven winters later, and later still to kill as many of our soldiers in South Africa as the Boers' bullets. It was a fever carried on the poisonous breath of the hospital itself. After the war, the mortality rate of any regiment matched the number of men who had been invalided to Scutari.

'Our registration of deaths is still lamentably defective,' was Miss Nightingale's response to the encounter. 'The only record kept is that a man died on such and such a day. We should know the ages, modes of treatment, appearances of the body after death. I calculate that I have already attended 2,000 deathbeds.'

'Tom Handshear imagines you more an Angel of Death than an Angel of Mercy.'

'That is unfair of Dr Handshear. It is simply that I have an instinct for the worst cases.'

We moved along the ward, the breathing, snoring, groaning like the rustle of leaves and creak of branches from a wind in a forest. A man began to swear loudly, saw Miss Nightingale, cut his oath on his lips.

'You see?' she said softly, with satisfaction. 'Amid these scenes of loathsome disease and death, there rises above it the innate dignity, gentleness and chivalry of the men. It prevents instinctively the use of any expression which could distress a gentlewoman. Look—' She was entranced. 'He is kissing my shadow.'

'Because you are one of the few women he has seen for many a month, and he is enjoying some satisfaction.'

'Save your cynicism for your salons, Mr Darling. A man hears, so far from home, in the nurse's voice that of the mother or sister who nursed him in childhood.'

'Believe me, Miss Nightingale, a woman's gentle touch feels the same to a man sick as a man well. Lady and rough soldier are joined in a relationship as complex and delicate as a spider's web.'

'Webs cause no trouble until they are discovered and must be removed.'

'You must talk more to the less ill patients,' I advised her earnestly. 'An enthusiastic letter in every soldier's home will be most useful if the Government falls. And it is tottering already. Lord Aberdeen will drag Mr Herbert down with him, you will find yourself without a champion in London and with a rival at Therapia.'

'But whenever a man opens his mouth with, "Please, ma'am, I want to speak to you," my heart sinks within me, for I feel sure it will end with flannel shirts, and we haven't got any.' She stopped, lamp aloft. The patient cowered under his blanket, eyes glittering like a frightened animal. 'Never be ashamed of your wounds, my friend,' she said. He stayed silent. 'Would you like a drink of water? Or of tea?'

'If it's all the same to you, ma'am, I likes a drop of brandy.'

'H'm,' said Miss Nightingale. 'Perhaps, Mr Darling, your view of the world is right,' she conceded.

The Government was out before the month. On January 26, Mr Roebuck, a Radical, won a vote of censure about the war by 157 votes in a howling House of Commons. Lord Palmerston became Prime Minister. He had known Miss Nightingale since her girlhood. The offices of Secretary for and at War were concertinaed, and embodied in the Scottish Lord Panmure. In January, four of our surgeons died of the new fever. So did Poor Old Ward and his poor old wife. Handshear seeing no necessity for a bravery which risked his own life without saving his patients', contented himself with shouting through the doors of fever-smitten wards, 'You people all right in there?' and hoping that he would not get deathly silence as an answer. Then one blowy afternoon in the middle of March, the inspired innkeeper astonishingly appeared.

I found two strange persons at ease before our messroom stove. One was a gentleman of colour, young and slight, in smart livery with bottle-green facings. The other was plump, about forty-five, heavy eyed, waxy faced, with a thick moustache and a beard like an exclamation-mark. His blue trousers were red-striped, resembling a guardsman's, his waistcoat magenta piped with pink, his jacket to match in heavy watered silk, on his dark hair a green silk tam-o'-shanter.

'Dr Newbolt, I am honoured,' he exclaimed as I entered. 'My card.'

Dress and accent indicated some latter-day Baron Larrey. Our French allies never paid us a visit, the squalor and pestiferousness of our hospital being famous. Correcting him, I looked at the card, of uncustomary diagonal shape.

Alexis Soyer

London   *Paris*

I exclaimed, 'You know Mr Wakley-Barlow at the Reform Club?'

'Certainly, I have cooked for Mr Wakley-Barlow and many famous Parliamentarians,' he said grandly. 'Though Monsieur Wakley-Barlow *est ami de coeur de la cave plus que la cuisine.* I have had the honour to cook for Lord Panmure, who said, "Go to the Crimea and cheer up those brave fellows at the camp! Your joyful countenance will do them good, Soyer!"' His voice began to gallop, his arms to fly. '"Teach them to make the best of their rations! I must make some arrangement for your expenses!" – an arrangement I accepted, or I should be giving offence to his Lordship and the Government. You read my letter to *The Times,* sir? February 2.'

The fluttering slip was instantly pressed on me. I later discovered that Soyer wrote to the Editor of *The Times* with the frequency and ardour of a lover to his lass. The correspondent had read of gross mismanagement in the hospital kitchens, and proposed proceeding at once to Scutari, if the Government honoured him with its confidence.

'That was written, sir, towards one in the morning, in the Wellington tavern at Drury Lane, while waiting for my scalloped oysters and pint of port wine.' He had a knack of making the most commonplace statements sound like a royal proclamation.

'I fear you will find Scutari a tattered canvas for your artistry.'

'*Merci, monsieur! Moi, je suis artiste.* And like all successful artists, sir, I am a practical one. Mr Thackeray – with whom I have long had the honour of friendship – said of me in his *Vanity Fair,* "The immortal Alexis Soyer can make more delicious soup for a halfpenny than an ignorant cook can concoct with pounds of vegetables and meat". During the Irish Famine, sir, my soup kitchens fed 26,000 every day!' he exclaimed explosively. 'And 10,000 London poor in Spitalfields have enjoyed the same benefit of my knowledge and experience. In that same year, I furnished the Reform Club with 30,000 dinners and forty banquets, besides receiving 15,000 distinguished visitors eager to inspect the renowned altar of a great Apician temple. My pen produced *The Gastronomic Regenerator,* of which you have doubtless heard – I am the author of half a dozen books, including *The History of Food in All Ages*, which was highly acclaimed last year – my cooking was a magnet to which all particles of the Liberal Party could cling. Though I fear that radicals seldom have good digestions. Mr Thackeray would cancel dinner engagements because of "an old friend", sir, appearing at the Reform Club – my beans and bacon! Everyone was utterly distressed by my resignation, and neither club nor party, I sense, has been the same since.'

'Have some brandy,' I said, offering the Turkish bottle. He sniffed his glassful, cried, '*Zut! Mon Dieu!*' poured it flashingly into the stove, and commanded his servant, '*Jullien! Le cognac. Le vieux.*'

A bottle was produced from a hamper at their feet. 'Cooking,' Soyer pronounced, 'is organization. The excellent and delightful Mademoiselle Nightingale took my point instantly. At six o'clock tomorrow morning, Mr Darling, as it becomes light, you and I are inspecting the hospital kitchens.'

I asked where he was quartered. 'But here, *mon ami*,' he replied in surprise. 'Perhaps I could inspect your *batterie de cuisine*?'

I had the best meal that night since leaving London. In the kitchen below, Soyer politely deflected Kipping, donned a huge white apron, turned back his cuffs like Newbolt preparing to amputate a leg, and with herbs, flavourings, wine and imagination turned our rations of hard biscuit and salt pork into a *ragoût* deserving of the Reform Club. He sat afterwards smoking a *tchibouque*, telling anecdotes of the English aristocracy, all of whom seemed his close and admiring friends.

Newbolt, Handshear and Wiley were lost. The man was even further beyond the circle of their experience than myself. Alexis Soyer was a theatrical Frenchman, as Thackeray wickedly drew him in Monsieur Alcide Mirobolant, the cook in *Pendennis*. It was the response of an individualist to a lifetime spent in England, serving English gentlemen.

'Have you visited Meaux-en-Brie, sir?' he asked Newbolt. 'This is my first excursion from England, monsieur, and I suspect my last,' Newbolt said, seeming offended at the suggestion.

Soyer sighed deeply. 'There I was born. So delightful! Wooded, cornfields, windmills on stilts, the Marne the width of the Thames at Henley.' His eye gazed longingly across a continent. 'I was destined for the Church,' he revealed, 'but I went on the stage instead.' He shook with laughter for several seconds. 'Then I was nearly murdered by the revolutionaries, so escaped with my twenty-two-year-old skin to London, where I had the honour to serve the Duke of Cambridge, who was always very agreeable towards me. Afterwards I married dear Miss Emma Jones. A brilliant artist, the English Murillo! How wonderful a wife I won! She filled me with a love which can never diminish.'

Wiley lit one of his cigarettes. 'You've left Mrs Soyer behind in England?'

'She is in Kensal Green.'

'Sounds a nice place.'

Handshear gave a burst of laughter. 'It's a cemetery.'

'I still cannot decide how fittingly to inscribe her grave.' Soyer wiped a tear with his yellow bandanna.

'How about *Soyer Tranquille*?' I suggested unsympathetically.

'I thought, "England gave her birth, genius immortality". Otherwise, people might think she was French,' he added revealingly.

At six the next morning, Soyer and myself met Miss Bancroft at one of the hospital's half dozen huge kitchens. Soyer ran his eye over it like Lord Raglan his battlefield – the cracked stone floor, the long deal tables and forms, the racks and ceiling-rings. A dozen soldiers under a sergeant were making the tea and coffee for breakfast. He strode up some steps to a long row of food-boilers encased in marble.

'Copper!' he cried in disgust. 'The worst metal, as I wrote upon my important visit to the Consumptive Hospital at Brompton. The wealthy alone should have copper, because they can afford to keep it tinned. Malleable iron is extremely clean and much cheaper.' I saw that Soyer had the same attitude towards cooking as Miss Nightingale towards nursing. He turned to Miss Bancroft, rubbing his plump hands. 'Mademoiselle, bring me the ration, and I shall start work on the midday dinner.'

'But that is impossible. Rations cannot be issued before ten o'clock.'

'*Mon Dieu!*' He clasped his wide brow dramatically. 'Even *I* could not manage in the time. And regard this charcoal – dusty, damp, useless. See that fire, in the roasting fireplace. Small trees, six foot lengths! The soup would boil too fast.'

'They throw pails of water to keep it down. Though it *does* fill the kitchen with smoke and steam.'

Soyer clasped his head with both hands. Unlike Miss Nightingale, his spirits rose and fell as his countryman Eugène Godard's hot air balloon over the undulations of the countryside. 'Such waste! Such inefficiency. Would that my kitchen in the Reform stood here in my country's service! All was powerful steam – that intelligent and indefatigable servant – turning the spit, drawing the water, carrying up the coal. Everywhere bubbling stewpans, savoury *rôtis* on my patent movable furnaces. Dutch ovens, marble mortars, gravies, sauces, stews, broths, fish on iced metal plates, as spacious as a ballroom, mademoiselle, and as white as a young bride. Where are the cooks?'

I told him, 'Cooking is a duty imposed on the soldiers, between their being well enough to stand up and being posted back to their regiments to be knocked off their feet again.'

He shook his head, as though over the ending of the world. 'They order this matter better in France, to quote my immortal Sterne.' He gave the impression of the author somehow being a valued friend. 'General Canrobert's cooks are as highly trained as his infantry, and as highly regarded. Would that I had some of my pretty female assistants from the Reform Club! Lord Melbourne – who often honoured my kitchen with a visit – once remarked on their beauty. "My Lord," I told him, "we do not want plain cooks here."' The end of the world was forgotten and he quivered with laughter for several seconds.

At noon, the kitchen was in its customary uproar. The orderlies waiting to draw food for their wards were jostling, swearing, banging their soup-cans, some grabbing double rations, some left with none at all. Soyer was aghast. 'The market at old Billingsgate is nothing to this. Look!' he cried. 'A wooden leg, boiled with the mutton!'

'That's a skewer, tied by the ward orderly to identify his piece when it's done,' Miss Bancroft explained patiently. 'Usually they use buttons, or a rag of red uniform, or an old pair of scissors or some snuffers.'

'The meat is issued *raw* to *each* orderly?' Soyer was on tiptoe upon the pinnacle of incredulity.

'That is so, monsieur.'

'*All* the meat is *boiled*?'

'The army knows no other method of cooking.'

'But one soldier may get all meat to eat, another only all bone to gnaw?'

'That is the system, monsieur.'

'Oh! I am living on the same planet which saw my great banquet for Ibraham Pasha of Egypt – with my meringue three feet high – or my repast for Lord Palmerston – who honoured me with so many fine compliments – when the band of the Coldstream Guards played, and my dear friend Mr Thackeray sang *Rule Britannia*—' He grimaced over a ladleful of soup. 'The fat must be skimmed, not thrown out, it is better for cooking than rank butter from Constantinople at fifteen piastres a pound. The gizzards, the heads and feet of the chicken and oxen, must not be taken out and buried, but turned into nutritious broth, which if poured over the serving of meat will keep it hot. Cooking is organization. Where are the vegetables?'

'Soldiers do not eat vegetables,' said Miss Bancroft.

'But they are part of a proper diet,' exclaimed Soyer in anguish. 'As Hippocrates says very justly, "What pleases the palate nourishes". *I* said exactly the same in my *Shilling Cookery Book*. The celebrated Leibnitz told us, "the experienced cook has made acquisitions in regard to the doctrine and theory of nutrition, surpassing all that chemical and physiological science have done."'

'If you, Hippocrates, and the celebrated Leibnitz are as one, Monsieur Soyer,' said Miss Nightingale, who had entered the kitchen behind us, 'I am sure we can be very reassured. Miss Bancroft, please have removed from the ward a carcass of a skinned sheep. It was apparently drawn by the orderlies too late this morning to be cooked for dinner.'

Within a week, Soyer had reorganized the cooks and the cooking. By a change so simple as drawing the salt meat a day earlier to soak for a day longer, by sprinkling it with pepper and flavourings as liberally as his conversation with noble names, Soyer turned the inedible into the desirable. He made delicious beef-tea, mutton-broth, arrowroot-water, calf's-foot jelly and cheap Crimean lemonade. He invented a Scutari stove and a huge Scutari teapot – 'Though admittedly it has no nourishing qualities, there is nothing yet discovered which is a substitute to the English patient for his cup of tea,' said Miss Nightingale. The men cheered him as he passed down the wards, three times three. There was to be a grand official opening of the kitchens. Lady Stratford de Redcliffe had promised to attend, to sample the soldiers' soup.

The night before, Soyer woke us all up, complaining that he was dying of brain fever. It was from seeing our immense number of wounded, and the number of dead bodies passing before the windows to be buried. Newbolt prescribed a purge. The next morning, he buzzed with health like a midsummer bee. At eleven o'clock, Miss Nightingale and Miss Bancroft, Major Sillery and even Newbolt, appeared respectfully in the kitchen. Lady Stratford could not come, but sent a kind message.

Like William Howard Russell, Soyer joined Miss Nightingale in making a new point to the world – that all men are important, even soldiers. We have entered the century of the common man, as I continually tell my readers of the *Daily Pioneer*. Miss Florence Nightingale was his midwife.

17

MAY CAME. Newbolt and Handshear were permitted by standing orders to change their trousers from blue cloth to white linen. On a Wednesday morning in the middle of the month, Miss Nightingale, Miss Bancroft and myself sailed in the steamship *Robert Lowe* from Constantinople to the Crimea.

The hospital had changed unbelievably, like a battlefield from the carnage of action to pastoral peace. The most terrible of the Czar's commanders, Generals January and February, had retreated from the defence of Sebastopol. Scutari had only a thousand patients, only a hundred of those bedridden. The hospital killed only twenty-two men from every 1,000. In January, it was forty-two in every hundred.

The day was warm, the air soft, Constantinople wore a vaporous golden tint, the foaming current of the Bosphorus seemed buried in its bed. Amid the skimming *caiques*, under the squawking gulls, we watched the gorgeously silk-hung *caique* of the Sultan leave the marble steps of Dolma Bachi Palace to the beat of a dozen oars and the bang of fifty guns. My excitement of quitting my pestiferous lodging for the seat of war was lessened only by Monsieur Soyer coming with us. I had the notion that he thought the Crimean campaign engineered only for his benefit. Though at least we should eat well.

'What a glorious mine of subjects for a Claude Lorraine, mademoiselle!' Soyer appeared on deck in gold braided waistcoat, blue-and-silver striped trousers, white burnous, and wideawake hat flowing with red and white ribbons. He looked more important than General Canrobert. The two ladies wore heavy shawls over their black dresses. My Mayfair clothes having disintegrated, I had written to uncle Peregrine and received promptly a box of shooting-jackets, leggings, comforters, boots and a gutta-percha coat from Gibbys & Haines. 'It is much to be regretted that Claude Lorraine never visited these Moslem shores,' sighed Soyer.

'We are near Therapia,' remarked Miss Nightingale, who saw the world with a different eye. 'Where the naval hospital is situated so beautifully and so very unhealthily.'

I said, 'I heard a shave today that Miss Stanley has gone home.'

Miss Nightingale's eyes flashed. 'That is perfectly correct. Miss Stanley has been very unwell for some time.'

Miss Stanley did not recur in our conversation.

'I bear an unofficial letter from the War Office to Lord Raglan,' announced Soyer, as though it would solve all our travelling problems, and even force the Russians into surrender. 'I had the honour of knowing his Lordship some ten years ago. He called me one of his great benefactors, for giving his Lordship's cook my receipt for *pot-au-feu*. I had of course the honour of sailing out with the distinguished Turkish commander Omer Pacha from Marseilles. He imagined that I was coming to open a hotel!' He quivered with laughter at so ridiculous a misconception. 'Hello! Here is your "man", mademoiselle,' he continued boisterously. 'A regular *enfant de troupe*.'

Miss Nightingale's latest adherent was Robert Robinson, who everyone called Thomas, a drummer invalided from the 68th Light Infantry. He declared often that he had quitted his instruments and sticks 'to devote my civil and military career to Miss Nightingale'. He was twelve years old.

'Bravo!' Soyer greeted him. 'Are you a good sailor? Are you, Mademoiselle Nightingale? You know, the Black Sea is called in French *La Mère Noire*, who safely bears her children upon her tranquil bosom in the morning, and at night rocks the cradle with such furious love that she changes the smile of comfort to sickness and tears.'

'*There's not a sea the passenger e'er pukes in, Turns up more dangerous breakers than the Euxine,*' I quoted Wakley-Barlow's favourite poem.

Our spirits stayed as bright all the voyage, though the ship was slow, crammed with officers, Government officials and 420 of Florence's convalescents, sent to be shot at again. On Saturday after breakfast we anchored at Balaclava. It was barely a creek between steep hills with a village at the far end, the water a picket-fence of masts. Every rigging was alive, every ship's side strained with men giving sporadic cheers, calling, 'Miss Nightingale! Miss Nightingale!' At Scutari, we felt her renown no more than celebrated explorers still in their jungle. That morning, I realized that she was truly famous. My catch-phrase *The Lady with a Lamp* was a trump to take a trick on the public imagination.

The smell of Balaclava was terrible. Everyone spoke of the storm the previous November, when the harbour looked like a forest in an earthquake, ten hours when no one dared go out for fear of blowing into the sea. The sailors of the *Prince*, lost with the supplies to Scutari, were buried so shallowly on the beach of Leander Bay that parts of them were still clearly visible, preserved by the shovelfuls of lime which constituted their interment. The army had power above the high-water mark. The navy's sway began beyond the low-water one. The tidal shore was outside the authority of everyone. The only beneficiaries of this mortal muddle were men pressed into reburial, who had an issue of brandy whenever the stench made them feel faint, which it did repeatedly.

We arrived to find that we did not exist.

Dr John Hall was still smarting from a slap by Lord Raglan's military glove. An officer had been so appalled by patients laid under a blanket in mid-November on the bare deck of the *Avon*, awaiting transport to Scutari, that he had galloped at midnight to General Headquarters. Hall tried shuffling blame on the Balaclava local medical officer, Lord Raglan clapped it round his own shoulders, in his Orders of December 13. Hall was further infuriated by the women intruding into the seat of war, as if into the Army and Navy Club in Pall Mall. His eye picked from Sidney Herbert's original instruction that Miss Nightingale's powers lay over the female nurses in *Turkey*. In the Crimea, he refused to provide any of us with rations, roof or riding-stable.

I borrowed a horse, and rode through the muddy, uneven streets of Balaclava to remonstrate. Hall lived in Kakikoi, a village where the plain, white little church with its fancy portico and lantern atop its red roof, had been turned from the service of God to that more immediate of man, as a hospital during the agonized winter. His house was tiny, the living-room hardly big enough for two sitting comfortably. This was the General Headquarters of the Army Medical Department, which conducted all hospital business between the trenches of Sebastopol and Scutari. Dr Hall was not at home.

We had to live on the *Robert Lowe*. It became Miss Nightingale's floating drawing-room, military and medical bigwigs pouring aboard. From over the hill, we could hear the cannonade and fusillade of the siege. We inspected the crammed hospitals. Mrs Davis at the General Hospital was rude, and greeted Miss Nightingale, 'I should as soon have expected to see the Queen here as you.' Mrs Shaw-Stewart (sadly, really Miss) at the Castle Hospital on the Genoese Heights was an enthusiastic martyr, wasting our visit with complaints of her ill-treatment by the army. We went to the war itself. We looked down at Sebastopol across the fascines of a mortar battery, a popular spot for the 'T Gs', including the feminine ones. An officer's field-glasses showed the white stone warehouses against the quays, Fort Paul by the main jetty, men of war stranded in the harbour, the double line of British and French ships blockading the mouth of the roadstead, the intimidating Star Fort beyond.

'I had always heard that Balaclava was pretty,' observed Miss Nightingale. She picked a few blades of grass. 'Fields watered by my soldiers' blood.'

The adhesive Soyer insisted that Miss Nightingale sat in her riding-habit astride one of the massive, squat mortars. 'Gentlemen, behold this amiable lady sitting fearlessly upon a terrible instrument of war!' he cried to the gunners. 'Behold the heroic daughter of England, the soldier's friend!' The men cheered three times three.

I had noticed uneasily the black fingers of guns poking at us from the Russian fortifications. Now black smoke puffed from a muzzle, and with the noise of a railway train, a shell passed over our heads, protected by nothing more substantial than Thomas's parasol. 'They have the range very well,' remarked the officer with the glasses mildly. 'Though they don't usually shoot at lady visitors.' Thirty years later, when his story *Sebastopol* was translated into English, I discovered that behind the embrasures opposite that morning was Leo Nikolayevich Tolstoy. Perhaps I had the honour of his trying to kill me.

We had been in the Crimea a week, when Miss Nightingale fell dangerously sick.

I had been riding round the camps all day, and returned to the *Robert Lowe* to receive Miss Bancroft's agitated greeting, 'Miss Nightingale was very poorly this morning – but being Miss Nightingale, hardly complained. Then at two, I had to send in a great hurry for Dr Henderson from the General Hospital. He says she has the fever, and must be moved at once to the Castle Hospital on the Heights. He's still with her.'

'Why not the General Hospital?' I asked impatiently. 'It's much nearer '

'It has the cholera raging '

As we spoke, Dr Henderson appeared up the companion-way, looking glum

'How ill is she?' I demanded.

'She is suffering, I assure you, from as bad an attack of Crimean fever as I have seen,' he told the pair of us. 'But I should say the chances are in her favour, because she does not fret in the slightest degree, but is perfectly composed.'

A procession was rapidly organized. Miss Nightingale lay almost motionless on a stretcher, with an escort of soldiers. Thomas the drummer-boy was on tiptoe holding his white parasol over her, weeping bitterly. The soldiers had to clear our path from the dockside. All Balaclava was in uproar at the news. Soyer was soon at the dramatic scene, galloping on a grey pony.

'What do the doctors say of the case?' he asked me breathlessly from horseback.

'That the lady is most seriously ill. No one must go near her except Miss Bancroft and myself.'

'*Mon Dieu!*' His fist beat his brow under his wideawake hat. 'She caught the fever from consoling that officer with it, up at the Heights. I warned her about the danger of exposing herself, several times.'

There had been a rainstorm, the roads were muddy, it took us an hour, the soldiers carrying the stretcher in relays. The Castle was hardly a hospital, just a few rough wooden huts, filled with wounded from the Sebastopol trenches. She was taken to the hut nearest the stream, its plain plank walls containing only bed, table and chair, with one small high window and a view from the door across slopes bright with spring flowers to the overcrowded harbour. I at once left her to Miss Bancroft, borrowed a doctor's horse, and hurried to the Balaclava telegraph office. I usually sent my dispatches to the *Penny Pioneer* by the mails. But I knew that Russell was visiting Constantinople. There was no other correspondent in the Crimea. I should get the news to London first.

I rode up to the hospital early the next morning. The sun was already burning, the long grass which caressed the chest of my horse was full of buttercups, bluebells, poppies and birdseyes, the wind was soft, the butterflies sported in clouds. It seemed a ridiculously unseasonable morning for anyone to choose for being ill, or for fighting a war. Miss Bancroft had stayed overnight with Mrs Shaw-Stewart, and I found her waiting outside the hut.

'How is Miss Nightingale?'

'Still in danger. Dr Henderson is attending her this moment.'

As I dismounted, I noticed her surly look. 'Why did you not remain and help me with her yesterday?' she asked.

'I had to telegraph the news home.'

'So fortunate for your reputation, Mr Darling, that Miss

Nightingale is so ill. I know that you came East only to send tales home about us. That you might find yourself less of a nobody when you return.'

'How can you so accuse me of that?' I asked resentfully. 'Haven't you seen enough of my work among the sick and wounded to know otherwise?'

She gave no reply. I was mystified at her bad temper, though having to admit that her charge was reasonably justified. I did not then foresee the journalistic glory from my telegraphed words. I learned this a week or two later, from copies arriving of the London papers. Not just Balaclava had exclaimed in distress. Not just in the wards of Scutari had men wept. The words of Fleet Street leader-writers fell like the beat of muffled drums. At Windsor, the Queen had asked Lord Panmure anxiously about 'that excellent and valuable person, Miss Nightingale'. In poor households throughout the country, the alarm and desperation of the past winter blew cruelly into the brighter spring days. Upon the health and safety of Miss Nightingale depended the health and safety of their sons and brothers, husbands and sweethearts.

'Then you only came out to be with Miss Catchpole,' Miss Bancroft continued slightingly. We strolled a few paces among the flowers, leading my horse. 'It was distressing for you that death should put an end to your sport with her.'

'I came out not even knowing that Miss Catchpole was of the party,' I returned patiently. 'She was a lively and pretty woman, who was happy in finding satisfaction where she least expected it. If you do not feel her death, it must be because your heart is enamelled with jealousy.'

'Jealousy? Of Miss Catchpole?' she asked contemptuously. 'In what single respect?'

The morning had darkened like our words, one of the sudden Crimean storms was blowing up. I conceded her turning upon me, her callousness towards Harriet, to the effect of emotions disturbed by Florence's sudden danger.

'I wish you had never come to Harley Street that day,' she said bitterly.

'Why? I wrote no tales about you then.'

'You wedged between myself and Miss Nightingale.'

This amazed me. The two women were always close – I sometimes felt that Miss Bancroft's adoration provoked in Miss Nightingale indifference or irritation. I was too wise unduly to favour one from a pair of female friends more than the other. My work was different from Miss Bancroft's, I saw Miss Nightingale far less. I was irritated, having put myself to such discomfort and risk at Scutari for both of them.

Dr Henderson in blue undress frock-coat left the hut. 'Ah, Mr Darling, there you are. Miss Nightingale wishes to see you.'

'How do you find her?'

He dropped his voice. 'Her mind is wandering. Please remember as much. She asks to speak privately, by yourself.'

I looked up at Miss Bancroft. She had turned her back.

The wooden room had the sour smell of fever. Miss Nightingale lay flaccidly upon a bank of pillows, her face was scarlet and sweaty, her hair shorn like a convict's, her eyes shining with white fire.

'Mr Darling, how kind,' she greeted me weakly, as though I were unexpected. 'Did you see the Persian gentleman?'

'Only Dr Henderson, Miss Nightingale.'

'The Persian gentleman who had a draft of £30,000 for me . . . but perhaps I was mistaken.' Her cropped head lay on one side. 'I am going to die, Tristram.'

My vehement denial went unheeded. It was the first time she used my Christian name. 'I want you to do me a service. But you must tell no one in the world I asked it.'

I nodded towards the door. 'Even Miss Bancroft?'

'I do not trust Miss Bancroft.'

I sat on the chair beside the bed.

'Take this—' She drew from under the bedclothes a gold cross set in a mother-of-pearl ring, suspended on a black ribbon. I remembered it round her neck, that turbulent breakfast at Embley House. 'Give it to Clarkey.' I frowned, for the moment puzzled. 'You met her in Paris. Madame Mohl.' I remembered the childlike Irish–Scotswoman with hair like a Yorkshire terrier's. 'She lives in the rue du Bac, No 120. You can go home by Paris, when the war is ended. Give it her with my fondest love. Say I sent it from my deathbed.' She handed me the pendant, her fingers hot. She added characteristically, 'Take care of the contagion.'

I wrapped the cross in my handkerchief, and put it in the pocket of my shooting-jacket.

'You must not tell Miss Bancroft,' she repeated. I promised. 'Should anything happen to you, Tristram . . . and I pray to God it may not . . . hand it on to Dr Newbolt, or some man you can trust. Perhaps they can take it. But I should like you to give it Clarkey yourself, and to tell her how you see me now, to pass her my love from my own lips.'

She fell silent. I wondered if I should steal away.

'I have loved Clarkey since I was eighteen. Since I first met her in Paris. That was when we lived in the Place Vendôme—' Her voice grew dreamy, she looked slowly round as though seeing it. 'In those splendid rooms, all gilt mirrors and crimson satin, and the statue of Napoleon outside the windows . . . they had just had a revolution. I loved Clarkey more than Mary Stanley. Much more. It was for Clarkey that I never married Richard Monkton Milnes, though the family were desperate I should.'

She stopped again. I waited patiently. Now I knew why Jane Bancroft hated me.

'I loved Clarkey more than Marianne Nicholson. I was twenty-five then, I felt I had never loved but one person with passion in my life, and that was Marianne. She was so beautiful. The face of an angel.'

She raised her large hand, but it fell back like a sick bird on her skimpy-bosomed chest.

'Marianne was my cousin. Her brother Henry proposed marriage to me, you know. I refused him. My family thought I was being haughty and vain, and Marianne left my life. She was cruel.'

As Florence talked of her younger self, she began to sound and look like a girl, the childishness which sometimes comes upon the dying. I realized with a shock that I had been chosen for her deathbed confession. I wondered if I should break off, and have Jane Bancroft send for the chaplain.

'I have an intellectual nature which requires satisfaction, and that I would find in a man. I have a passionate nature which requires satisfaction, and that I never would. I can hardly find satisfaction for any of my natures . . .'

She was breathing quickly, her eyes were shut. I told her that I understood my mission, that I must leave her to sleep.

'We must all take Sappho's leap, one way or another, before we attain to her repose,' she said faintly. 'Some take it to death, some to marriage, and some to a new life, even in this world. But no more childish things, no more love, no more marriage . . .'

She turned her head, feverish eyes suddenly looking at me searchingly. 'My experience of women is almost as large as Europe. And it is so intimate, too. I have lived and slept in the same bed with English countesses and Prussian *Bauerinnen*. No Roman Catholic *supérieure* has ever had the charge of women of the most different creeds that I have had. No woman has excited passions among women more than I have. Yet I leave no school behind me. My doctrines have taken no hold among women.'

'Have they not?' I protested comfortingly. I had read Gautier's *Mademoiselle de Maupin* and Diderot's *La Religieuse*. 'When you recover, as the doctors assure us—'

'The doctors being wrong is surely a usual experience?'

'You must not feel condemned to loneliness, as a woman loved only by women.'

'Women crave for being loved, not for loving. They scream out at you for sympathy all day long. They are incapable of giving any in return.'

I told her gently, 'Men don't think that.'

'Men think it all but playful sport between two beings of amusing inferiority to themselves. It makes me mad.'

The room was gloomy. Through the open door it was already raining hard. I cursed having to get wet, riding back to the harbour. But it would repay Miss Bancroft's petulance with a good soaking outside. I looked back to the bed, and Miss Nightingale had dropped abruptly into sleep. I tiptoed to the door, eager to get the acrid stink from my nostrils. There was the noise of horses. A loud voice demanded, 'Which hut's Miss Nightingale's?'

'Hist, hist! Don't make such a horrible noise as that, my man.' I found Miss Bancroft making quietening signs with both hands to a pair on horseback, wrapped in gutta-percha cloaks already running wet. One jumped from his horse, pushing her aside. 'What do you want?' she asked, frightened. They could have been Russians, come to kidnap a prize hostage. 'Pray, who are you?'

'Oh, only a soldier. But I must see her. I have come a long way. She knows me very well. My name is Raglan.'

I recognized him. Square-jawed, toothless, wrinkled, sad eyed, hawk nosed, grizzled grey, pale, tired, sixty-six. He hated pomp and processions. He wore his rank with the modesty of the civilian frock-coat and muslin-wrapped straw hat which he adopted out of battle. He was shy, and so thought arrogant. His left arm carried a telescope mounted on a rifle-stock. His right had been cut off at Waterloo, when he had called after the surgeon, 'Hey, bring my arm back. There's a ring my wife gave me on the finger.' Had his own endurance been less, his Crimean army would have had less to endure.

He strode past me, leaning against the doorway with legs crossed.

'Oh, Lord Raglan!' Miss Nightingale had woken with the commotion. 'I have a very bad fever, it will be dangerous for you to come near me.'

'I have no fear of fever or anything else.'

I stood with Miss Bancroft and his *aide-de-camp*, in the rain and in silence. After a few minutes Lord Raglan came out. He said to us, 'I hope that Miss Nightingale will soon be able to continue her charitable and invaluable exertions, so highly appreciated by everyone, as well as by myself.'

Miss Bancroft curtsied as though in a drawing-room, and begged to apologize.

'No, no, not at all, my dear lady. And who's the boy?' Thomas, coat collar up, had walked from the harbour.

'I am Miss Nightingale's man, your honour. I heard the Russians are to attack this way.' There was a shave in Balaclava. 'I have come to guard my sick mistress, and I am ready to die in her defence.'

The Commander-in-Chief laughed, patted the boy's head, mounted and was off. Exactly a month later Lord Raglan was dead, of the cholera.

18

THE WAR got off to a fresh start. The French had already replaced General Canrobert, of the twirled moustaches and curly imperial, for General Pélissier, fat, bull-necked, rude, up from the ranks. Lieutenant-General James Simpson, aged sixty-three, last in action at Quatre Bras, was given command of the British army, and hated the task as much as he hated his French allies. Raglan's death was a surprise to everyone. It was a surprise to him. 'I shall soon be all right,' he had told his *aide-de-camp*, from his green-curtained camp bed.

'Alas, sir, I fear not,' was the discouraging reply. 'The doctors have a very bad opinion of you, sir, and have desired me to tell you, and ask if you would like the chaplain sent for.'

'They are quite mistaken. They are making a mistake altogether. Yesterday I was very bad, but now I am easy and comfortable. I do assure you that they will find they are mistaken.'

The man who had sent the Light Brigade to charge the wrong way could not even direct his own soul to Heaven.

'Not a *very great* general,' Miss Nightingale recollected, 'but a *very good* man.'

It was now mid-August, and we had been back in Scutari over a month. Our journey had been dramatic, as everything involving Monsieur Soyer. Miss Nightingale was brought down from the Genoese Heights by eight soldiers on a stretcher and taken aboard the *Jura*, sailing within the hour with 400 horses and 500 troops. The ship stank. Soyer complained to the captain. The captain told him shortly that his ship always stank in port, it would blow away at sea. Miss Nightingale fainted. Soyer insisted on her moving to the *Baraguay d'Hilliers* alongside. That night, Soyer turned his intimacy with the aristocracy to use, and cadged us berths on a visiting lord's steam yacht. After sailing, we learned that the *Jura* was bound not for Scutari, but directly for England. It was Hall's plot. Crimean fever having failed to free him from this turbulent nurse, he had slyly passed sentence of banishment.

Miss Nightingale sat outside the chaplain's house at Scutari, where she was still convalescing. Her hair had grown into fair boyish curls, she was gaunt, in her usual black dress. Across the Bosphorus, Constantinople burnt in the setting sun. There was a terrier barking about, sent by Sidney Herbert, but she was not interested in animals, whose deaths were unremarkable.

Catching the fever was Miss Nightingale's most valuable accomplishment in the Crimean peninsula. Howard Russell was stranded in Constantinople, unable to prise a passage from the surly military. Every evening, I telegraphed home news of her condition. The Crimean was the first war on the wire. It was invaluable, if unreliable – Lord Panmure's immediate recommendation on becoming Secretary for War, that the Commander-in-Chief might advantageously employ his Lordship's favourite nephew Dowbiggin, became condensed to 'Look after Dowb' and an army catchphrase.

I deliberately made my readers hold their breath. My wire that Miss Nightingale was out of danger had almost the impact at home of the news from Trafalgar. I was still twenty-two, and had lived out the unfulfilled dream of so many old Fleetstreeters, commanding the headlines of the world.

Miss Nightingale sat at the head of British public opinion as surely as Joan of Arc led the Dauphin's armies. Everyone at home with a pen seemingly started writing about her. The *Spectator*, *Punch*, the vapid, evaporating poets of the universities offered their verses. There were songs – *The Shadow on the Pillow*, or *Angels with Sweet Approving Smiles*. Another had a chorus ending,

159

So forward, my lads, may your hearts never fail,
You are cheer'd by the presence of a sweet Nightingale.

From the printers of Seven Dials came, *The Only and
Unabridged Edition of the Life of Miss Nightingale, Detailing
her Christian Heroic Deeds in the Land of Tumult and Death,
winning the Prayers of the Soldier, the Widow and the Orphan,
Price One Penny.* Her likeness appeared in woodcuts, in the
watermark of writing-paper, on greengrocers' bags, in
appalling vivid pottery. Streets, children, waltzes were stuck
for ever with her name, at a race meeting Florence Nightingale beat Barbarity and a field of nine. Someone hugged
himself with the discovery of her anagram, *Flit on, cheering
angel.* She was idolized in wax at Madame Tussaud's, a dis-
tinction lost to me but shared by Disraeli and the rogue
Charlie Peace.

But she was really the heroine of the humble. Though
the Crimean officers were as brave as the men, after duty
they had a change of clothes, a bed, food hot and sent out
from home, a servant. They were sick seldom compared
with their soldiers, to whose sufferings they were indifferent
not through inhumanity, but through tradition. Soldiers
diseased or drunk were soldiers unfit for action, and beneath
the interest of their commander. Their families were the
unconsidered trifles of the Queen's subjects. They loved
Florence Nightingale, and Fleet Street puffed the fire of
their adoration with its usual opportunistic compassion.

The Queen sent a nice letter, and a diamond brooch saying *Blessed are the Merciful*, designed by the Prince Consort.

'Look at this, Tristram,' said Miss Nightingale that
evening in Scutari. She handed me a cutting from *The
Times*, a month or so old. 'I missed it through being ill. As
you may be sure, it fell into the wrong hands. Dr Sutherland
has just received it in a letter.'

With Miss Nightingale and the terrier, sitting on a
wooden chair outside the house, was the man who would
follow me at her side. Mr Roebuck's bringing down the
Government had produced in Scutari the Roebuck Sanitary
Commission, which consisted of two Liverpool sanitary
inspectors and Dr John Sutherland. He was forty or so,

slight, frailly handsome, with thick dark hair and moustache, wearing a high collar, black trousers and waistcoat, and with a long jacket of gaudy tweed check, a shiny-peaked military cap like that I was quickly shamed to abandon. He was a doctor from Edinburgh, for seven years a government inspector at the Board of Health. He had gone straight to Balaclava, missing us there by a few days, and been in Scutari a week.

I read the cutting, startled to find Newbolt's name. He had sent in his papers and returned to London, in exasperated disgust at the muddle which, after a year, stood like uncleared bramble in the path of his work. Many officers, medical or combatant, reacted as bitterly, and never understood why they were cut in their clubs as cowards.

The item was headed, *Blunders at Scutari. A Surgeon's Strictures*. Newbolt had celebrated civilian status by lecturing to the Marylebone Medical Society, attacking the Army and its senior doctors, praising as forcefully Miss Nightingale and her nurses.

'How will Lord Panmure read *that* in the War Office?' Miss Nightingale asked. 'He'll conclude I sent Dr Newbolt home to fight my battles against the Army Medical Department. That battle is what I exercised such self-restraint, such tact, to avoid, since I first refused to let a nurse into the wards here unless requested by the doctors.'

'And *this* is what the wrong hands wrote of it,' said Sutherland in his quiet Scots voice.

He passed me the covering letter. It was from Hall, in the Crimea.

Dear Dr Sutherland,

When one reads such twaddling nonsense about Miss Nightingale putting a hospital containing 4000 patients in order in a couple of days with The Times' *fund, one cannot suppress a feeling of contempt for the man who indulges in such exaggerations, and pity for the ignorant multitude who are deluded by them.*

'Dear me,' I murmured. I had met Hall in Balaclava, once. He was short and pigeon-chested, with low, straight eyebrows, a quiff, a white imperial and a look of petulance. I had spoken of Miss Nightingale's illness, and he asked heartily if she would be concealing her cropped head with a woman's wig or a soldier's helmet.

Miss Nightingale simply does not know what to do with her boasted Free Gifts. Like those she sent to the Russian hospitals by mistake, and the wine and arrowroot thrust on the French after it had been refused. They are simply a matter of absurdity on the part of the kind-hearted well-intentioned contributors, and a piece of silly ambitious vanity on her part to have the European reputation of being the guardian angel of the sick and wounded.

I recalled her sister's angry words across the Embley breakfast-table. Were Parthe and Hall bedfellows in spite, or insight?

Sister Bridgeman, a very superior and conscientious person, has positively refused to acknowledge Miss Nightingale's authority, and I cannot blame her after what is past, and she will go home, taking the only real nurses we ever had. Thus the Government loses the free service of these estimable women, and the soldiers the benefit of their administration, to gratify Miss Nightingale.

I was told, when I declined to interfere, that right or wrong, Miss Nightingale's friends were powerful enough to carry her through. My reply was, 'So much the greater pity'.

> *I have the honour to remain, sir,*
> *Your obedient servant,*
> *John Hall, M D.*

'A fossil of pure Old Red Sandstone,' Miss Nightingale said disparagingly, as I handed the letter back to Sutherland.

Hall had been resentful for months of the money lavished on her by *The Times* when he had none from the Government, insulted that it bought items lacking through his own incompetence, fearful of her passing directly to Sidney Herbert a confidential report about himself – which he had so often used to assassinate the careers of his own officers – angry at her insinuations of his negligence and perhaps guilty that they were true.

'In London there was a shave – it was more than a shave,' Sutherland revealed, 'that Dr Hall is shortly to be Sir John Hall. He's in line for a K C B.'

Miss Nightingale snorted. 'Knight of the Crimean Burial-grounds.'

'Mr Darling, what's your opinion of Miss Salisbury?' Sutherland asked abruptly.

Miss Salisbury was one of the nurses, put by Miss Nightingale in charge of the 'Free Gifts' which inflamed Hall's correspondence. She was pretty, against the plain and coarse flattery of the others.

'It's all to do with those "Free Gifts",' Miss Nightingale sighed. They were parcels pouring from England for distribution among the troops. 'Those frightful presentations! Dr Hall's strictures are the least troubles they arouse. There is not a parish from which we have not received contributions, and not one worth its freight. The trouble of landing, unpacking, acknowledging! The English nobility must have emptied their wardrobes, and sent out bandages for the wounded in the shape of the finest cambric sheets and the most beautiful underclothing, with monograms beautifully worked. They give the rats a fine nest. The good that has been done here has been done by *money*,' she said forthrightly. 'Money to spend in Constantinople. And now this stupid Miss Salisbury – of course, it *had* to be Mary Stanley who took the kindness to bring it to my notice – Miss Salisbury wrote home accusing *me* of using the free gifts for my own gorgeous adornment. Her family passed the letter to Miss Stanley, who is *quite* certain there is *no atom* of truth in the charge.' She stopped, weak and breathless. 'I believe she's a pilferer, trying to shift the blame.'

I suggested, 'Why not get Major Sillery to search her belongings?'

Sutherland was against it. But Miss Nightingale showed the persevering malice which she could turn against women, but never men – not even, two summers later, Dr Hall. I was charged to see Major Sillery.

I wanted to leave Scutari. Wiley was packing up for Boston, Handshear itching to send in his papers and go home for a winter's hunting. However happier the inmates' lot, our shadows still fell on illness and death, who waited for us ourselves like patient coachmen outside the door of our convivial mess-room. I saw it my duty to stay and serve Miss Nightingale, but I was tired of her pointless squabbles, peevish feuds, touchy resentments and trivial pets. I saw the world through a wider glass than anyone at Scutari – particularly Miss Nightingale, who since arrival had seen it through the wrong end of a sanitary telescope.

About noon the following day, feminine shrieks rang from Major Sillery's office on the landing above our mess. I ran up the flight of stairs, to find the major red-faced, open-mouthed, and incapable of controlling events or his aspirates. Miss Salisbury lay on the tiled floor, clasping the ankles of the impassive Miss Nightingale.

'This girl is a thief,' she said to me unpityingly. 'A thief from two people at once – the poor cottagers who themselves went cold, and the sick soldiers who would have blessed their warm clothing.'

I recalled her remarks about the aggravating 'Free Gifts'. I was to enjoy watching Tartuffe played by Mrs Siddons.

'Not only mittens, and that,' complained Major Sillery with outrage. 'But she 'ad wine, bottles of brandy, preserved sausage and six 'ole Stilton cheeses. And a couple of water-beds, sent by the Queen.'

'Don't put me in prison!' screamed the girl. 'Send me home. I'll never do it again. Honest to God, never, never, never! I'm a decent woman, Miss. It was a moment of temptation, that anyone could fall for.'

'Government stores!' said Major Sillery more wrathfully. 'That could be an 'anging matter, I'll 'ave you know.'

The prospect of the rope incited the poor child to wordless screaming. Miss Nightingale took no notice. 'Mr Darling, pray do not write of this disgrace to the newspapers.'

'As you like. But if you hang, or even gaol, Miss Salisbury, someone else will write of it. It is surely best to pack her off home, and no more said?' The rats would have gobbled six Stiltons much quicker than she.'

The three of us argued the girl's fate. She lay clasping Miss Nightingale's feet, sobbing and moaning. Miss Nightingale announced that she would be merciful. It was sensible, to slip the girl away rather than pass fresh ammunition to Dr Hall in Balaclava. Major Sillery objected about the sanctity of government property, but Miss Nightingale did not appear to hear him, and the major appeared relieved that she did not.

The miserable, squalling, hypocritical scene decided me. The next morning, I went to Miss Nightingale's office behind the curtain in the Sisters' Tower. She was writing at her table, Miss Bancroft beside her.

'Miss Nightingale, I am going home.'

'Oh? Like the Reverend Mother Brickbat? You know my opinion of officers who resign their commissions.'

'But surely! What is the shame of quitting when the battle is over? The survivors are only extra mouths to be fed.'

'*My* battle is not over.' She jabbed her pen back into the pewter pot. 'My battle is with the War Office and the Horse Guards. I have started by nursing the British army, by clothing it, by feeding it, by writing its letters home, by making its wills and by burying a good proportion of it. What do you expect me to do when the war is over? Go back to Embley House with Mama and Parthe, whose whole occupation is to lie on two sofas and tell one another not to get tired by putting flowers into water?'

This was my first whiff of a burning ambition. I objected, 'You cannot expect to direct the welfare of an entire army. In time of peace, everything will quickly return to normal.'

'Normal? We all know what "normal" means at the Horse Guards. We all know what the "normal" system produced here last winter. How can anyone forget? *I* shall never forget. Our rate of mortality from disease exceeded that of the Great Plague in London.'

'And now the mortality is little more than among healthy men in barracks at home,' Miss Bancroft said proudly. 'The result of Miss Nightingale's untiring efforts and expostulations.'

'But there may not be another war for a hundred years,' I pointed out. 'Perhaps for ever. Mankind is creating a world of so many good things, so much wealth, it becomes every year wilder madness to smash at it, like an ill-tempered child with its nursery globe.'

'War will always come, like illness.' She shifted on her

camp-stool, elbow on table, as though lecturing me on rustling nurses' dresses in Harley Street. 'And success in war depends upon preparation in peace. You cannot improvise an army. You cannot improvise the sanitary care of an army in the field. Dr Andrew Smith searched St James's in vain for precedents. Under the "normal" system, if he wished to supply Scutari with arrowroot or sago, he had to request the Horse Guards to ask the Ordnance Department, who would pass it on to the Admiralty, who would mention it to the Transport Office, who would correspond with the shipowners, if they ever got to hear of the matter.'

She looked up at me indignantly. 'What does the soldier know of your good things, your world's wealth? Or care? His capital is his courage. You cannot expect a soldier to become his country's hero in war if he becomes his country's victim in peace. I intend to change completely the way he is treated, and more importantly the way he is thought of.'

'You will fail,' I told her bluntly.

'Why?'

My attention was distracted. Something moved in a small, apparently empty, straw-filled box in the corner. I thought for an instant that she had made a pet of a snake. But it was a tortoise, called Jimmy. 'Because you are for once letting your heart drive your mind. The only item in the world you feel in the slightest sentimental about is the British soldier.'

'How can anyone sentimentalize a man who enlists only for three causes – being either out of work, in a state of intoxication or jilted by his sweetheart? I suppose for a better army, the country needs more poverty, more drink and more faithless women? The officers may tell me that I am "spoiling the brutes", but the men are more respectful to me than to them.'

'And how do you suppose that advances you in the opinion of the officers?' I was vexed with her conceit. 'You will only break your finger-nails against the stone walls of official indifference. I have seen the shabby mechanism that changes things in our country – a word or two in salons and clubs, between men who owe and repay favours as the coin of their own advancement. There is a clearer view from a newspaper office than a hospital ward.'

'I stand by the altar of murdered men. While I live, I fight their cause.'

'You may fight the good fight with the righteousness of St Paul himself, if you care. But I'm going home.'

'Miss Bancroft, kindly leave us.'

The sharpness of her exit indicated her irritation. Miss Nightingale waited for the footsteps to fade. She smiled. 'You still have my pendant, Tristram?'

'May I keep it? A memento of you.'

She looked arch. 'A keepsake from a woman a dozen years your senior?'

'A bewitching woman – after her fashion.'

'I take heart you think me open to flattery, like any other woman. After my confessions about my English countesses and Prussian peasant girls . . . I am not ashamed of them. You shall have the names of the English ladies if you like. Those of the farm girls I fear I have forgotten. What should be shameful about it, in the least? I am far less disreputable than the society ladies in your newspaper, who repeatedly share their bed with different *men*.'

She nodded towards the door-curtain. 'Jane is fearsomely jealous of any person I take a fancy to, feminine or masculine. Which would be flattery of the most delightful sort, were she not so unintelligent. But she is pretty, and a competent player of Sappho's lyre. You may keep my little gold cross. Should I remain here for eternity—' She nodded now towards the cemetery. 'And you know the chances of that, please carry out my instructions. Go home if you must. Call at my bootmakers in St James's, and order me another stout pair. Tell them the last went quickly at the seams.'

Jane Bancroft was waiting near the far door of the kitchen. 'So you're going home, Mr Darling? Think of me in London between waltzes, won't you? I shall envy you, when winter comes again to us in Scutari.'

'Perhaps I shall envy *you*? I shall be living among trivia, but every hour of the day you are useful to Miss Nightingale, or to your country, which is the same thing.'

'She calls you "Tristram" in private, doesn't she?'

'I'm known to her family.'

'You've got that cross she wears, the one on the black ribbon.'

We were walking down the narrow stairs, twisting in the barracks' massive walls.

'If the Queen gives Miss Nightingale a jewelled brooch, surely Miss Nightingale can recognize my own services on a comparable scale?'

'She gave it you, that you might give it to Madame Mohl,' Miss Bancroft said blackly.

'Only in the unfortunate event of Miss Nightingale's death.'

'I want it.' We stopped. She was close to me, eyes afire, breathing heavily. 'Give it me.' I tried to move down the stairs. 'Give it!' Quick as a serpent, her hand was in the pocket of my coat. I seized her wrist, and pushed back her fingers hard. She gave a cry, stifled it, stood looking at me, scarlet, two tears in her startled eyes. 'That's not the behaviour of a gentleman.'

'It is, towards a lady who is robbing him.'

'Florence is mine, not yours. Nor Madame Mohl's. Nor Mary Stanley's. Nor Marianne Nicholson's. Nor anybody's,' she said furiously. '*I* possess her.'

'Then why do you complain? I'm leaving her to you.'

'I *can* complain. Because . . . because now you know about us, Flo and me. And anyone who knows, intrudes.' She began to repossess herself. 'Well, give it to Madame Mohl. Give it to any crossing-sweeper. I don't care. If Flo died, it would be a puny thing to bear her memory. Even the greatest memorial in London could not.'

'Oh, I agree. But the world generally forgets its martyrs quicker than it remember its heroes.'

I dropped her hand. We descended the stairs looking reasonably composed. She gave me messages for the Harley Street nursing home, which was continuing in business despite the absence of its proprietor abroad.

Soyer had moved to a house in a village lane renamed by the army Cambridge Street. He complained that it overlooked the *Grand Champ des Morts*, but so did everything in Scutari. Three nights later he came to dine, making us superb *rognons à la brochette*, apologizing for the lack of a proper silver skewer, which held the heat better, and which any Reform Club *gourmet* would insist on. 'Partaking over-done kidneys at night is the forerunner of the nightmare,' he warned us solemnly. He mixed his Crimean cup of maras-chino, cognac, curaçao and champagne. Handshear gave me messages to countless young women in Haymarket. Wiley sang *Alabama* with Soyer's frying pan as his banjo on his knee, several times. Soyer talked about his dead wife, cried, laughed, gesticulated, sang. Had the shell over the Balaclava mortar-battery blown his head off, only that would have simmered down his ebullience. He declared us three capital fellows, whom he would remember to his dying day, though as we had no titles I doubted it.

The next morning, I sailed from the Golden Horn in the *Himalaya*, feeling that I had just recovered from a terrible illness.

19

I ARRIVED in London on Saturday, September 1 1855, to find that my uncle Peregrine was dead. He had cut his hand badly while operating, and contracted the hospital gangrene, which had slaughtered so many who were wounded on his surgical battlefield. He had died while I was at sea, and I learned about it from his obituary in the newspapers which came aboard with the pilot at Plymouth.

'I think he would have been content with his funeral,' decided my uncle Humphry, now the Right Reverend Sir Humphry Darling Bt., a baronetcy being heritable sideways. I had presented myself for thin tea and thin bread-and-butter on the Monday afternoon. 'I took for the text of my sermon St John, 5, 8 – "Rise, take up thy bed, and walk".'

'It is a sharp blow, sir. It knocked from my head any delight at coming home from Scutari. You must have observed, sir, how uncle Peregrine and myself had a close feeling for each other? He was always ready with a kindness in my direction, and he saw my scurrilous occupation only as amusing.'

The bishop leant back in the horsehair-stuffed, buttoned-leather armchair of his study, well brushed head on antimacassar, gaiters crossed on footstool. 'I must confess, you hid it from me most successfully. Were you as careful with other people's secrets as your own, you would not have gone very far.'

I was uneasy. He said this without his usual acidity. There was a slight smile on his fleshy lips. I should have thought him twinkling, had he not been as incapable of it as some cold, dead planet.

'I am done with parlourmaids' whispers, sir. I find to my surprise that I have landed from Scutari on a high tide of reputation.'

'When Miss Nightingale was ill with the fever, your name was on everybody's lips hardly less than hers.' I grew more puzzled. He was treating me with affability, almost equality. Perhaps the loss of both brothers left him with feelings of paternity. 'So what are your plans?'

'Towards my career, indefinite. First, I must buy some clothes. I apologize for my tweed.'

'Why apologize? It is the equivalent of an officer's tunic.'

I decided that he wanted me to edit his collected sermons. 'I must move from my hotel in Jermyn Street to inexpensive lodgings.'

'Why inexpensive?'

'Well, sir, I saved money in Scutari, because for once I had nothing to spend it on. But it will not last for ever, and I need a long holiday.'

The bishop bit a triangular sandwich with precision. 'You may take a holiday for the rest of your life, if you care. You were not appraised by your late uncle of his will?'

'He never mentioned such melancholy matters.'

'He has left his entire fortune to you. There is of course the estate in Berkshire, a large number of houses in London and Ascot – I never believed him a landlord on such a scale, he could be irritatingly secretive – shooting and fishing in Scotland, a good sheaf of securities at his brokers and a solid balance at his bankers. I had no notion that surgery was so profitable.'

He finished his sandwich.

'Is this a jest, sir?'

'I am not a jester. You have an appointment with his lawyers at Lincoln's Inn, ten tomorrow morning.'

I sat forward like a jockey winning the Derby. 'But what am I to do with such wealth?'

'Give it to the Church,' he replied promptly.

I planted but one seed in the cold fields of ecclesiastical

charity. On the south wall of Brompton Church, you may see a marble plaque which says in gold,

Harriet Catchpole
1834–1854
Nurse at Scutari
RIP.

If my world wore a Panglossian lustre, I did not care to risk the uncomfortable disenchantments of Candide. My fortune was substantial but not ducal. I could have lived a country gentleman in Berkshire, but my reasons for refusing the job of the steward applied equally to that of the master. I could have travelled the world, but Scutari would have put Marco Polo off voyaging for life. I could have spent it on gambling, drink and women, which would have been agreeable. But Scutari was a classroom which taught severe lessons. I had seen misery imposed by incompetence and ignorance, and I itched to cure all three human afflictions.

From Miss Nightingale I had learned the danger of good intentions. Unweighted with thought or information, they spread more hardship than they seek to relieve. My best start would be founding a weekly paper – liberal, humane, reforming, providing the Government with a weekly thrashing, like the policy for keeping the boys on their mettle at Rugby, but with amusing articles, theatre reviews, and a page of scandalous gossip to ensure that it sold.

I hit on a title – *Candour*. I should shoot my shaft in the air on Saturday, December 1 1855. Miss Nightingale was to be its arrowhead.

At the end of September, when the people who matter come back to Town from the moors and rivers, I dined with the Herberts in Belgrave Square. It was for my news of Miss Nightingale, but the invitation was an important indication. I was making my way in the world, down the ringing grooves of ambition.

I foreran myself with a letter.

'That notion you wrote me was admirable,' I was greeted by Sidney Herbert. 'The country must certainly mark in some public manner its appreciation of Miss Nightingale's services and devotion.'

'I did not mean, sir, a personal testimonial of the teapot and bracelet kind. Miss Nightingale, I am sure, would accept only a gift which she could apply to carrying on her work for others.'

'Some institution for the training and protection of nurses, Mr Darling,' suggested Liz Herbert. We were standing in the upstairs drawing-room. I was startled how a year had marked her husband. His body was wasted, but his face puffy, the contrast between its tints of pink and white too sharp for health. 'Always in Miss Nightingale's mind was some English Kaiserwerth.'

Sidney Herbert smiled. 'But only if Miss Nightingale were its autocrat. Obviously, she cannot leave her work in the East to lay such plans now. We must let your idea rest until the end of the war, Mr Darling.'

'May I disagree, sir?' I ventured. 'Miss Nightingale stands so high in the eyes of the whole world at this moment, it is the one to seize. The end of this terrible conflict is mercifully in sight.' Sebastopol had fallen on September 8, but not to the glory of British arms. The enemy, like the hunter of the Snark, softly and silently vanished away. 'The bubble reputation is easily pricked, away from the cannon's mouth.'

His brow frowned disagreement, his eye acknowledged political truth. I suggested forming a committee. He shortly agreed. 'I think I can get the Duke of Cambridge in the chair.' He was the Queen's cousin, then aged thirty-five. 'And of course we must have the Duke of Argyll.'

'And Lord Stanley, and Lord Lansdowne,' said Liz Herbert.

He nodded. 'And I shall be a member. We need a secretary—'

'Might I suggest myself, sir?'

'You?' He gave the look which had acknowledged my presence in Lady Canning's reception-room the previous October.

'I only dare to suggest it, because my close association

with Miss Nightingale, which the whole public knows, would almost create her presence at the meeting. I should be happy to relinquish the task to one more worthy immediately afterwards.'

'Yes, that's a sound move, Mr Darling. But what meeting is this?'

'At the Willis Rooms in St James's, on Thursday, November 29. I took the liberty of provisionally engaging them. They are booked long ahead at this time of year.'

So I had enmeshed myself with four of the land's most powerful noblemen – I had naturally no intention of ever relinquishing the job, unless it was commandeered by Miss Nightingale herself. I wondered if Sidney Herbert agreed through thinking me a simple, pure-hearted young man – though whether that was flattering or unflattering, in his eyes or in mine, I do not care to decide.

'I have known Miss Nightingale since we met in Rome, the year Mr Herbert and I were married,' Liz Herbert recalled sentimentally, as her husband was drawn aside for deep discussion with a grave-faced man.

'Yes, I knew that.' I knew also that Sidney Herbert had been living the previous five years with Caroline Norton, who had already seen Lord Melbourne brought to court by her dissolute, green-eyed husband for her adultery.

'You know how devoted I am to Miss Nightingale, how I helped her at the Harley Street nursing home.' I nodded my appreciation. 'And it is so delightful to witness my husband's devotion to her, and to share her noble work by observing the assistance he is able to give her from official quarters.' I murmured my approval. 'But you know, Mr Darling—' Her laugh was small and dry. 'Mr Herbert's family sometimes joke that he does not love his wife! They say that he loves only Miss Nightingale.'

Should I join her with a laugh of reassurance? But it would ring mockingly in her heart. She meant what she said. She did not know that a man who loved Florence Nightingale was a dog barking at its reflection in a millpool. Sidney Herbert and Dr Sutherland were both convinced they loved her, when all they felt was awe, fascination, fright, a longing to be part of her, to creep comfortably under those arms which incessantly and painfully punched and pinched. When I followed Florence's coffin, carried by six sergeants of the British army to a Hampshire grave, I felt only that she was a woman with the predominant quality of being immutably unlovable.

'Will you take down Lady Violet Conquest, Mr Darling?' Liz Herbert broke into my meditations. It was dinner-time. Lady Violet was the Earl of Gravesend's youngest daughter, pretty, talkative and incalculably rich. I spoke all the meal about Scutari, to the fascination of us both.

All society was at my meeting in the Willis Rooms, furred, silken, diamonded in the flaring gaslight. Even *The Times* had to concede it 'the most brilliant, enthusiastic and unanimous gathering held in London'. The Nightingale family themselves remained in the Burlington Hotel. They feared overcoming by emotion.

I had seen more of them, and the more disliked them. W E N was like a worm threaded with whalebone. Mother Fanny and Sister Parthe were like two cold-blooded lizards basking on Neapolitan rocks, inanimate save for the sun of Florence's fame. Florence Nightingale herself wore her reputation like her plain black dress, not for decoration but practical use.

'Too much has been made of Miss Nightingale's sacrifice of position and luxury,' said Sidney Herbert from the platform, between the crimson plush curtains, amid the aspidistras and maidenhair fern. 'God knows that the luxury of one good action must, to a mind such as hers, be more than equivalent for the loss of all the pomps and vanities of life. I contrast the crowded and brilliant scene before me with the scene which met the gaze of that noble woman, now devoting herself to the service of her suffering fellow-creatures on the black shores of Crim Tartary, overlooking the waters of the inhospitable sea.'

He held up a soldier's letter home, with which I had furnished him. ''What a comfort it was to see her pass, even,'' he read out. ''She would speak to one and nod and smile to as many more, but she could not do it to all, you know." Miss Nightingale had taken my advice, offered on her night round. "We lay there in hundreds, we could but kiss her shadow as it fell, and lay our heads on the pillow again, content. Before she came, there was cussing and swearing, but after it was holy as a church."

These rough sentiments strongly stirred polite hearts beneath delicate linen and muslin.

'There is no part of England,' Sidney Herbert continued, unhealthy face uplifted, 'where some cottage household has not been comforted amidst its mourning for the loss of one who had fallen in the war, by the assurance that his last moments were watched, and his worst sufferings smoothed, by that care, at once tender and skilful, which no man, and few women, could have shown. True heroism is not so plentiful that we can afford to let it pass unrecognized – if not for the honour of those who show it, yet very much for our own. The best test of a nation's moral state is the kind of claim which it selects for honour.'

Sidney Herbert was one of the most elegant and most heeded orators in the House of Commons. Such beautiful sentiments, beautifully expressed, were tarnished for me by remembrance that Herbert shared responsibility for throwing good lives into a wickedly unnecessary war, and then ensuring through his mismanagement that an excess of them were lost in conditions as wretched and painful as possible.

He ended, 'With the exception of Howard, the prison reformer, I know no person besides Miss Nightingale, who within the last hundred years within this island, or perhaps in Europe, had voluntarily encountered dangers so imminent, and undertaken offices so repulsive, working for a large and worthy object, in a pure spirit of duty towards God and compassion for man.'

Everyone left feeling participation in Florence Nightingale's mission, without the inconvenience of having to miss their suppers. The only sourness came from the self-important gentleman I had last seen at the Cannings' talking to my uncle Humphry, and whose name for the instant I forgot.

He touched my elbow as I was leaving hastily to write my copy. 'A silly fad, sir, raising the status of the nurses. Lady Pam thinks so, anyway,' he confided, referring to the Prime Minister's wife. 'She thinks the Nightingale Fund great humbug. She says the nurses are very good now. Perhaps they do drink a little, but poor people, it must be so tiresome sitting up all night.' He nodded towards Herbert, who was delightedly defending himself against congratulations on the platform. 'Newcastle was ignorant of military affairs, and not equal to his post. Sidney Herbert was not much better.'

But everything would read inspiringly in the maiden edition of *Candour* on Saturday morning.

We got £44,000. I arranged a concert with Jenny Lind, which brought another £2,000. I was becoming an indispensable young man, a most prized status. Through Sidney Herbert, I contrived that Lord Panmure in the War Office should proclaim the fund in Sir William Codrington's General Orders to the army in the East. (The reluctant, red-nosed newly-promoted General Sir James Simpson had resigned, succumbing like everyone else in the Crimea to diarrhoea.) All ranks would volunteer a day's pay. Dr John Hall refused.

Then I began to read with disquiet in the newspapers that Miss Nightingale, like all saviours of mankind, had fallen for the temptation of improving her handiwork. She had nursed, clothed, fed and buried the army. Now she would educate it. Corners of the horrendous hospital became reading-rooms, there was the Inkerman Café without wine or women, lectures, classes, schoolmasters sent from England, amateur theatricals, dominoes, chess. She encouraged the men to send pay home instead of drinking it where they were, and Panmure growled, 'The soldier is not a remitting animal.' The repatriated Miss Salisbury complained of ill-usage to the War Office – incited by Mary Stanley, hell having no fury like a woman scorn'd by another woman. The War Office sent an accusing letter to Miss Nightingale, which encouraged Hall to describe her in his confidential report as a dishonest and insubordinate female, heading a rabble of rude, shifty, drunken, immoral and useless others. The enemy was retreating, the fusillade of the British army could be concentrated upon Miss Nightingale. She had ceased to be essential, and became only useful.

Two springs buried the bleak vestiges of Balaclava and Inkerman. The ranks were full, the hospitals empty. The arcades of agony at Scutari bore only vestiges of the British, a few shelves and bed-numbers, the lingering names of surrounding streets. The barracks was claimed back for the Orient, Monsieur Soyer's kitchen cooked pilaff for the Turkish Imperial Guard.

Peace was signed in Paris on May 30, 1856. It had been a war of few heroes. Three of them were doctors, with the new Victoria Cross. Miss Nightingale sailed from Constantinople in the *Danube* on July 28, as Miss Smith.

I was preoccupied in *Candour* with blood-chilling reports of murderous mutiny brewing among Her Majesty's Indian subjects. But I busied myself and my Lords Stanley and Lansdowne to stage-manage a fitting welcome. There were to be triumphal arches, addresses from mayors and corporations, her carriage drawn by massed orphans, the Coldstreams and the Grenadiers with their bands, a man-of-war at her disposal.

Our difficulty was Miss Nightingale's concealment of her timetable. Fanny, Parthe and W E N were in their dear little fifteen-bedroomed house at Lea Hurst in Derbyshire, excitedly discussing my florid plans, when a slight, pale lady in a black dress with lace at the cuffs came wandering into the garden from the railway station. After two years, Miss Nightingale was home.

20

'BUT your *Candour* is an absolute *succès de scandale*, Mr Darling,' exclaimed Lady Violet Challenger. 'Everybody is talking about it. In the clubs, in the House, even – so I hear – in the Palace.'

I sighed. 'I fear that the readers swallow my camel of gossip, but spit out my gnat of political edification.'

'On the contrary, the only way to make people think is by deceiving them that they are being amused. The British feel no guilt over pleasure, but are horribly embarrassed by the taint of philosophy.'

It was early in the New Year of 1857. We were in the same party at a ball.

'But how do you find these items you print, which public men hardly dare to utter?' she asked, eyes wide with admiration. 'Or sometimes, I believe, hardly dare to think?'

'An easily-recruited battalion of spies, working for the wages of spite. They eat with guiltless appetites at powerful dining-tables, some soldier more daringly in boudoirs. I employ a bruiser on my office door, and I have a card engraved, "Mr Darling thanks you for your challenge, and is placing you on his waiting-list".'

She laughed. We were crushed together in a corner at supper. As Lady Violet seemed to move everywhere amid a crowd of swells, conversation alone with her was valuable. We drank our champagne and ate our eggs with truffles, which I mentioned as a favourite creation of Monsieur Soyer.

She looked at me, puzzled. 'Why do you always speak about the war, Mr Darling?'

'Do I? Then I'm sorry. But it was an experience which I cannot shake off as easily as a terrier which has fallen into a river.'

'But it's over! And Miss Nightingale is dead.'

I raised my eyebrows. 'If so, her ultimate task was her most difficult, in keeping the event from the notice of Fleet Street.'

'But isn't she? Everyone seems to think so. One never hears a single word about her these days. It's like those other people – Lord Lucan, Lord Cardigan, whose names were on our lips every breakfast-time two years ago. Of course, I was dreadfully sorry for the soldiers – you know how mama and I knitted and sewed – but it is all past, like a bad dream. There are much more important things to think of.'

'What things?'

She looked amused. 'Well, there's the *dreadful* spread of Puseyism. The whole country is shaking in its shoes about that. Or there's . . . the persistence of the crinoline? Should clerics wear beards? We cannot be deadly serious for ever. That's why everyone prefers listening to the scandal rather than the speeches of Cabinet ministers.'

'Were Miss Nightingale to enter this room this moment, Lady Violet, would you not stare at her?'

'Only as I should stare at last season's fashionable opera singer.'

I nodded. 'The Crimean war was a disaster, a textbook for every succeeding British general of how *not* to fight a war. Its end would seem a disaster for Miss Nightingale. I agree, when a quarrel is over, everyone has a healthy eagerness to forget it. Except for the vengeful few who keep grudges like vampires in the nooks of their souls, the dull few who find in war the only excitement and importance of a lifetime, and the few clever enough to learn its lessons. I don't think I am any of those. But I cannot forget Scutari. Its sights are mixed with the quicksilver of my shaving-mirror.'

'You were brave to go out there, Mr Darling. But you still suffer from one terror.'

'What is that?'

'Of being thought a compassionate man.'

To be young, good looking and talked about, opened doors and hearts to me all over London. I tentatively courted Lady Violet – an outrage upon our difference of station, but she seemed amused with the upstart, and I had a deft tongue to lap the cream of society.

I consorted with other ladies whose company was more accessible and intimacy more immediate. I supped extravagantly in private rooms with actresses whose performances upon the boards were considerably fewer than upon the bed-springs. One midnight that January, Handshear's charge at Scutari flitting into mind, I wandered curiously into a deeper pool in London's underground rivers of vice. I had barely turned the corner of Pall Mall into the Haymarket, when a voice shrilled urgently, 'Sir! Sir! Mr Darling!'

An alarming greeting for a man in that place at that hour. The girl who knew my name was faintly familiar. She hurried up, ashen and rouged in the gaslight, pale hair straggling under her bonnet, her body so slight I thought her one of the children pressed into this work by their satanic families.

'Sir! You remembers me? Don't you, sir? Down in Brompton. You used to call me "Little Nell".'

I could say nothing for several moments. 'How long have you been at this game?' I asked shortly.

'About a year, sir. After Mr Larderton sent Miss Harriet packing, there was another lady. But we didn't get on, sir. And one day she dismissed me without a character.' She told me as cheerfully as recounting some misfired childish prank. 'Mr Larderton would have kept me on, sir, I'm sure. He was such a nice gentleman.' She giggled. 'Don't you remember, sir, that afternoon, when he caught you with Miss Harriet—'

'Miss Harriet is dead.'

'Oh? Fancy that. Well, it's a surprise, upon my word. What did she die of?'

'She died in the war. She went to nurse the soldiers in

Scutari, had the cholera and died of it in a day. I put her in her grave.'

'To think of Miss Harriet nursing soldiers!' she giggled again. 'More likely, she'd be up to something else with them.'

'Aren't you sorry?'

My irritated tone surprised her. 'Course I'm sorry, sir. I'm sorry when anyone's dead and buried. But it's all over and done with now, ain't it, sir?' She hesitated. 'Come home with me, sir? I've a nice place.'

'What are you intending to do with yourself? This? For the rest of your life?'

'I might find some nice chap.'

'You won't, and you know it.'

'Oh, well, a girl has got to live. What else is there? For me?' We stood looking at each other in silence. She said pathetically, 'Why are you so angry with me, sir? I didn't think you was the sort to read a sermon.'

I had been needlessly callous. If I condemned her, I wore the shadow of the condemnation myself. 'I could find you a respectable position in a good household,' I offered.

Little Nell wrinkled her nose. It reminded me of Harriet. 'I don't think I should care for it, sir. A servant girl can't call her soul her own these days. There's plenty of them to be found up and down the Haymarket.'

I put my hand in my pocket. Her eyes lit. For the second time in a London street, I handed a woman all the money on me. I hurried away. It would give her a week or two in idleness, if some bully was not waiting to take it off her.

So Harriet was washed from living memory by the lethal currents of the Bosphorus. And Miss Nightingale was a diamond which had been tossed back down the mine. I walked preoccupied across Piccadilly, to my chambers in Albany. A woman who could run the Barrack Hospital that first winter of the war had a genius for administration and diplomacy outrivalling Downing Street. *Candour* would say as much. I needed a cause, a cast-iron case for the furnace of public anger. If my weekly degenerated into a popular gossip-sheet, my career would be following Jack o'Lantern down a familiar path in the wrong direction.

Two weeks or so later, Miss Nightingale arrived from Derbyshire at the Burlington Hotel. I had not seen her since saying farewell in the tiny room behind the curtain in the Sisters' Tower. I wrote seeking an interview, granted by return of the messenger.

It was a customary fog-soaked London winter's afternoon, my hansom clopped warily from Fleet Street, horse snorting steam, others emerging and disappearing in the choking yellow billows like sea-serpents. Link-boys with flaming faggots, coachmen in cockaded hats waving oil-lanterns, cleared a path for their masters with curses. The citizens risked coughing out their lungs, or knocking out their brains on lampposts, the omnibus drivers swore more colourfully than usual and the pickpockets did brisk business. I arrived at the Burlington Hotel with my linen specked by soot as though suffering an attack of black measles. London prides itself on its fogs, as upon Big Ben. I wish some scientific person could puff them into the middle of the Atlantic Ocean for ever.

Miss Nightingale was with Mother Fanny and Sister Parthe. They had as usual taken the first floor, overlooking Burlington Street. I had been asked to tea.

The valet showed me into a small sitting-room. Two gentlemen in the middle of the Turkish carpet stood deep in conversation. One was Dr Sutherland, who had renounced his tweed coat for seemly black. The other was Mr Arthur Clough, who had seen us off at London Bridge. He had a large brown-paper parcel under his arm.

'Miss Nightingale is ill,' imparted Sutherland solemnly, after the reminiscent greetings of old campaigners.

'Dear me, yes,' said Clough, miserably, bald head shaking above a high shirt collar. 'Most ill.'

'But this is sudden?' I exclaimed. 'I was invited only yesterday.'

'The onset of symptoms was shortly after she returned from the East.'

'Six months ago? Then it is hardly as dangerous as Crimean fever.'

'It is an illness of remissions and relapses,' explained Sutherland, with his professional expression. 'Only a woman of Miss Nightingale's spirit and constitution could stand it. I am led to believe there must be a foundation of truth under the old myth about the Amazon women somewhere to the East. All I can say is, that had she been Queen of that respectable body in olden days, Alexander the Great would have had rather a bad chance.' He smiled, elevated by his elegance.

A bell tinkled briefly behind an inner door.

'It is hard to diagnose exactly the condition,' Sutherland continued in a reverential whisper. 'There is involvement of the cardiac and respiratory systems, which were exhausted by her unsparing work in the East. Sometimes she seems nigh unto death, at others her recovery is miraculous.'

'The bell!' Clough's face was a mask of terror.

'Was it? Dear me, I didn't hear. I am getting so deaf—'

The handbell rang again, noisily and urgently. Without a word to excuse himself, Sutherland shot through the door.

'I must take Miss Nightingale's parcel to the post.' Clough set it on an imitation ormolu table, augmenting the substantial knot.

'You are one of Miss Nightingale's household, Mr Clough?'

'Being of use to this inspired lady gives the only purpose to my existence. I lost my faith, you know.'

'I am extremely sorry, sir,' I said, as though it were his umbrella on the Great Western Railway.

'The Oxford Movement was to blame. I became greatly vexed by the vortex of philosophism and discussion about religion. I should have taken Holy Orders, then I could have held my fellowship, my *toga tutoria*, at Oriel. But I was too scrupulous, too sensitive. Instead, I went into the hard world, a wilderness with small hope of manna, quails or water from the rock, where I found a place at the Education Office.'

184

I consoled him, 'Your name was mentioned at Rugby only with reverence.'

'Yes, I did well at Rugby. I kept goal, too, you know. But at Balliol I missed my First. I missed my First.' His voice could have escaped from Lot's wife as she felt her limbs undergoing salination.

The bell gave an insistent little ring.

'I must fly, I must catch the post,' he said nervously. 'I hope you will find Miss Nightingale passably well today. How terrible if her efforts in Scutari killed her! Say not the struggle naught availeth, the labour and the wounds are vain.'

He had the indefensible habit of quoting his own poetry – though perhaps, like many poets I have known, he simply gave the impression of doing so.

Sutherland opened the door. He saw me into the sick-room, bowed, and left us alone.

21

IT WAS DARK, heavy damask curtains drawn against the fog, the fire a dull glow, the gas in a single globe turned low. It was a bedroom, but the bedstead was pushed in the corner, and there were extra tables covered with books and papers. A small table had an inkpot, and a chair hurriedly pushed aside, where I suppose Sutherland sat writing industriously to her dictation.

In the middle of the room was a black horsehair sofa, packed with pillows and covered with shawls, under which lay Miss Nightingale. I could see in the dim light that she wore her black, lace-trimmed dress and white cap. I put down my hat, and at once picked a volume from a low table beside her, squinting at the title *Little Dorrit*. 'I see you have Mr Dickens' latest.'

'Dickens! What did he write about the war? One little story about seven travellers at Chatham. Something to amuse children at Christmas. He never bothered to write, even to think, of the filth, disease and death at Scutari. Because Charles Dickens is a sentimental humbug. All his characters who die either deserve to, or appear to enjoy it. Had he come out East, he would have shocked the world more than you or Mr Russell. But he preferred to stay at home, where the warm fires and the money are. I've no time to read it, I'm alternately too ill and too busy. What did Dr Sutherland say of me?'

'That sometimes you were near death, at others as fit as a flea.'

'Dr Sutherland has an incurable looseness of thought. Did he compare me to the Queen of the Amazons? He does to everybody. He is infuriatingly flippant. He is also untidy, forgetful and unpunctual, and far more preoccupied with his own health than the best of doctors with the health of his patients. He feigns deafness, to annoy me. He is a man born without a soul, like Undine.'

'But a useful disciple.'

'Dr Sutherland is an extremely able sanitary expert,' she said more generously. 'I'm only a humbug. I know nothing about sanitary matters except what I have learned from him.'

'And Mr Clough is a handy postboy.'

'Mr Clough does the work of a cabhorse. And he is incurably lazy.'

'You always despise the people who are useful to you. The more so, the more unselfish their attentions.'

'Did I despise you?'

'No, because I am the urchin who might laugh at you. Which you would find appalling. May I sit down, Florence?'

She motioned impatiently to a chair. 'You don't seem to believe that I am ill.'

'I think you are suffering from lack of occupation.'

There was a knock. The waiters brought our tea, which relieved me because the gas could be turned up. She was fatter, and pale from living indoors. I noticed how her hair had recovered from its crop in the Castle Hospital above Balaclava. 'I still have your pendant,' I said, as they had infused the tea and left us.

She smiled. 'Keep it.' The atmosphere was more cheerful, or perhaps it was the brighter light. 'I often see Madame Mohl these days.'

'What happened to Miss Bancroft?'

'Oh, she's out shopping. She is here with me in London.'

I was surprised. 'In the hotel?'

'I keep her because she does everything I tell her with the meekness of a nun and the thoroughness of a Prussian.'

I poured the tea. I said, 'I do not care to see your experience rusting like the abandoned weapons outside Sebastopol.'

'I arrived back at Lea Hurst eager to write, speak, do

whatever might be asked of me. The War Office gave me plenty of tinsel and plenty of praise, which I do not want, and did not give me the real business of soldiers' welfare, which I did.'

'As I warned you plainly in Scutari.'

She disregarded this. 'Lord Panmure, "The Bison—"' It was one of her many unaffectionate nicknames. He had a huge head of bristly tufts, which he moved slowly from side to side, as if he pawed the prairies, 'was in Scotland shooting grouse. Mr Herbert was in Ireland fishing for salmon.' She seemed to wonder how they dared. 'Herbert wrote to me simply, '*Ni lire, ni écrire, ni réfléchir* – the prescription of some mad doctor in Carlsbad. He thought that I was *overwrought*. I had nothing to do in Derbyshire except settle the nurses' wages, answer begging letters and turn down invitations to garden parties.'

Teacup in one hand, I reached for the piles of manuscript in Sutherland's handwriting beside the inkpot. The top sheet read, *Notes Affecting the Health, Efficiency, and Hospital Administration of the British Army.*

'If the War Office refused you work, you gave it to yourself. This would make almost a thousand pages of print. How long did it take?'

'Six months.'

'Write articles for *Candour*,' I suggested. 'I could use so trenchant a contributor. Your letters have vigour and incisiveness, which cut like the blades of scissors through commonplace literary embroidery. And I pay well. You need money, I expect? Five hundred a year is not a fortune.'

'Oh, money,' she said contemptuously. 'I disregard it. Though mama sends me my share of the hotel bill every week, so I *must* retrench. But I want to act, not to write.'

'You will not start to act until you start to forget the Crimea.'

'How can I forget?' she asked angrily. 'The trenches cold and damp, the starved and frozen camp, the deficient rations, the stores which might have served the great army of dead lying unused! I cannot sleep at night without thinking of those I could not save. Oh, my poor men! I am a bad mother to come home and leave you in your Crimean graves.' She paused. 'Seventy-three percent in eight regiments in six months died from disease alone,' she added with characteristic descent to pragmatism. 'Who thinks of that now?'

'You were at the war for 632 days, which is not long from a lifetime. We must use them as a battery for your vital electricity, and skilfully produce sparks to your advantage. But first we must galvanize the people. They may forget the war, but never the Lady with a Lamp.'

She was sitting up straight, sipping her tea. I saw no trace of illness on her. It could have been one of her grumpier afternoons in Scutari. 'The people . . . yes, it was the artisans of Sheffield who sent me knives and forks, not the master cutlers. It was 1800 workmen of Newcastle who sent me an address, not the Duke. You know that women are mistaken for me in the street? Folk crowd to touch their shawls or stroke their arms?' I nodded. 'Rouse them if you can, and wish to. But what for? I have the Nightingale Fund already.'

'That can stay where it is for the moment, earning very nice compound interest at £1,426 per annum. I want to force on the Government a Royal Commission.'

'About Scutari?'

'No. On the whole condition of the Army Medical Department. Barracks, hospitals, doctors, orderlies, supplies, transport, all must be inspected. The mistakes of the past must be chopped into faggots and publicly set ablaze, to raise a mighty head of steam for the engines of reform.'

She was straighter, eyes gleaming. 'Exactly! The bad health of the British army in peace is hardly less appalling than before Sebastopol – when those who fell by disease were above seven times those who fell by the enemy.'

Her voice took the old enthusiasm of a complaint against Dr Hall or Major Sillery. 'The only way to prevent those disasters in war is to maintain efficient general hospitals in peace. The army are *picked lives*, Tristram. But do you realize that the army dies during peace at twice the rate of the general population? In the parish of St Pancras, the civilians die annually at the rate of 2.2 per thousand. The Life Guards in St Pancras Barracks at 10.4 per thousand,' she quoted readily. 'Among a thousand ladies and gentlemen of Knightsbridge, 3.3 die a year. Of the soldiers in Knightsbridge Barracks, 17.5. Our soldiers simply enlist for death in barracks. Neglect kills 1,500 good men every year, as surely as if the War Office lined them up on Salisbury Plain and had them shot.'

'That's the copy I want,' I told her with equal warmth. '*Candour* will work up a public outcry. There are plenty of Conservative MPs to shout with the wind blowing into a Liberal Government's faces.'

She looked doubtful. 'Yes, but I must find a mouthpiece. I am greatly detested by officials. I need a *man*, one high enough in the world to work the question of reform, someone who could talk to ministers and commissioners, which I cannot. But I should have to tell him everything to say, of course,' she added.

'Mr Herbert.'

'He is no longer interested in me.'

'I can make him be.'

The door burst open. It was Fanny and Parthe, with three or four hotel servants carrying shopping and sheaves of winter's costly flowers. They talked immediately about London in January, which they found as dull as a funeral.

'Poor Flo! Don't you see such a change in her, Mr Darling?' asked Parthe, enthusiastically poking chrysanthemums into a crystal vase.

'You're so much better in the warm here, Flo dearest,' said her mother, with the same energy undoing the ribbons of a hat-box. 'That fog! How Parthe and I managed to brave it, I can't *imagine*! We had to have *two* ragged boys running ahead of the coach, it was so thick.'

'I hope Miss Nightingale will brave it tomorrow. I should like her to see my offices in Fleet Street.' I had to get her away from them, from the cloying Sutherland and creeping Clough. I had a plan, but unless conceived in secret, it would be stillborn.

Fanny looked at Florence, aghast. 'But we shall need the

coach all tomorrow. Parthe and I have a dozen visits to return.'

'Then I shall take a hackney coach,' she said.

'Oh, you must not sit in a draughty, jolting cab in your state,' objected Parthe.

'It would be more comfortable than the baggage cart in which I spent my second visit to the Crimea, after being thrown from my mule. Well, I shall use an omnibus.'

'Flo! You cannot be seen in an omnibus,' cried her mother. 'Even out of the season.'

'I shall walk.'

'Florence, dearest—' Her mother's voice ran creamily with compassion. 'Why stay here in horrid, foggy London? Why not go back to Embley?' She sighed deeply. 'We are both of us so tired, looking after you up here. You must get away from all this writing, all these visitors, all the people you *will* keep round you. You must rest—'

The fuse touched the gunpowder. 'Rest!' Florence screamed the word. 'I am lying here like my dead owl, without my head, without my claws, and you both peck at me. It is *de rigueur, d'obligation*, like saying something into one's hat when one goes into church, to say to me all that has been said to me a hundred times a day during the last six months. It is an *obbligato* on the violin, and the twelve violins all practise it together, like the clocks striking twelve at night all over London, till I say like Xavier de Maistre, *Assez, je le sais, je ne le sais que trop*. I am not a penitent, Mama, but you are like the R C confessor, who says what is *de rigueur*.'

'Parthe and myself are victims of our self-devotion to you,' cried Fanny, equally hysterically.

'Oh, you lead a very amusing life,' Florence threw back. 'This is a scene worthy of Molière, two people in tolerable and even perfect health, who lie on the sofa all day and persuade themselves of their exhaustion by another who is dying of overwork.'

Florence was bolt upright on the sofa, arm rigid with accusation. Suddenly, it was at her own throat, her mouth open, her eyes turned up. 'My heart!' she cried. She fell back, limp, panting like a dog in the sun. 'A palpitation . . . you have made me talk myself into a palpitation . . .'

The room exploded with panic. Sal volatile, water, brandy, pillows and towels were flying everywhere. Fanny cried that she was killing her loving daughter, or that her daughter was killing her loving mother, I was not clear. Parthe threw open the window, admitting much disagreeable fog, gasped, choked and howled terribly. Sutherland appeared, urgently professional, and started slapping Florence hard on both wrists. Clough occupied the doorway, clasped his hands and uttered elegantly poetic expressions of distress. I reached for my hat and withdrew.

As I was leaving the hotel, Miss Bancroft came through the front door with a miasma of fog.

'Well, Mr Darling! I wondered how long before we encountered one another. If we ever did.' She smiled warmly under her bonnet. She seemed to have forgotten my assault upon her on the stairs of the Sisters' Tower. 'I'm glad we have met this moment. To see you lightens this dreadful day.'

'To see you makes me forget it completely,' I said with vapid politeness.

'But you're famous,' she said accusingly, as those do who knew you when you were not. 'Everyone in London who can read seems to be talking about *Candour*. And many who cannot, I think. The cabman was asking me what *Candour* said about Mr Gladstone and . . . oh, I could not tell him, of course.' She put her hand to her mouth laughing. 'Those ladies of the unfortunate class. In the streets!'

She seemed livelier than I could remember, but perhaps it was the effect of escape from the vast dead-house of Scutari. 'You must hurry upstairs. Miss Nightingale is having one of her attacks. Dr Sutherland is there.'

'Oh, there's no haste. Miss Nightingale always recovers in her own time.'

There was a pause. We stood looking at each other. We both knew that if we parted with an unqualified farewell it would be final, separation for ever. If I wished to see her away from Miss Nightingale's shadow it was my moment to decide. Had the lamps of a waiting hansom shown through the windows, I would have left. Instead, I said, 'I have a small party to the opera on Saturday week. Would you care to join us? Miss Nightingale's health obviously precludes her own invitation.'

There was another silence, I suspected more formal than decisive. 'Thank you, Mr Darling. I should like to, very much.'

'It's *Cosi Fan Tutti*. Will you please tell Mrs Nightingale that I shall be arranging a coach from the Lord Mayor's own stables to fetch her daughter at two o'clock tomorrow afternoon?'

22

THREADS OF THE WEB I spun from my editorial chair reached from the pot-houses of Seven Dials to the Palace. There was a young Lord – whose name I cannot give, as he shares my talent for longevity – who in the Royal Household exercised small functions and large ears. He sought my patronage because he wanted my help to win power and fortune from financial jugglery, for which his slyness and graspingness fitted him better than for life at Court.

In February, I asked him, 'Is the Queen still interested in Miss Nightingale? Nobody else is, who matters.'

'Oh, frightfully. They were the fondest of correspondents. "Dear Miss Nightingale," he mimicked, ''How warm my admiration for your services, which are fully equal to those of my *dear* and *brave* soldiers. *No one* takes a greater interest or feels *more* for their sufferings than their Queen, day and night she thinks of her *beloved troops*.'' Oh, and I forgot. "So does the Prince." You know the line.'

'Could you manage Miss Nightingale an invitation to Windsor? Preferably when Panmure happens to be there?'

We were eating cutlets in the Reform Club. Soyer had left Turkey after Miss Nightingale, returning to his everyday business of creating feasts for noblemen. He had brought home triumphantly his purchase of the baggage cart which trundled her shakily round the Crimean battlefields. I had already suggested to the lord that lunchtime he might volunteer to me the offer of club membership – canvassing for election being strictly forbidden.

'Windsor?' He screwed up his full, bright pink lips under

his silky fair moustache. 'Yes, I should think so. Clark, the Queen's physician, might make a useful go-between.'

'I want to re-establish Miss Nightingale as a national heroine, which after all is her rightful position. The common people of the country would cheer themselves hoarse at her name, but officials and society, comfortably shut up in Whitehall and Mayfair, would not be disturbed in the slightest by the noise. If the Queen cheered with the people, they would be forced to open the windows.'

'What's your real game?' he asked.

'To use Miss Nightingale's wasted talents as a big stick to beat Pam and his cabinet about India. Look what's happening in Lucknow, Delhi, Meerut. The sepoys are furious at the War Office's new cartridge, which is greased with the fat of the sacred cow and the abhorred pig. And they have to bite the ends off, to use them! What block-headedness, what bungling! Just like the war. There'll be an explosion in India, unless Panmure feels even faintly the warmth of their feelings. But they're cold fish in the War Office. They never lost an hour's sleep over an army ragged, shivering, hungry outside Sebastopol.'

'By jove! You *sound* like Miss Nightingale.'

'Oh, I expect I do. She's a boa-constrictor, who leaves indelible marks even on lucky victims who escape the coils. A boa-constrictor who can hypnotize men with fright, knows precisely when to nip them in the neck, then swallows them whole. I have discerned the outlines of many distinguished doctors, soldiers and politicians in her interior. As there is comfortable capacity for many more, I intend to throw her the square meal of a Royal Sanitary Commission on the army.'

'With which *Candour* will be identified, and have all the confidential information?'

'Of course.'

'I'll see what hints I can drop. I believe that Sir James Clark's figure has shown in Miss Nightingale's stomach for some time.'

Miss Nightingale's audience with the Queen had been plotted between us at the *Candour* office in Fleet Street. She insisted it must be her last attempt to grasp the trailing reins of public affairs. If my plan failed, she would go back to Embley House and write books. *Suggestions for Thought to the Searchers after Truth among the Artisans of England* was already started. She would rectify philosophical affairs rather than sanitary ones. The Church was misinterpreting God's word to artisans, though she was beginning to wonder if God's words themselves were sometimes ill-chosen. She had written to Mr John Stuart Mill about it, and Mr Mill had replied most kindly.

Many men make great heroes of themselves in action and bigger fools of themselves on the deceptive battlefields of ideas. I assumed that Miss Nightingale was inspired to un-block the world's theological drains because God was to her a mighty sanitary engineer, with the commonsense to advise directly into her ear. From philosophy I hastily drew her to photography. Her likeness should be our battle flag. But she refused a sitting. She had already turned her back on a forest of academicians' brushes. 'I do not wish to be remembered when I am gone,' she told me. To which there was no answer.

I had no qualms of Miss Nightingale's feebleness pre-cluding the journey to Windsor. I did not need call at the Burlington Hotel until it had been accomplished. 'From the very day of receiving Her Majesty's command,' Sutherland greeted me excitedly, 'Miss Nightingale's health improved rapidly. She said she could have walked with springy step all the way from Balaclava up to Sebastopol. Now alas, she is a little poorly, and unable to take a turn in the Park these fine afternoons.' His voice grew hushed, as everyone's at the Burlington exchanging the latest on Miss Nightingale's health, like secret passwords. 'But she mends by degrees.'

'In front the sun climbs slow, how slowly,' said Clough, 'but westward, look, the land is bright.' Two sharp tinkles of the handbell rang behind the inner door. 'My signal!' He hurried from the room.

'I simply didn't hear it.' Sutherland shook his head, finger in ear. A double desk had been installed, the two men sitting opposite like clerks in the ante-room of a great banker.

'This deafness! Miss Nightingale finds it so annoying that she threatens to send Mr Clough to the instrument-makers for an ear-trumpet. It is *nervous* deafness, from the strain of work. I sent my wife from Highgate to corroborate my point, but Miss Nightingale didn't see it.'

He glanced at the inner door. 'She *can* be so dreadfully demanding. Last week, late at night, a message to me at Highgate, come at once – teeming rain – I arrived in a temper, a terrible scene, poor Miss Nightingale fainted, indeed had a *fit*.' He sighed. 'Miss Bancroft and I had to sit up all night with her. Can you imagine my sorrow, my distress, at almost causing her death? She makes me work on Sundays. I see so little of my wife. When she is angry with me, she passes me little notes from her room. Look—'

He thrust at me from his pocket torn scraps of writing-paper, the edges of newspapers. This débris of contention was scribbled, *Where is the Tulloch Commission Report? Where is the Sanitary Minute? Why did you write me a lie this morning? Must you linger so long over lunch? No I will not be friends.*

'She compares herself to her dead owl, but I assure you, her little beak is of the sharpest.' He looked self-conscious, but confession is compulsive. 'Other times, she calls me her "sick baby".' He sighed more deeply. 'She is a wonderful woman, who could do what men could not, and who would dare suffering knowingly where men would shirk it. Did you know, I gave up £1,500 a year from the Government to be with Miss Nightingale? That was part-time, too.'

I tried to cheer him. 'You're as lucky as an Ottoman. You have two wives.'

'Miss Nightingale is not one of my wives. I am better described as one of hers,' he responded sadly.

Clough reappeared, with a shopping-basket. 'Calf's-foot jelly,' he murmured anxiously. 'Where might I find calf's-foot jelly?'

'Messrs Crosse and Blackwell of Soho Square,' I told him.

He thanked me with deep relief. 'And pens, indelible pencils, blotting-paper, tagged tapes . . .' He left, head shaking at the complexities of the quailless wilderness.

The bell rang loudly. 'That's you,' said Sutherland.

There was rearrangement of the hospital which Miss Nightingale was creating for herself in the hotel. Fanny and Parthe were dislodged to the floor below, where they could arrange flowers until overcome with exhaustion without criticism. The bed had been removed, the heavy curtains were open to a bright winter's day. Miss Nightingale lay with her pillows and shawls on the couch, Miss Bancroft sat on a stool beside her. I supposed Miss Nightingale knew about the opera. I was curious whether she resented it. But we had more serious conversation to exchange. I tossed my hat on a table and sat down, flipping coat-tails over thighs. 'And how was it?'

'The Queen and Prince Albert's whole thoughts were on things of importance. The fine folk about them were occupied with trifles. The Queen is a remarkably conscientious person, but so mistrustful of herself.'

'And the Bison?'

'Miss Nightingale has tamed him,' smiled Jane Bancroft.

'Oh, his mane is absolutely silky, and a loving sadness pervades his whole being. His eye for detail is as useless as a short-sighted man for Rembrandt's brushwork, his sense of system is that of a sluttish housemaid, he is excited only by three items, all north of the Border – grouse, salmon and the Church of Scotland. But he has one supreme attribute. He is bullyable.'

The door flew open. There was no knock. Miss Nightingale looked aghast. 'Mr Herbert!' cried Sutherland.

I had seen the key in Liz Herbert. I suspected that she sniffed pungent memories of Caroline Norton. The Peace of Paris had divorced Miss Nightingale from her husband, now he must rest well away from her, in their country house at Wilton in Wiltshire, fishing and shooting to his heart's content.

I suspected also that Liz Herbert was horribly insecure. I could myself readily envisage Sidney Herbert bursting the bonds of matrimony, becoming a denizen of the Burlington Hotel like Sutherland and Arthur Clough. I called upon her at Belgrave Square, on some excuse about the

Nightingale Fund, and flew this black kite in a delicate breeze.

Miss Nightingale could do much more for the country, I insisted, and Mr Herbert could do a little more for Miss Nightingale. Was not persuading him so Mrs Herbert's *duty* to husband and nation? Would not Mrs Herbert shine in the golden light when Mr Herbert relit Miss Nightingale's lamp? And surely he must be growing terribly weary of trout and pheasant? She agreed. Once I had Mr Herbert in Miss Nightingale's presence, the tail of the boa-constrictor would shortly be round his ankle.

'My dear Miss Nightingale, I am shocked to see you again laid low.' He was as impeccably dressed and as impeccably handsome as ever, though smouldering fever glowed through his cheeks as a winter fire through a darkening cottage window. The three of us were shortly alone. 'Lord Panmure told me you were so full of vigour at Windsor.' He laid hat and gloves amid the papers on Sutherland's table. 'He was much surprised, you know. He expected some vain and fierce virago, some scolding tyrant. Instead, he found a petticoated philosopher.'

'The Bison is a reforming animal, if not an organizing one. You know that the Treasury, the Horse Guards, the War Office and the Medical Department are like a rickety, clumsy machine, with a pin loose here and a tooth broken there, and a makeshift somewhere else. The force of Hercules may be exhausted in needless friction before they all move together. But *I* know you are only lukewarm to reform, Mr Herbert,' she chided him. 'You pensioned me off with £40,000 and forgot me.'

'But Miss Nightingale! I needed a rest,' he excused himself.

'Rest!' The word sounded like de Quincey's laudanum.

'I too have not been well, so I stayed down at Wilton. And my tenure of office as Secretary at War was not one to inspire a man who is beginning to find great exertions difficult . . .' His voice fell away for a moment, but he resumed more vigorously, 'The Queen was most impressed by the defects present, and the reforms needed, in our present military hospital system, which you put to her so modestly. The Queen has expressed a wish to the Duke of Cambridge, as Commander-in-Chief, that you hold an official position at the War Office.' She sat up straight, in surprise at such regal flattery. So did I. 'That would be impossible, I fear. But the very suggestion made it seem high time I paid you a visit, even unexpected.'

'I am glad you chose today,' she said briskly. 'Mr Darling – those files. Mr Herbert, the Report of the Tulloch Commission on Supplies to the British army in the Crimea . . .'

Never was a war sat upon so heavily by commissions. Never were so many facts unearthed for decent reburial in Blue Books.

Miss Nightingale held it up. 'This report was laid before Parliament a year ago, but everyone knew its contents perfectly well months earlier. It castigates Lord Lucan, Lord Cardigan and Dr Hall, all three of whom got decorated. Why?'

'Lord Panmure disliked the report.'

'Lord Panmure sent the Commission out. He may dislike the taste of his own medicine, but he still has to swallow it. Lord Panmure now orders a Board of Generals to sit at Chelsea Barracks, to give officers criticized in the report an opportunity of defending themselves. Why?'

'Because Lord Panmure would otherwise have the infuriating bother of acting on the report,' Herbert told her cheerfully. 'I know from experience that the War Office presents its Secretary of State with unending and complicated work, which Lord Panmure finds easy, through the simple process of never attempting to do it.'

'The army put whitewash to better use on the barrack walls of Scutari. Next, the new military hospital, building at Netley—'

'Is anything the matter with it?' he asked, concerned.

'The windows all face the wrong way, so the bad air will waft from one ward to another. It is nothing but one huge corridor, to serve row upon row of uncomfortable and ill-ventilated patients. Why?'

'Because the design cuts a dash when seen from Southampton Water.'

'It must be pulled down.'

'But that would cost £70,000! Parliament would set upon your Bison like picadors. You know the realities of politics as well as I.'

'It is impossible to scrutinize in too fine detail the building of a hospital. Kitchens, laundries, washhouses, the movement of hot food, soiled linen, sick people, all is interdependent. What books should there be in the recreation rooms? Who should carve the meat, and where? What colour for the walls? I prefer pale pink. It's all in my book on the health of the British army. You had better take this and read it.' She thrust a sheaf of papers at him. 'It is my treatise on hospital sinks.'

He accepted it, smiling. 'Now, Miss Nightingale, I have something to tax you with. I have just come from Lord Panmure. Lord Panmure has just come from the Queen. A Royal Commission is to investigate every part of the Army Medical Department. You were right. The Bison is a reforming beast – or Her Majesty and yourself have goaded him to be. The Royal Warrant will be issued in the beginning of May, and the commission sit shortly afterwards. Your sex precludes you from being a commissioner, but your movements behind the scenes will be more important than the dramatics upon the public stage. That is another reality of politics which you know as well as I. So you have much work to do.'

The coil of the boa-constrictor was already up to his calves. I did not know then that it would steadily squeeze him to death.

23

IT WAS THE LAST Friday afternoon in March, 1857. It was my next call at the Burlington. As my coachman pulled up – I had succumbed to the dignity of my own carriage – the black-clothed, squat form of the Bison, silk hat pulled low over ox head, followed by a black-dressed secretary, was bowed reverently from the hotel with their cluster of scarlet dispatch boxes into the black official coach. I found the rooms upstairs ringing with jubilation.

'The Bison was here *three hours*,' exclaimed Miss Nightingale from her couch. 'You see, Mr Darling, my lying here a sick woman demands that even Secretaries of State pay court to me, and not I to them. He could not shelve me for ever as a bothering woman, a "turbulent fellow" as he called me, sweetening me with his hampers of game, saying he could not write because of gout in his hands – gout is a very *handy* thing, he always has it in his hands when he is called upon to do anything. But I shall never let him alone until *this* thing is done.'

This was a terrible curse on the poor Bison, I recognized.

'Miss Nightingale nominated nearly all the royal commissioners she wanted,' said Miss Bancroft, with Sutherland fluttering like a butterfly on a lovely day.

'The Bison *will* have three army doctors,' said Miss Nightingale. 'Not fair! But like a sensible general in retreat, I named a military doctor who will do less harm than most others. The Bison was amazed at my condescension in naming another military doctor as secretary, so I concealed the fact of the man being a dangerous animal and obstinate innovator. I failed on one point. Unfairly. I wanted the Queen's physician. It would be agreeable for the Queen to have him, and agreeable for us to have the Queen. I was so good to leave the Bison Dr Andrew Smith, the more so as I could not help it. Of course, Dr Smith will say, in equal parts lachrymose and threatening, "I do not understand why we are to enquire into all this." Oh, I had a tough fight of it.'

'Lord Panmure really *does* have such an inconveniently bad memory for names, facts, dates and numbers,' complained Sutherland.

'Convenient, you mean,' Miss Nightingale told him. 'Mine will serve us both, though I know too well what discipline means, to claim a better memory than my chief. He does not wish the world to suppose he takes suggestions from me – which crime indeed is very unjust to impute to the man.'

'Miss Nightingale presented him with a list of seven points,' continued Jane Bancroft excitedly, ticking them as usual on her fingers. 'A scheme and financial estimate to be prepared for an Army Medical School—'

'I won,' said Miss Nightingale.

'The Netley plans to be reported to myself privately,' interrupted Sutherland delightedly.

'I won.'

'Commissariat to be put on different footing, as in India—' said Miss Bancroft.

'I lost.'

'The camp at Aldershot to kill cattle, bake bread, build, drain, shoemake, tailor and generally do for themselves—'

'Lord Panmure will consider,' said Sutherland.

'Which means he will do nothing,' said Miss Nightingale.

'Sir John Hall will *not* succeed Dr Andrew Smith as Director-General,' imparted Sutherland, hugging himself.

'I won!'

'Colonel Tulloch to be knighted—' said Miss Bancroft.

'I lost. It would have wiped off some of the whitewash down at Chelsea.'

'Statistics—' began Miss Bancroft.

'Vague promises. In the end, the Bison contradicted himself and everything. Thus I entertain the most sanguine expectations of success.'

'And I sit on the commission as sanitary expert.' Sutherland wriggled as though his undervest had caught fire.

'Every one of these names I have been obliged to carry by force of my will upon the Bison against his. Mr Herbert will be chairman, of course. I could do nothing without him. My only fear now is the Bison seeing this visit as a sop, and shelving the commission as soon as he dares.'

'In that case, *Candour* will print your full Crimean experiences, with your suggestions for improvements. Publicity will get what you want in the long run. People won't stand for their sons and brothers joining the army for the army itself to kill them.'

'No one can feel for the army as I do,' said Miss Nightingale, with sudden ferocity. 'These people who talk to me now have all fed their children on the fat of the land and dressed them in velvet and silk. I have had to see *my* children dressed in a dirty blanket and an old pair of regimental trousers, and to see them fed on raw salt meat, when we knew the stores were bursting with warm clothing. Living skeletons devoured by vermin, ulcerated, hopeless, speechless, dying like Greeks as they wrapped their heads in their blankets and never spoke a word . . . Nine thousand of my children are lying, from causes which might have been prevented, in their forgotten graves. I can never forget. Never.'

I made my excuses and left. Miss Nightingale talking about the Crimea was becoming torturingly tedious.

Miss Bancroft saw me downstairs.

'Thank you for your letter. I am so pleased that you enjoyed the opera,' I said.

'I am very fond of music, but not very fond of society.'

'Why should you be frightened of society? You have better looks and better manners than many society ladies, and much more intelligence.'

'You think me intelligent?' She was artlessly surprised, not flattered. 'Miss Nightingale thinks I am foolish.'

'As she thinks that of cabinet ministers, you should not feel downhearted. Did she know about our meeting?'

'No.'

'You won't keep it from her long.'

'Shan't I?' She gave a crafty smile. 'It's remarkable how the cleverest people will believe a good tale told by an idiot.'

We walked in silence down half a flight of stairs.

'The things you know about me and Miss Nightingale,' she said, eyes on the treads. 'They were childish things. Any girl of my age would have done the same under *her* domination.' She gave a flick of the head upstairs. 'They are the affairs you may see in any seminary or convent, and which nobody thinks about. Only Miss Nightingale strains to raise it to the passions of Daphnis and Chloe. You know how everything she touches instantly becomes the most important matter in the world's progress? And at Scutari, of course, we were all on top of each other, the Barracks was so grim and there was nowhere to escape. It was a forcing house for those sort of relations, just as the tendrils of flowers meet in a hot-house. There were plenty more than Miss Nightingale and myself among the nurses, believe me.'

We reached the hall, occupied by a family of six, all red-faced, tweeded, furred, just arrived from Yorkshire, scattering the staff with a fusillade of complaints behind fortifications of stout leather portmanteaux.

'Would you leave Miss Nightingale?'

'Where for? The nurse is still either a slut or a nun.'

'Haven't you a home? Your father's a farmer, isn't he?'

'A poor one and an ill-tempered one. I could not feel dutiful towards my parents. Like Miss Nightingale, I escaped from them to this work. Unlike her, I have not the character to return and face them.'

'You would give me great pleasure by taking supper with some friends tomorrow.'

She smiled. 'Innocence is one of the most irritating things to be accused of. The supper would materialize, but not the friends.'

'After Scutari, a chaperone seems an extravagant luxury. Well, a box at the opera?'

'Much more acceptable. How fortunate for me that you enjoy the opera.'

'I can't stand it, but we shall go.'

The Bison called once again at the Burlington Hotel. He bore the official Draft of Instructions to the Commissioners. Miss Nightingale was graciously pleased to alter it before its forwarding to the Queen. The Commission sat on Tuesday, May 8 1857. Three days passed. It was overwhelmed in the newspapers, and about to lose its guiding genius.

The electric telegraph brought news of the Indian uprising in Meerut. England was shocked, outraged, bewildered, angry and sorrowful, as though the inmates of a ragged school, saved from the gutter and from themselves, clothed, civilized and given pocket-money, had without the slightest reason turned upon their philanthropic betters and cut their throats.

Lady Canning had now risen from Postmistress-General to Mrs Viceroy. At once, Miss Nightingale telegraphed an offer to go at twenty-four hours' notice, were there anything in her 'line of business'. An encore by popular demand would have pleased her as much as it pleased Miss Jenny Lind, but the mountain of work for the Royal Commission would have become a melting iceberg.

While we waited for a reply, Miss Nightingale began to see the mutiny as a stroke of luck, in directing public attention again towards the army. I saw it as justification of my unheeded cautions. *Candour* was right. I had warned that I heard in a splintering corner of the Empire the creaking fragility of the whole structure. *Candour* was right again, half a century later, when another corner was shot to bits by the rifles of a few Boer farmers. If we find ourselves cowering behind it from the Kaiser's Krupps' howitzers, it will not be for equally grave warnings equally flippantly disregarded.

To everyone's relief Lady Canning declined. There was a plenitude of natives for use.

We advanced only to another crisis. Miss Nightingale refused to appear before the Commission and give evidence.

This seemed to me an anticlimax as ludicrous as burning Joan of Arc with damp faggots.

'It would only make bad blood, my bringing up past delinquencies,' she told me in the Burlington.

'Can't you go along and say *something*?'

'What on? An indifferent matter like hospital construction? Leaving untouched the great matters which have affected our sick more than any mere architecture could do? That would be unconscientious of me.'

'But the absence of your name from the list of witnesses will diminish the weight of the final Report, and will give rise to unfounded rumours,' I counselled her impatiently. 'It will be said that you made suggestions about the Crimea, the responsibility for which you were reluctant to incur in public.'

'It would be treachery to the memory of the dead,' she said flatly.

I suggested a compromise. She agreed to give written answers to written questions. The arrangement was anyway superfluous because she saw every witness herself and told him what to say. Their testimony was often printed in *Candour* before they uttered it.

The summer was as stifling as three years before. I became a regular caller at the Burlington. Sidney Herbert was there every morning, iller and iller, to take his orders for the day. Fanny and Parthe came up to do the season. Miss Bancroft seemed to enjoy the excitement. Clough went out for the india-rubbers and postage stamps. With terrible coyness, Sutherland called the hotel 'The Little War Office', Miss Nightingale 'The Commander-in-Chief', the indifferent meals served by indifferent waiters, 'our mess'. 'She is one of the most gifted creatures God ever made,' he told me in the ante-room. Then the bell tinkled beyond the inner door, and one of God's creatures had to jump like a flea for another.

In August, the weather was heavier, the streets stank. The season was over, Fanny and Parthe bored. One afternoon I found Miss Nightingale alone with Miss Bancroft, the windows again shut, the curtains drawn, the gas low.

'I am dying,' groaned Miss Nightingale from the couch. 'I cannot breathe, I cannot sleep, I cannot eat, I have lived all week on nothing but tea.'

'Then I must get Miss Harriet Martineau to post your obituary notice up to the minute for *Candour*.'

'You think I am *une malade imaginaire*?' she accused me indignantly. 'Dr Sutherland is convinced that I have congestion of the spine, brought on by incessant worry and overwork, and that leads straight to paralysis.'

'Dr Sutherland is a drain-doctor.'

'You have caught the unpleasant disease of flippancy from him.'

I pulled back the curtains. I had become powerful in the Burlington Hotel. With the newspapers preoccupied over the siege of Lucknow, *Candour* kept the Royal Commission before the public. Languid on her pillows, Miss Nightingale held a hand over her eyes. 'There is one service you can do a dying woman. My association with my children makes me wish to be buried in the Crimea.' I glanced at Jane Bancroft, but she was expressionless on her stool, hands folded in lap.

'It amounts to what I never should have expected to feel – a superstition.' Her voice was low as a moan. '*For they are not there*. But for every one of my twenty thousand children, I have expended more motherly feeling and action than my mother has expended on me in thirty-seven years.' She dropped her hand. 'It is for you, Tristram, to employ the deep grief of the public to see that, is done. I hope you will spread no chivalrous ideas of what is "due" to my "memory". The Government will insist on the Abbey.'

'Particularly if the Royal Commission's report fills them with shame.'

Her deathbed was disturbed by the appearance of Sutherland, brisk and smiling. His eye fell instinctively on a pillbox in the middle of his table, which he picked up, rattled, and opened.

'Tell me what those pills are,' Miss Nightingale ordered faintly. 'One of the maids here, attending the world's greatest authority on nursing, takes quack remedies.'

'The nearer to Rome, the less the religion,' he replied lightly. 'The Commission today made its most important and beneficial decision.'

'What was that?' she asked feebly.

'We shall adjourn for two months from August 8.'

Miss Nightingale sat bolt upright, raised like Lazarus by the miraculous touch of fury. 'What? The Commission *must* make its report the moment Parliament reassembles. Otherwise, it will be shovelled aside by a dozen willing hands, as impedimenting the train of legislation.'

'*I* should work on, all summer,' said Sutherland, deflated. 'But alas, my will is stronger than my legs—'

'Lord Panmure wants to go north to shoot grouse, and Mr Herbert wants to go to Ireland to catch fish,' Florence said, as though accusing them of unspeakable crimes.

'Mr Herbert is ill,' Sutherland told her more forcibly.

'His neuralgia is fancy, all fancy. Doesn't he inhale that prescription I gave him, cotton soaked with chloroform and camphor?'

'It makes him sick. He has violent headaches, and the most crippling feelings of lassitude. I really feel there is something wrong with the poor man, though I cannot put my finger on it,' Sutherland confessed. He looked even more guilty. 'This morning, Mr Herbert felt so ill that he had to go home to Belgrave Square, to bed.'

'Bed? Idling! He ought to be ashamed of himself. His only disease is in the mind of Mrs Herbert. He is essential to me. He is a man of the quickest and most accurate perception, his very manner vital in engaging the most sulky and recalcitrant of witnesses. He is my mouthpiece, without him I can do nothing. And here I work double tides, labouring day after day until I am almost fainting. Well, I had just as soon wear out in two months as two years. The Commission *will* not adjourn.'

'You can't adjourn with Sir John Hall about to give evidence,' I objected. 'That will be like Lucifer summoned for judgement in Heaven, with Miss Nightingale sitting, if not on God's right hand, just without the blaze of His glory passing Him instructive little notes.'

'I do not want the old man badgered in his examination,' she said startlingly. 'Oh, I have the proofs of his incredible apathy by heart, back to his fatal letter to Dr Andrew Smith in 1854, the month before my arrival at Scutari, when he expressed his satisfaction that the whole hospital establishment "was now put on a very creditable footing." '

I said, 'I did not imagine that mercy droppeth as the gentle rain from thunderclouds.'

'My own belief is that Hall is a much cleverer fellow than everyone takes him for.' She seemed to overlook being interrupted in the act of dying. 'We want to make the best out of him for our case. He was much afraid of the Commission at first, but now thinks it is taking a good turn. He should not be put too much on the defensive, but allowed to slip quietly into the current of reform. I am turning the quality of mercy to practical effect – had I not at Scutari, I could have done nothing but wept. Though if he proves obdurate, he must of course be put in a corner,' she added forthrightly. He was to die peacefully ten years later, thirty miles from her birthplace.

Soon we were alone.

'You are killing Sidney Herbert.'

She glared at me. 'What an absurd charge. Though admittedly, he would gladly kill himself for me. Look at him – a statesman, past middle age, absorbed in politics for a quarter of a century, through *sympathy* towards me remodels his whole life and policy. That is what I call real sympathy.' She hesitated. 'But no woman has ever altered one hour of her existence for me, even those with a passion for me. *Women have no sympathy.* All these women have influenced me, more than I have them. Parthe always told me, as a reproach, that I was "more like a man". Indeed, it was true.'

'Hasn't Miss Bancroft remodelled her existence for you?'

'Miss Bancroft has no *appris à apprendre*, which I attribute to want of sympathy.' She drew her shawl round her shoulders, sitting up against the pillows. 'Like my own family, her want of the commonest knowledge of contemporary history makes her quite useless as a secretary. She doesn't know the names of the Cabinet ministers. She doesn't know the offices at the Horse Guards. She doesn't know who of the men of today are dead, and who are alive. She doesn't know which of the churches has bishops and which do not. Now, I'm sure when I went to the Crimea I didn't know a colonel from a corporal. But there are such things as Army Lists and Almanacs. Yet I never knew a woman who, out of sympathy for me, would consult one. Sidney Herbert and I are together exactly like two men. Of him, I can truly say, O Jonathan, my brother Jonathan, my love for thee is very great – passing the love of women.'

She smiled. 'People often say to me, you don't know what a wife and a mother feels. No, I say, I don't, and I'm very glad I don't. And *they* don't know what *I feel*. I am sick with indignation at what wives and mothers will do of the most egregious selfishness. And people call it all maternal or conjugal affection, and think it very pretty to say so. I wish I could tell the truth from my own experiences. It makes me mad when people talk about "Women's Right", when the world won't even open its eyes on our right to love one another. Ezekiel went running about naked "for a sign". I can't run about naked, because it is not the custom of the country. You are wasting my time as usual, Tristram, by inviting my confessions. I have work pressing upon my feeble chest like *la peine forte et dure*.'

She reached for the pile of papers which Jane Bancroft had left on her stool. 'I have the momentous affairs of Robert Robinson in my hands.' I frowned, puzzled. 'Thomas the drummer boy,' she reminded me. 'I am sending him at my own expense to school, and he is going to agricultural college. A reasonable reward for one prepared to defend me single-handed from the Russians on the Genoese Heights. Please give this other document to Miss Bancroft, to be kept carefully. Sutherland would probably lose it. It's stolen goods. To besiege the Army Medical Department, no Lancaster gun could be more formidable. But I cannot fire it.'

I glanced at the paper. 'Mr Wakley-Barlow!'

'A scoundrel, but he is a distant relative.'

It was a report to Dr Andrew Smith, on Wakley-Barlow's furnishing the Army Medical Department with medicines, dressings and comforts below standard, rotten, wrongly labelled, or simply charged for and never seen. 'Up to his old Harley Street tricks?'

'Dr Smith suppressed the report. He wished less to give Wakley-Barlow his deserts than expose his own officials' incompetence.'

'I should be happy to see Wakley-Barlow walking his way to salvation on a treadmill.'

'Why? Because he sent you to me on a fool's errand?'

'Because he sent a man to me with a knife on an errand far from foolish.'

'I've heard ugly tales of him.' She reflected a few moments. 'Would you not give your source of information?'

'I should go on the treadmill myself first.'

'Oh, very well. The dog shall have its bone.'

I folded the paper and put it in my pocket. It would be at Bow Street in the morning.

The Commission did not adjourn. The grouse and salmon were each spared an extra adversary until the beginning of September, when it finished its work. To the surprise and relief of the *habitués* of the Burlington, Miss Nightingale succumbed to Sutherland's advice to take the water cure at Malvern.

'All her blood wants renewing,' he explained to me in the ante-room when I called *faire mes adieux*. Clough was fussing with timetables, tickets, small change and luggage labels. 'Miss Nightingale must have new blood, or she cannot work. And new blood can't be made out of the tea on which she is living. At least, as far as I know.' He twinkled.

She was carried to Paddington Station in a litter borne by Crimean veterans, paraded like a deity. The streets were crammed, there was the reverent shedding of hats, as though she had succumbed to stale blood already. The stationmaster received her, the passengers forgot their trains, she involuntarily inspected a guard of honour of curious porters.

Only Clough accompanied her on the Great Western. Sutherland went back to Highgate, to dig a pond in his garden. Sidney Herbert went back to Belgrave Square, struggling to write the Commission's report. Jane Bancroft was left to tidy up the Burlington, to follow two days later with the luggage. The next morning, we were married by my uncle Humphry in a chapel of Chelsea Cathedral, by special licence. I decided that it did not really matter whether she knew the names of the Cabinet ministers and the offices at the Horse Guards.

24

EARLY ON an icy Sunday morning in February 1860, my uncle Humphry went to preach at a new church in the swelling suburb of Sydenham, south of the Thames. At the top of steep Sydenham Hill, beneath the transparent vaults and towers and educative animals of the Crystal Palace, where I had once invited Harriet to pass an afternoon, one of his fine four horses slipped, his smartly-liveried coachman lost the reins, the splendid, emblazoned carriage careered over fifty yards of slippery cobbles, tottered, crashed, splintered and stopped under the wheels of an omnibus. My uncle's coachman jumped clear, but my uncle lay looking up to Heaven in the lap of a washerwoman, his neck broken.

The funeral was on the Thursday. When we reached home in Berkeley Square, the afternoon mist was thickening into fog, the gaslamps pale, square suns. I told my coachman to wait.

'You're going out again?' asked Jane.

'Of course I am. The funeral's something I must write up myself. Otherwise, it'll hold no interest for anybody.'

I had just bought the *Penny Pioneer*. I was under thirty, rich, and already infuriating the rest of Fleet Street with my artful miracles.

We went up to the drawing-room, still in our funeral clothes. The curtains were drawn across the tall windows, the gas was bright, the fire leapt in welcome like an affectionate dog. I stood before the grate, coat-tails apart. 'This'll get rid of the chill of the graveside.'

'Didn't the will take an age to read?' Jane was unpinning a black hat swaddled in a black veil.

'You had to listen pretty carefully, to avoid missing my legacy of a pair of cufflinks '

'It's strange, the three brothers each meeting an untimely death.'

'Uncle Peregrine killed himself with his knife as surely as a Borgia pricked with his own poisoned ring But the only accident about my father's death was his picking the wrong horses. Well, you're a baronet's wife. How long before you get used to it?'

'That's of no importance, when I'm indifferent to it.'

'No woman can remain indifferent to suddenly being called "My lady". No more than her friends who are not can remain unenvious.'

'I *am* indifferent. I have seen the real world, and it's a squalid, sickly place, full of misery, agony and death. Its titles are ridiculous, they're like decorating with gold leaf the tenement houses of Cholera Court in Soho.'

'You mean only that you are indifferent to marriage.'

'Oh, that accusation again!' She fell wearily into an armchair. 'You make it as often, and as falsely, as the Puritans against the witches of Salem. I do everything for you that a wife's duty demands. Or would you prefer to burn me at the stake and get another?'

'On the contrary, you do not perform the only duty that a wife must.'

'Must?'

'I could employ an extra housekeeper, and there are a hundred women in society eager to share my invitations to dinners and balls.'

'Fill both vacancies. I shouldn't mind.'

'But *I* should. If we separate, people will talk.'

'Why worse than of any other couple in London who can't get on? Since going into society, I've learned that unhappy marriages are highly regarded, as providing lively conversation. Happy ones are mentioned as scathingly as a dull pudding.'

'Everyone in London knows that Florence is a lover of women. They would laugh at me as her rival suitor. I don't mind scandal, I live on it. But I cannot take ridicule.'

She sat in her mourning silk, looking sulky, feet stuck out, arms ungainly. She had lost her habit of standing with hands clasped. She no longer flavoured her conversation with a *bouquet garni* of French phrases. But she was still the woman whose wrist I had bent back on the stairs at Scutari.

'You shouldn't have taken me away from her.'

'That was apparent on our honeymoon.'

'Oh, don't start about that,' she said crossly.

'A man less considerate than myself would have left you in that hotel in Vichy.'

'It isn't my nature to play the woman. I can no more change my nature than a Mussulman the colour of his skin.'

'You can play the woman with a woman. Perhaps you still do? You have a pretty lady's maid.'

'Stop! You are making me cry. And the servants will be in with the tea.'

'Cry as much as you wish. It is appropriate this afternoon. They will think you more tender-hearted than you are. Why did you marry me?' I often asked, though often less angrily. 'Why did you leave Florence? Why did you choose to spoil my life, for no better reason than to spoil your own?'

'Because I wanted to prove to myself that I was a normal woman, like all other women.'

'You mean you wanted to prove it to Florence? Out of spite.'

'Perhaps I did. We quarrelled a lot that summer at the Burlington. I thought because she suspected our secret meetings.'

'You quarrelled because she was wearying of you as a partner in her miserable tribadism. Oh, I've read my Juvenal.'

She was furious. 'You *will* not understand this is *not* just a physical connection, like two animals in a field. I loved Florence, ever since she first took me to Harley Street. And she loved me. You know that perfectly well, from everything she wrote when you took me away from her. Pathetic, terrible letters. I can still hardly bear to read them, but I do. Other women have children, or someone inspiring to live for, but she lost husband and children and all. She said I was killing her, and I nearly did. For weeks, her life hung by a thread.'

'Miss Nightingale is a valetudinarian fraud.'

The footmen brought the tea. The upper classes enjoy the pacifying advantage of servants, who are liable to interrupt any conversation, and usefully prevent our fury mounting until it bursts the thwarting restrictions of intellectual disputation into the satisfaction of assault. Were it not for their butlers, we should see more duchesses with black eyes.

By the time they had infused the tea and served the buttered toast, our tempers had cooled above the steam of our cups.

'I am travelling to Geneva this summer. Will you accompany me? It is only right that my mother should look upon the face of her daughter-in-law, and she cannot show her own in London.'

'It is my duty to accompany you,' Jane said irritatingly.

'I can offer the attraction of Count Arezzo's cook, a disciple of the late, loved Monsieur Soyer.'

Two summers before, Soyer had opened his model kitchen at Wellington Barracks, gone home, spat blood and died. Florence was employing him in the sanitation of barracks, I was employing him for cooking articles in *Candour*. He was buried with his beloved wife at Kensal Green, to be joined there within the decade by the faithful admirer of his bacon and beans, Thackeray. He left the Soyer stove, still to warm the soups and stews of the British army.

'You know I am as indifferent to food as to titles. I would far sooner manage the dinners of a thousand hospital patients than eat a single rich one myself.'

'Or would you prefer to go back and live with Florence?'

'She wouldn't have me. Remember, she never saw Mary Stanley again.'

'Then I shall sleep every night beside cold chastity, until death parts me from it.'

'You make too much of my one deficiency. In all other

respects I do my duty as a wife, as I did it as a nurse in Scutari.'

'Scutari and our marriage is hardly a flattering comparison.'

I stood up. It was time to describe my uncle's funeral so that it would interest a workman next morning in an omnibus.

Miss Nightingale was then intent on becoming sanitary Empress of India. Having set the Army Medical Department in order, she would perform the same service for Indian dungheaps. Her ambition and enthusiasm for salubrity were boundless. One of the many times she fancied herself dying during the sultry summer of the Commission, she remarked to Sidney Herbert, 'Perhaps He wants a "Sanitary Officer" now for my Crimeans, in some other world where they are gone.'

She had published *Notes on Nursing*, a combination in style of Soyer's practical cookery instruction and God's word, which sold 15,000 copies at five shillings. She was preparing *Notes on Nursing for the Labouring-Classes*, at sevenpence. I was still secretary of the Nightingale Fund, though my lords had long ago withdrawn their interest, for more fashionably worthy affairs. There was still no promised nurses' training school. There was nowhere to put it. All the great London hospitals had been built with accommodation for their nurses no more generous than a mattress in a corridor. I heard secretly that spring of 1860 about the South-Eastern Railway wanting to build a line through the middle of St Thomas's Hospital. They would give £75,000 for the land. I wrote to Miss Nightingale, desiring an interview. I said nothing to my wife.

She was still at the Burlington Hotel, almost in sight of my front door. She now had a suite in the annex, with a sitting-room downstairs, in which I found Sutherland, deafer than ever. He greeted me cordially, explaining that Miss Nightingale's health still saw its good days and its bad ones.

'There is more work for us in the legacy of the Royal Commission than in its birth or keeping it alive. Five sub-

Commissions were founded, you will recall, Mr Darling –
Oh! I do beg your pardon, Sir Tristram. One, to put the
barracks in sanitary order,' he enumerated. 'Two, for
founding a statistical department. Three, to institute an
Army Medical School. Four, completely to reconstruct the
Army Medical Department, revise the hospital regulations
and prepare a new warrant for the promotion of medical
officers.' He gave an arch smile. 'Miss Nightingale names the
last her "Wiping Commission", because she can wipe the
wrongs of the past and draw anew. And not only in England. I have myself been invited to inspect the barracks in
Malta and Gibraltar.'

'An agreeable voyage at this time of the year.'

His face fell. 'Miss Nightingale will not let me go.' A
servant's bell on a spring, added to the sitting-room wall,
gave a brief clang. Sutherland looked heavenwards. 'Miss
Nightingale is ready.'

I did not ask after Clough, supposing he was on an errand
in Mayfair. But he was dying in Italy.

The room was light. She looked well. She was fatter. She
lay in her usual black dress and lace cap on a brand-new
couch. Blue Books, letters, and reports were as usual in
tidy piles everywhere. There were cats.

After greetings, condolences, congratulations, all exchanged without warmth, she said, 'This couch was given
to me by an East End upholsterer – everybody now knows
I am too ill to stand on my own two feet – as a token of the
esteem in which I am held by the working classes. His
workmen made it without pay.'

'Very civil of them.' I took the indicated chair, dislodg-
ing a cat. 'And how is Mr Sidney Herbert?'

'Haven't you heard? A sad change has come over the
spirit of my . . . not dreams, but too strong realities. Mr
Herbert is said to have a fatal disease.'

I started to say something gravely sympathetic, but she
interrupted, 'You know I don't believe in fatal diseases. But
fatal to his *work* I believe this will be. He was just here to
see me, to discuss what part of his work had best be given
up. I settled that he should abandon the House of Commons,

but continue in office as Palmerston's Secretary of War, at least until some of the things are done which want doing. He is particularly forbidden damp, so cannot see me at night, which is irritating.'

'He is surely attended by the best physicians available?' I would not accept her airy trivialization of Sidney Herbert's health. 'Supposing he really is ill? I heard of his long-lasting weakness in the kidneys.'

'In London, almost all the doctors are charlatans,' she dismissed them. 'They sell articles called prescriptions or operations *said* to be good for the health. I know more about Mr Herbert's illness than any medical man. I sorrow to see that he is weaker and thinner than he was, but he is not materially worse in his general health. He has many years of usefulness left in him. He *cannot* give up office now, when we have every card in our hand to reform the War Office—'

'The War Office! You are surely not seeking to reform the entire War Office?'

'Why not? The War Office is a very slow office, an enormously expensive office, and one in which the Minister's intentions can be entirely negatived by all his subdepartments, and those of each of the subdepartments by every other.'

I wondered if she would shirk reforming the Cabinet or the Court. One of the cats rubbed against my trouser-leg, and she ordered it away. It was called 'Bart's'. She had named her pets after London hospitals.

'I am glad the railway particularly wished to bisect St Thomas's,' she said, when I explained my plan for adding £75,000 to the original £44,000. 'Mrs Sarah Wardroper is matron there. A gentlewoman and a doctor's widow, who became a nurse at forty-two. Straightforward, true, upright, free from artificiality and self-interest, her whole life and strength in the work she has undertaken. She is the only matron of any who I would recommend to form a school of instruction.'

I thought that Florence's mind had drawn a replica of herself. 'I shall write to her,' she agreed, 'though of course I have no secretary. Clough has deserted me, and Sutherland always has some *pond* to dig in his garden. I have inter-minable correspondence about Netley, which will be built with a single disadvantage, that it is utterly unsuitable for the housing of patients. It may be a strange principle to enunciate, but the first requirement in a hospital is that it should do the sick no harm.'

We had reached the real reason for my visit. 'I did not realize the pain my marriage would give you.'

'You left me alone to this dreary, hopeless struggle,' she said bitterly, her hand indicating a roomful of work. 'To this desperate guerrilla warfare, ending too often in too little, which makes me impatient with life itself. I, who could once do so much.' She had no self-pity in Scutari. But the Bar-rack Hospital was a gentler taskmaster than her own emo-tions. 'I have felt these last three years the extreme weakness of not having one single person to give one inspiring word. I was glad to end a day which never can come back, gladder to end a night, gladder still to end a month.'

'How could I know that Jane had such great value? Your affections are a strange currency to me.'

'The currency wasn't strange to Ben Jonson. *Light Venus with thy tribade trine, invent new sports . . .*' Her eyes grew blank, as though she saw Jane in the room.

'Would you have her back?'

She said nothing for a moment. 'The things that are deepest in our hearts are perhaps what is most difficult to express.'

'Now the law is changed, I could let myself be divorced by her. Or have our marriage declared void through failure of consummation.'

'So? She did not bring you the happiness which she took from me?'

'People would laugh at me, but I suppose I am young enough for them to forget before I need cut a dignified figure.'

'Console yourself with Swift – "Censure is the tax a man pays to the public for being eminent." '

'Florence, I understand you better than do your other courtiers. I am a clever little devil, and you are a cleverer big one. We are both industrious and unscrupulous, and contemptuous of the unfortunate people on whom we bring these qualities to bear. Jane is a stupid girl. I married her because I thought her a quick and clever one. I ask you to take her back, because she would be exchanging a bad marriage for a good one. She is no wife to me. All her attributes are anyway superficial, stamped on the blank of her mind by yourself. It may be said – to stretch a point – that I married *you*.'

She was now more kindly. 'But you would have to oust a rival, Tristram. The Regius Professor of Greek at Oxford.'

'What! Mr Benjamin Jowett? That erudite owl with the piping hoot? Oh, he'd never do!'

'He has asked me. But he is a great Platonist, and perhaps it is an expression of *amor platonicus*.'

'Platonic love is Platonic nonsense. It is usually an expression of maudlin sentiment between the sexes.'

'I would not have him, in any event.' She thought a moment. 'He always talks to me as though I were someone else. Please ask Lady Darling to call for tea.'

25

Oxford was delightful at the end of that June. The under-graduates had scattered to a trimester of flirtation disguised as travel, the dons to one of idleness disguised as contemplation. The dozing spires beneath a soft blue sky housed the annual meeting of the thirty-year-old British Association for the Advancement of Science. Bishop 'Soapy Sam' Wilberforce would be attending, 'to smash Darwin'.

I was comfortably lodged at All Souls, one of whose dons wrote secretly for *Candour* under a classical pseudonym. The wretched savant needed money, his other secret being marriage, which disgraceful state would have immediately lost him his fellowship. I was developing my gift for finding men with the golden link of big ideas and the ability to implant them into little minds. Mr Karl Marx, still living in Soho, still writing articles on the Crimean War and the Eastern Question for the *New York Tribune* at a guinea a time, was doing me weekly pieces on political economy in place of those on cookery by Monsieur Soyer.

That summer, I printed in the *Daily Pioneer* selections from Mr Charles Darwin's long book with the long title, *On the Origin of Species by means of a Natural Selection, or the Preservation of Favoured Races in the Struggle for Life.* When published the previous November, its first edition of 1,250 had sold out in a day, which was even better going than Florence's *Notes on Nursing* at 15,000 a month. Darwin, Marx and Florence Nightingale were a trio who never met, but I met all three. They were three fire-crackers which went off together and roused the middle of the last century. It was I who lit the touch-papers.

The Oxford meeting started on June 28, a Thursday which was exceeded in soporific dullness by the Friday. Admiral Fitz Roy, Captain of the *Beagle* which had conveyed Mr Darwin for five years to the land of scientific speculation, read a paper – on *British Storms*. Mr Darwin was not there. He was ill, as usual.

Saturday was Soapy Sam's day. Everyone stranded in Oxford by the academic tide wanted to see the show. The meeting was hastily rehoused from a lecture-room to the New University Museum, by the Parks. An American professor was drearily concerned with *The Intellectual Development of Europe Considered with Reference to the Views of Mr Darwin and Others*, when Wilberforce entered, dome-headed, wide-mouthed, black-browed, gaitered and aproned, surrounded by a bodyguard of equally fearsome black-suited consciences, bowing greetings with unctuous liberality. It was a performance often seen in the theatre, when a famous actress arrives in the auditorium deliberately late, to the distraction of the audience and fury of the actors.

His speech was a Niagara of soapsuds, swamping the little *Beagle* from truck to keel with slippery ridicule. Mr Darwin had no proofs, only opinions. Whose did they accept, Mr Darwin's word or the Word of God? Listening on the platform was a man I knew distantly, Thomas Henry Huxley. He was a lecturer on natural history at the Royal School of Mines, a doctor of medicine and a Fellow of the Royal Society. A dry, perky, snub-nosed, profusely dark-haired man of thirty-five, so unsusceptible to academic hysteria that he was giving the meeting a miss. I met him in the Broad, and dragged him along. Bishop Wilberforce slipped into his peroration, then turned. 'Is it through Mr Huxley's grandmother or grandfather,' he enquired smoothly, 'that he claims to be descended from the apes?'

Huxley jumped up. He jammed on his intimidating pince-nez. 'I should most certainly rather be descended from an ape than from a man who prostitutes his education and his eloquence to the worship of prejudice and falsehood.'

For a respected man of science to insult a distinguished

bishop in public in mid-nineteenth century Oxford seemed at first like Lord Cardigan's charge at Balaclava. The canons volley'd and thunder'd demands for an apology. Then the scientists cheered on their champion, while the ladies dabbed desperately with their handkerchiefs and the wife of the vice-chancellor of Edinburgh University fainted away, to be carried out by a pair of analytical chemists. I had unknowingly seen Huxley switch the points for the world's train of thought. The home of lost causes was to house another. Mankind shed its terrified reverence of dogmatic religion. There would be a restless grave in the crypt of Chelsea Cathedral that night.

A month later, the Nightingale Training School was founded. It would be opened with fifteen probationer nurses in the new St Thomas's beside the Thames, under the paragon Mrs Wardroper. Miss Nightingale drew up the rules. The probationers had to be sober, honest, truthful, trustworthy, punctual, quiet and orderly, cleanly and neat, and to become skilful in dressing blisters, applying leeches, administering enemas and managing trusses. They would learn only a little medicine, which would otherwise make them intolerable in the hospital from airing their knowledge, or miserable from not using it. They would keep a daily diary, read by Miss Nightingale every month. Nurses would venture into London only in pairs, as they did into Scutari. And as at Scutari, flirtation meant the sack. The course took a year, for which they would get £10. They would all be ladies doing a maid-of-all-work's job. Miss Nightingale had squashed Mary Stanley's 'Lady System' flat. That was her accomplishment in nursing, so simple that it needed a genius to do it.

I was busy with the Fund, to which I noticed the medical profession's contribution stood as low as Miss Nightingale's opinion of doctors. As I passed most of my life in Fleet Street, and Florence all of hers in the Burlington, I did not see her again until Christmas, 1861. Clough had then been dead a month, Sidney Herbert four.

My wife was alone in the sitting-room downstairs. She was in her old lace-trimmed black dress. She greeted me smilingly. 'Why exactly have you come to see Miss Nightingale?' she asked pleasantly. Our marriage could have been made of dreams.

'Because I have an urgent message from the Secretary at War in Washington. He wants Miss Nightingale to take charge of the hospitals which serve the Northern States' armies. Will she rise from her couch and repeat for President Lincoln in Virginia~what she accomplished for Mr Herbert in Turkey?'

'Miss Nightingale is too ill to travel.'

I noticed Jane was busy at the table with a silver spoon and a saucer, rolling a tiny pellet of grey putty. 'What's that?' I asked.

She gave the mischievous smile which often met me in the hotel during our summer of secret meetings. 'Opium.'

'Indeed? Does Florence smoke it in a pipe like a Limehouse Chinaman?'

'I slip it under the skin of her thigh with a little silver knife. It's a curious little new-fangled op. which some doctors try. It relieves her.'

'From what?'

'She has backache, which I massage without effect. She likes opium, though she complains that it does not improve the vivacity or serenity of her intellect. By which I think she means it lets her forget herself for a while.'

'Like an old nurse's gin-bottle?'

'In a way,' said Jane gently. 'But Miss Nightingale has already been asked for advice from America, by Miss Dorothea Dix, Superintendent of Nurses at Washington. I sent our annotated report of the Royal Commission. Miss Nightingale is horrified at the news of suffering among the wounded.'

'Are you happy?'

'I think so. We are moving soon. This hotel is becoming quite unsuitable for Miss Nightingale. They never open the windows or shut the seats of the water-closets, and the cistern upstairs burst with a bang and flooded us. Miss Nightingale suffered a severe chill. We have acquired a house in South Street, nearer the Park.'

'Do you need money?'

'Miss Nightingale does, for her causes. Otherwise, it is not an important commodity with us. Are you going to marry your lady in Berkeley Square?'

'Yes, once the lawyers have done their job. I need a wife. I am standing for Parliament.'

'I look forward to reading your speeches in the newspapers.'

The bell rang.

Upstairs there were even more cats.

I started about the American war, but Florence interrupted, 'Didn't Jane tell you about Canada? Oh, she is as stupid a girl as ever. After the *Trent* affair—' The Northern States had taken Confederate prisoners from a British ship. 'We are reinforcing the Canadian garrison. Lord de Gray at the War Office consulted me personally on the sanitary arrangements, the defects and dangers to be feared, the name of a suitable Principal Medical Officer. I have a thousand details to master, the distances which might be covered by sledges, the relative weights and warming capacity of blankets and buffalo robes . . . the War Office *still* does not define with sufficient precision the manner in which meat is to get from the Commissariat into the soldier's kettle, or clothing from the army medical general store on to the soldier's back. I have told Lord de Grey that he must define all this, or they will again have men shirking their responsibility. The Government will do everything I say, because they are terrified of the national indignation if they lost another army as they did in the Crimea.'

She had not changed. 'My other reason for calling today was the expression of double condolences.'

'Oh! I am so distressed at the death of Mr Clough, that I cannot open a newspaper for fear of seeing his name. He was a man of rare mind and temper, who helped me immensely by his sound judgement and constant sympathy.'

'You once said he did the work of a cab-horse. But he was a racehorse harnessed to a coal truck. If that did not kill him, it hastened his end.'

227

'Now you are accusing me, like his family,' she said petulantly. 'You do not think of *my* feelings. Hardly a man remains – that I can call a man – of all those I have worked with these five years. I survive them all. I did not mean to.'

'And Lord Herbert—' He had been ennobled seven months before dying. 'When he was examined by the doctors after death, he was found to have terrible kidney disease. You attributed to infirmity of will what was due to infirmity of body. Even when he struggled to the War Office under your whiplash, blinded with headache, fainting, surviving only on gulps of brandy. You told him not to judge too hardly of himself from the doctors' opinion – with which you disagreed – that you cannot absolutely mend a damaged organ.'

'Sometimes, I said *sometimes*. Why, I know a very active intellectual man with the same albuminous symptoms as Herbert, who by sleeping in the country gave himself fifteen years of good life, and may have fifteen more ahead. Sidney Herbert suffered from thorough London ill-health, with poverty of blood, which deposits albumen.'

'You refuse to believe in kidney disease. You refuse to believe in germs, when every scientific doctor in the world can see them like houseflies. Your little learning is a danger to the public.'

She looked at me angrily. 'It is impossible, for an old nurse like me, to see a man every day without knowing him off by heart. Of Sidney Herbert's constitution I could speak with confidence.'

'You did, but also with misjudgement and I think self-deceit.' I took a paper from my pocket. 'I have been consoling Lady Herbert, who passed me her husband's notes of your last conversations. "There is no evidence that disease is getting the upper hand with you,"' I quoted. '"Let me see your prescriptions. At least I can give you an opinion upon them. You need not take them. I do hope you won't have any vain ideas that you can be spared the War Office. There is no one else to take your place there. You know that as well as everybody else. You cannot be the only person

228

who does not know that you are necessary to the reorganizing of the War Office. One fight more, the best and the last." You were like Lord Raglan, throwing troops dying of cholera against the Russian ramparts on the Alma.'

'God should never have let him die,' she cried. 'God should have set aside a few trifling physical laws to save him. Do you think I cannot see death when it is written on a man's face? Me, of all women! But for him to give up the War Office was like myself feebly packing my portmanteaux in the middle of that terrible winter in Scutari and going home. I understood him better than Liz Herbert, whose claim upon him compared to mine was as tenant to landlord.'

She was bolt upright on the couch, eyes ablaze, voice wild. 'The thing wanted in England to raise women, to raise men too, are those friendships without love between men and women, and if between married men and married women all the better. I think a woman who cares for a man because of his convictions, and who ceases to care for him if he alters those convictions, is worthy of the highest reverence. Women in love with men without any reason at all, and ready to leave their highest occupations for love, are to me utterly wearisome, wearisome as a juggler's trick, table-turning, spirit-rapping. How happy widows are! Because people don't write them harassing letters in the first week of their widowhood, and yet I know of no widow more desolate than I . . . Poor Flo! Poor Flo! I shall mount three widows' caps on my head, yes, three, one for Sidney Herbert, one for Arthur Clough, and one for the loss of sympathy from you, the only man I have opened my heart to. Oh, I am pains, pains, pains all over, I must have my dose—' She reached for the bell handle, working it violently.

I told her, 'You are more jealous than Othello, more intolerant than Cassius, more resentful than Lady Macbeth and more cruel than Regan.'

She was silent. A moment passed. Her voice came wearily, 'How can you say such things to the woman who found the British soldier a brute, and left him – for all his faults – a noble creature?'

'Because like every British general in the past, and doubtless in the future, you drew public esteem from his nobility, which he cannot express in fine words and great schemes, but only by dying.'

'Tristram, sometimes you muddle me,' she said sorrowfully. 'Though sometimes I am frighteningly muddled by myself.'

I left. I never went back.

Now Miss Nightingale is dead. On Saturday, August 13 1910, at her little red brick house in South Street, Mayfair, of heart failure, in her afternoon sleep, at ninety. She tyrannized important men for half a century with the fearsome power of her impending death. Her couch was attended beseechingly by generals and viceroys, physicians and politicians, sanitarians and ecclesiastics, the propagandist apostate Manning, the amorous don Jowett. She reformed the drains of India, but never the War Office. That would need the hand of Sidney Herbert in his supernatural condition. She found nursing a trade and left it an art. I suppose Soyer did the same for English cooking.

She ended fat and moon-faced, petting, weeping over, sentimentalizing the young girls sent up to her from St Thomas's. With the delicacy of timing rather than taste with which the British Government distributes such twinkling lustres, in late 1907 Campbell-Bannerman sent Sir Douglas Dawson from Downing Street to South Street with the Order of Merit. 'Too kind, too kind,' Miss Nightingale said. She was the first, the only, woman to have it, a woman half-blind, half-mad and half-dead. The Kaiser was visiting his cousin Edward, and remembering Kaiserwerth sent a bouquet.

The release of Miss Nightingale's soul from her body releases the diaries of my years with her, their pages as yellow and loose as old teeth, from their locked desk in the library of my country house. The diaries themselves are far more interesting than this memoir which I have written from them over the past eighteen months. They give the names, the occasions, the details of her loves among many noble and princely ladies, and among many ignoble and plebeian ones. As I may prove as deaf to the call of Heaven as she, I am depositing them beyond intrusive British eyes in the library of Harvard University, to which my wife and myself will be crossing with our friends the Astors next month, on the maiden voyage of the much-trumpeted *Titanic*.

Postscript

The massive 18th century Selimiye Barracks still stands four-turreted against the Bosphorus on the Asian shore of modern Istanbul. Now Headquarters of the Turkish 1st Army, the corridors where a British one died on the floor are rubber-tiled, warm, spotless and smelling of soldiers' lunch. Beyond the officers' library, two rooms are preserved in the Sisters' Tower, one above the other, 15 feet square, filled with Victorian furniture, their deep windows overlooking the Bosphorus and Sea of Marmara. From here, Florence Nightingale nursed, fed, clothed and buried her Crimean children, and quit them for immortality.

Scutari has become Üsküdar, a suburb with a busy ferry pier and the grandiose terminus of the Kaiser's Baghdad Railway. White, red-roofed middle-class villas overwhelm its cypress-striped slopes, dominated by the only bridge joining Europe to Asia. The domes of the Covered Bazaar in the Old City, where Miss Nightingale bought soldiers' lives with *The Times'* fund, canopy little shops selling carpets and antique *tchibouques* to tourists. The domes of mosques and delicate fingers of minarets burst through the same tangle of alleys, which have suffered only the flea-bites of World War I air-raids.

Turkish society has been Western for over fifty years. The *muezzin's* call to prayer is still heard, electronically amplified. The *araba* which transported the wounded, slightly sprung, delivers ewe cheeses and cases of raki. Lord Stratford de Redcliffe's glorious reception room has become the British Council library. The Golden Horn is polluted.

The bones of the Turkish cemetery beside the Barrack

Hospital have been cleared for a children's playground – a cheerful reassurance for mankind. Almost a mile away, among the British graves where no Harriet is buried, surrounded by the headstones of half a dozen surgeons lost to Crimean fever, a raised marble tomb is inscribed—

Sacred to the Memory of
LUCAS WARD ESQ
Purveyor to the Forces
who died at
SCUTARI, JAN 1st 1855
After Serving His Country 46 Years
also
To the Memory of
JANE WARD
Wife of the Above
who died at the same place
Jan 3rd 1855
This Monument was Erected by the Members of his Department as a Tribute of Esteem and Respect for an Old and Faithful Public Officer.

Exactly opposite, a towering memorial with Florence Nightingale's name dominates for ever Poor Old Ward and all he lived and died for.